PRAISE FOR THE NOVELS OF
RANDY WAYNE WHITE

"Randy Wayne White and his Doc Ford join my list of must-reads. It is no small matter when I assert that White is getting pretty darn close to joining Carl Hiaasen and John D. MacDonald as writers synonymous with serious Florida issues and engaging characters." —*Chicago Tribune*

"Enough twists to satisfy any hard-boiled but intelligent detective fan." —*The Dallas Morning News*

"One of the hottest new writers on the scene."
—*Library Journal*

"Great action scenes, terrific atmosphere, and a full-bodied hero add up to a pleasure." —*Booklist*

"Packed with finely drawn characters, relevant social issues, superb plotting, and an effortless writing style ... The best new writer since Carl Hiaasen."
—*The Denver Post*

"White is the rightful heir to joining John D. MacDonald, Carl Hiaasen, James W. Hall, Geoffrey Norman ... His precise prose is as fresh and pungent as a salty breeze."
—*The Tampa Tribune*

"A series to be savored." —*The San Diego Union-Tribune*

TITLES BY RANDY WAYNE WHITE

Sanibel Flats
The Heat Islands
The Man Who Invented Florida
Captiva
North of Havana
The Mangrove Coast
Ten Thousand Islands
Shark River
Twelve Mile Limit
Everglades
Tampa Burn
Dead of Night
Dark Light
Hunter's Moon
Black Widow
Dead Silence
Deep Shadow

NONFICTION

Batfishing in the Rainforest
The Sharks of Lake Nicaragua
Last Flight Out
An American Traveler
Tarpon Fishing in Mexico and Florida
(An Introduction)
Randy Wayne White's Gulf Coast Cookbook
(with Carlene Fredericka Brennen)

FICTION AS RANDY STRIKER

Key West Connection
The Deep Six
Cuban Death-Lift
The Deadlier Sex
Assassin's Shadow
Everglades Assault
Grand Cayman Slam

NORTH of HAVANA

RANDY WAYNE WHITE

THE BERKLEY PUBLISHING GROUP
Published by the Penguin Group
Penguin Group (USA) Inc.
375 Hudson Street, New York, New York 10014, USA
Penguin Group (Canada), 90 Eglinton Avenue East, Suite 700, Toronto, Ontario M4P 2Y3, Canada
(a division of Pearson Penguin Canada Inc.)
Penguin Books Ltd., 80 Strand, London WC2R 0RL, England
Penguin Group Ireland, 25 St. Stephen's Green, Dublin 2, Ireland (a division of Penguin Books Ltd.)
Penguin Group (Australia), 250 Camberwell Road, Camberwell, Victoria 3124, Australia
(a division of Pearson Australia Group Pty. Ltd.)
Penguin Books India Pvt. Ltd., 11 Community Centre, Panchsheel Park, New Delhi—110 017, India
Penguin Group (NZ), Cnr. Airborne and Rosedale Roads, Albany, Auckland 1310, New Zealand
(a division of Pearson New Zealand Ltd.)
Penguin Books (South Africa) (Pty.) Ltd., 24 Sturdee Avenue, Rosebank, Johannesburg 2196,
South Africa

Penguin Books Ltd., Registered Offices: 80 Strand, London WC2R 0RL, England

NORTH OF HAVANA

A Berkley Book / published by arrangement with the author

PRINTING HISTORY
G. P. Putnam's Sons hardcover edition / 1997
Berkley Prime Crime mass-market edition / May 1998
Berkley mass-market edition / December 2005

ISBN: 978-0-425-16294-1

BERKLEY®
Berkley Books are published by The Berkley Publishing Group,
a division of Penguin Group (USA) Inc.,
375 Hudson Street, New York, New York 10014.
BERKLEY is a registered trademark of Penguin Group (USA) Inc.
The "B" design is a trademark belonging to Penguin Group (USA) Inc.

PRINTED IN THE UNITED STATES OF AMERICA

30 29 28 27 26 25 24 23 22 21

Author's Note

I have visited Cuba several times, including a long stay in Mariel Harbor during the extraordinary and tragic 1980 refugee boat lift. Even so, writers whose knowledge of Cuba far exceeds my own have unknowingly contributed to this novel through their work. Highly recommended are *Castro's Final Hour*, by Andres Oppenheimer, *Fidel Castro*, by Robert E. Quirk, and the *Cruising Guide to Cuba*, by Simon Charles, a book that revealed Sanibel Island's topographical twin. Any factual errors or misrepresentations of fact in this novel are entirely my fault, or of my own creation, and their fine books played no role.

I would also like to thank the great people of Useppa Island, Florida, who allowed me room to work, particularly my friend Ginny Amsler, who read the early drafts and provided advice and support. I would also like to thank my buddies on Cabbage Key—Bob, Thea, Kim, Terry, Joleen, Jerry, Angel, Mike, and Judy—who always welcomed me with a cold beer and warm attention when, after a withering day of work, I came zombie eyed up the mound. Finally, I would like to thank Rogan White—a lifelong friend—for helping me finish this book.

For friends who are equal to Marion Ford's tough definition of the word: Dr. Brian Hummel, Rob Wells, and Debra Jane White. Also: Robert Bunk Fizer, a proud fellow member of the jumping-out-of-the-boat-at-night club, who bailed a final time.

I had never seen primitive man in his native place till then.

—H. M. Tomlinson
The Sea and the Jungle

Our worst enemies are not the ignorant and
the simple, however cruel; our worst enemies
are the intelligent and corrupt.

—Graham Greene
The Human Factor

The islands of Sanibel and Cayo de Soto exist, but they are used fictitiously in this novel. Havana, Mariel Harbor, and the Cuban countryside are, I hope, accurately described and reflect my own observations and experiences there. In all other respects, this novel is a work of fiction. Names, characters, places, and incidents are either the product of the author's imagination or are used fictitiously. Any resemblance to actual persons, living or dead, or to actual events or locales is entirely coincidental.

NORTH of HAVANA

1

Tomlinson telephoned at three minutes before ten Friday evening, December 20, to tell me that he was stranded in Havana, broke, frustrated, sailboat impounded, seriously discommoded, wholly bummed out and if I wasn't too busy, if I wasn't right in the middle of boxing a shipment of sea anemones or if my manatee research project could be conveniently interrupted, maybe, just maybe, I could get my butt to a neutral country and catch a plane to Cuba.

I thought: Cuba? Nope; no way. I will *not* go back to Cuba.

Tomlinson was talking: "You heard of a person being held against his will? I'm being held against my *bill,* man. Like they're holding *No Más* hostage until I can float the nut, plus charging me storage to boot! As in *muchos* simoleons, *comprende*?"

"The government?"

"These guys dressed in baby shit brown. Like storm troopers—"

"Who confiscated your boat, I mean." I was beginning to get a sick feeling in my stomach.

"Aren't you listening? *Yes*. The *cubano*-damn government. Man, it pains me to admit it, but socialism has gone to hell since I left the loop. I just thank the good Lord that Chairman Mao isn't alive to see it. Talk about a reality check! These pud duckers give me any more crap, I'm going to contact my old comrades from the SDS, Boston cell, and raise a serious stink. Who do they think came down here and cut their goddamn sugarcane in nineteen seventy-one? Wouldn't you think they had my name on file? Jesus Christ, we ate nothing but beans. We slept in barns. They had donkeys that bit like dogs! A machete scar *meant* something in those days."

Tomlinson was ranting—conduct out of character. Lately, though, he had been doing many things out of character. As his neurosurgeon, Maria Corales, had told me, "You can expect some odd behavior. He's been out of the hospital only what? A year? The beating he took, his brain was so traumatized that it could be another year—or more—before he's back to normal. So be kind to him. Be understanding."

So I listened kindly. And I tried to understand. But I kept thinking: Jesus, *Cuba* . . .

Tomlinson was calling, he said, from the Hotel Nacional, the old Meyer Lansky casino and brothel in downtown Havana, built during prohibition to service America's thirsty leisure class. It was his fifth night in the hotel, but he was thinking of switching to the Havana Libre up the street. At a rack rate of two hundred bucks a night, neither he nor his female companion could afford the Nacional much longer, and it had taken him that long to figure out a way to contact me.

"The phone system here," he said, "is not unlike whacking off. It's a hell of a mess and leaves something to be desired."

Not long ago, an American communications conglomerate received a lot of press about opening direct-dial phone service to Cuba. It was one of those hands-across-the-water events that implied a new relationship with our island foe of the old Cold War years. It also implied that Cubans had the freedom—never mind the financial means—to reciprocate. Not so, according to Tomlinson. You couldn't just pick up a Havana pay phone and dial your friendly AT&T operator. So what he'd finally done was find a guy who helped him work out a phone patch through the Vancouver British Columbia Marine Operator, a bit of satellite pinball that now had our digitized voices ricocheting through the ionosphere, then back and forth across the continent. Person-to-person. Collect.

"Did I mention bring money?" Tomlinson asked. I could hear the muted equipment clatter and conduit roar of the Third World communication system; Tomlinson's voice sounded as if he were yelling to me from the bottom of a stone well. "Lots and lots of money, cash American," he said. "Ten thousand, minimum."

I told him, "You keep me on the phone much longer I won't have any money left to bring," not because I meant it, but because saying it seemed a necessary courtesy to the woman who waited a few feet away, lying on my bed. With the phone against my ear, I looked at her, smiled, then I made a great show of being patient to illustrate my impatience with Tomlinson . . . an act that a perceptive, tough-talking woman such as Dewey Nye wasn't likely to buy.

She didn't. Dewey rolled gray-blue eyes heavenward, used a lopsided, cynical smile to accuse me of stalling, kicked off the covers, stood, and released a lanyard of butterscotch hair that fell heavily across her bare shoulders before she froze me with those sled dog eyes and mouthed the word "Coward!" Then she began to survey the room, searching for her shirt and jogging bra, which I had folded neatly over the Celestron telescope by the north window of my little house that stands in water, Dinkin's Bay, Sanibel Island, Florida.

A peculiarity of the intimate male-female relationship is that each small gesture is a specific communication which, in sequence, creates a discourse so constant and telling that words do little more than outline what is expected or reaffirm what has already occurred. When one partner says, "We don't talk enough," it is usually much, much too late for talking. So I watched Dewey to see what she had to say. Watched her glide to the telescope, ropy thigh and calf muscles contracting like cables with each stride; a tall, big boned, slim-hipped woman who, naked except for bikini panties, moved with the lazy immodesty of the shower room jock. Noted that she turned her back to me before toweling off the body oil I had been using on her neck and shoulders—less a gesture of modesty than of rebuke. But just when I was beginning to read that she was genuinely peeved, she did a casual quarter-turn so that she was illuminated by the reading lamp: face, pale sweep and weight of breasts, the muscle-patched symmetry of abdomen as she wiggled into the jogging bra and latched it tight, a performance designed to be shared. When she caught me staring, she used long fingers to comb hair from her eyes and mouthed another word: "Asshole!"

Through the phone, I heard Tomlinson say, "Look'a that—cockroach the size of a damn chipmunk just tried to hump my shoe. Dirty little bastard! Hang on. . . . Hah! Killed it!"

I thought: Killed it? Tomlinson?

Then he was barking at me: "Yoo-hoo! I know you're there 'cause I can hear you breathing like a bear . . . or maybe it's . . . hey, wait a minute. How could I be so stupid!" Inexplicably, his tone became guarded, his enunciation careful, as he said, "Mother of God, it just dawned on me! The ucking-fay ommie-cays got the phone bugged, right? We're being ape-taed? The proletariat scum!"

"Pig Latin? For Christ's sake, Tomlinson."

"Don't make it easy on them. Let the pink bastards wrestle with the code books. What gall! I was fighting for the collapse of capitalism when these twerps were abusing themselves with bootlegged Sears catalogues. Who do they think organized the Berkeley Expeditionary when Che Guevara was nabbed in sixty-eight? Was it my fault the Bolivian pigs shot him anyway? Is that what this's all about! Okay! Okay! Boycotting alpaca sweaters didn't carry the political juice I'd hoped. Turned out the whole firing squad owned llamas. But who knew with those Bolivians? Their sphincters are so tight, it'll be another ten generations before they can actually walk upright. Even howler monkeys consider Bolivians a bad risk as breeding stock! AM I GOING SLOW ENOUGH FOR YOU, COMRADE?"

I raised my voice: "Tomlinson! Take a deep breath and calm down." Paranoiac tangents were, in Tomlinson, a symptom of heavy stress . . . or of long-gone drug bingos . . . or it could be the residue of the beating he had received at the hands of goons on an island called Sulfur Wells a year earlier. With him, the borders were always clouded. Nothing could be assumed. Even though I knew the conversation was probably being monitored, I said, "Nobody's listening. We're not being bugged. Relax. Okay?"

"You sure?"

"Why would they bother? Look, you sailed too close to Cuba and had your boat confiscated. It happens all the time. Take a deep breath and tell me about it, then I'll see what I can do."

"You just sounded, you know, for sure distracted. And then I thought . . . hey!" His tone became hopeful. "Maybe my call interrupted something, huh? Holiday romance? A game of lock-'n-load?"

Close, but not quite. I looked at Dewey, who was now standing at the mirror. It had been more than a year since I'd last seen her. In that time, she had abandoned the mannish pageboy cut and let her hair grow, perhaps in an attempt to appear more feminine. It seemed unnecessary . . . and a little sad, too. Why is it that we find the small failed gestures of others so endearing? Dewey has one of those California unisex beach girl faces: pale-lipped, high-cheeked, smile bright, but without the delicate, vacuous leer. There is nothing vacuous—or delicate—about Dewey. She has a square chin, a nose broken by a grade school hockey stick, luminous deep-set gray eyes with a webbing of smile lines at the corners, a right forearm that is nearly as thick as my own, and the sort of knobby wrists and knees more commonly seen on gawky fourteen-year-olds. But Dewey is a dozen years past fourteen, and she is neither gawky nor adolescent. She was once rated among the world's best tennis players; she is now working her way onto the Ladies Professional Golf Association tour. She is a superb athlete with all the endurance and grace that that implies. Perhaps it is because she also happens to be one of my best friends that I find it less easy to note that her body is unmistakably female, though she herself often jokes about it. "With my pelvis, I could foal a pony, no trouble." Even though she is lean-butted and muscular. "I hate this! I get cold, anyone standing chest high should wear safety glasses." That, at least, is true.

Sitting there watching her—she was now combing her hair—I allowed the slow swell of physical wanting to recede, holding emotion at bay with perverse logic: because she was my friend, we couldn't be lovers.

Besides, Dewey already had a lover—a fading star on the professional tennis circuit named Walda Bzantovski, known to her close friends as Bets. A Romanian woman.

Over the phone, Tomlinson was pressing the issue. "That's it, isn't it? Romance. Jesus Christ, Doc, it's not like I called about the weather. So my timing's off. I interrupted."

"Not at all," I told him. He was more like the cavalry. Just in the nick of time.

Dewey had arrived that afternoon, Friday afternoon; flew in from New York on the cirrus fringe of December's first cold front. West Florida's cold fronts are something you won't read about in the travel brochures. They begin with a musky southeast wind that blows warm out of the Bahamas until the air congeals into an oily calm. For Christmas newcomers, it must be strange to see storefront holly wreaths and plastic snowmen baking in the winter heat, yet it's ideal tourist weather. Ideal weather for shelling and sunbathing and snook fishing and drinking margaritas on restaurant patios where snow-dazed midwesterners can lounge around in summer clothes and congratulate themselves on their balmy vacation choice.

But then it all changes and it changes quickly. Palm trees begin to clack and clatter in a nervous breeze. The breeze grows and builds, and then, as if guided by the boom of a sail, it swings compass-hard out of the northwest, hunkering there while a high-pressure system slips into the void. Then the wind blows Minnesota cold, roiling the green Gulf of Mexico until it's the color and texture of jagged marl, leaching the heat out of an ineffectual sun, sending the tourists scrambling and skittering back to their heated condos and expensive motel rooms to brood about money and their rotten luck.

Dewey had arrived unexpectedly with the first freight-train swing of wind. I'd been working on my thousand-gallon fish tank out on the deck of my stilthouse, fitting a new Styrofoam cover to insulate it from the predicted cold snap. Nearly a year before, my place had been all but destroyed by an explosion and I was still putting on finishing touches, rebuilding this, fixing that, trying to get things back to normal. No easy job. The problem with the Styrofoam cover was that I had sufficiently changed my new tank's PVC piping configuration—the raw water intake, exhaust, and overflow systems—so that the old cover could no longer serve even as a template. So I had spent the whole morning building a cover from scratch, measuring and fitting, cutting Styrofoam to size, then bracing the thing with marine plywood stripping. Every so often, someone from the marina would wander over to inspect, then comment on my handiwork, usually as prelude to some new bit of marina gossip or an invitation to a party on the mainland or up on Captiva—this was the holiday season, remember?—and they would generally finish by observing that I was being way too fastidious. The cold front wouldn't last for more than a week, so why didn't I just throw a tarp over the damn tank? It would save a helluva lot of time.

I listened to them. I smiled. I went right on working. One of the great frauds promoted by New Age mystics and other mind-control profiteers is that we are exactly what we envision ourselves to be. Imagine success, they tell us, and success will beat down our doors. Visualize big goals and big money; don't sweat the small stuff. But I think it is far more likely that we are directed less by our dreams than we are steered by our fears. We don't run to success—

whatever success is—we flee in its general direction until success hits us in the face. The best executives, best salespeople, best tradesmen, builders, promoters, and professionals all have, at the bedrock core, a healthy fear of not living up to their obligations. The obligations vary—each craft and discipline creates its own—and they range from the great and grand to tiny little nit-picking details that demand long hours, short weekends, and a full ration of stubbornness. The duties of obligation are not flogged on the late-night infomercials because there is nothing flashy about commitment. Hard work without shortcuts or excuses just doesn't sell on cassette, disc, or video.

I wasn't about to throw a tarp over my fish tank because I am one of those people who sweats the small stuff. "Anal retentive" is the current euphemism. I am compulsive about details. I am a neatener and a straightener. Whenever I try to cut corners by slopping together some makeshift remedy, I suffer a nagging anxiety at belly-button level. The solution? I don't cut corners or slop together makeshift remedies. There are "What if?" people who are nostalgia junkies. I am a "What if?" person who is driven by fear of the future. What if I covered the fish tank with Pliofilm and the temperature dropped below freezing? My tank contains immature snook, tarpon, and sea trout, all carefully collected and painstakingly maintained. Most of them would die. What if the nor'wester blew a gale? The Pliofilm would be ripped away in strips and the wind would damage sea squirts, tunicates, anemones, and the shrimps and squid that live among them. Odds were that it wouldn't freeze and it wouldn't blow a gale . . . but what if it did? Sanibel Biological Supply, purveyor of marine research specimens, is a small company but it's my company, my obligation, so I sweat the details. As Jeth Nichols, one of the local fishing guides, has told me more than once: "You big dumb shit, what with all the tah-tah time you spend looking through a microscope and cutting open fish, no wonder you live alone. What woman's gu-gonna put up with that?"

Jeth's stutter doesn't affect his powers of observation; he's probably right on all counts.

• • •

So I was squatting over the cover, barefooted and dirt-streaked, when I felt the earthquake-tremble of footsteps on the dock that connects my house to the mangrove beach. Looked up expecting to see one of the marina regulars, but there stood Dewey instead. Her hands were shoved into the pockets of her Day-Glo red warm-ups, her blue visor cap was tilted back. She gave me a long look of appraisal, then shook her head solemnly. "Jesus Christ, I've been gone only, what? A year? That fast, you've gotten fat and let your personal hygiene go to hell."

Meet a friend out of place in terms of space and time and it takes the brain a few beats to reshape the unexpected into the familiar. "Dewey?"

She made a face. "How many six-foot blondes you know? Now your memory's turned to mush. Just fucking sad!" She came striding up the dock, over the water, where I met her in a back-slapping bear hug. Picked her up, swung her around, gave her a brotherly kiss on the forehead. Stepped back to look into those good eyes, then hugged her again. Into my ear Dewey said, "Playtime's over, fat boy. Strap on your shoes. Coach Nye is back for the holidays. First we run, then we lift, then it's swim time."

"What the hell are you doing here?"

"We can talk while we run. Get your Nikes on."

"Can't. Not till I'm done working."

"Don't start with that stuff. You're always working."

"Give me an hour."

"Whine, whine, whine. Act your age!" She held my face between her hands and grinned at me. "Damn, it's good to see you, Ford!"

"And you, Dewey."

"The world just keeps getting crazier and faster and meaner, but you don't change. You and this rickety old fish palace of yours."

"You should have called. I could have picked you up at the airport."

"And ruin the surprise? Besides, I did call. Never got an answer, so I finally called the marina. Mack said you and

Tomlinson were off sailing someplace. That was what? October?''

''We sailed to Key West. I helped him get his boat in cruising shape. Tomlinson wanted to stick around for Fantasy Fest. That's a freak party; Halloween in Key Wasted. I caught a ride on a sports fisherman. A couple of buddies and I fished our way home.''

''And left Tomlinson.''

''Sure. His doctor said he was ready. He's getting better, I think. Slowly. Still a little weird. That lightning strike did more than just burn a scar into his temple. I expected him back last month. But the next day or two for sure.''

''The scar I haven't seen. But Tomlinson's always weird.''

''True . . . but not like this.''

''And you still don't have an answering machine.''

Nope, I didn't have an answering machine. No fax, no cellular phone, no beeper, no E-mail either. At the root of all technology is the human drive to triumph over isolation. Most people have a horror of being marooned. Sometimes I believe that I am not among them—a mild deception that has simplified my lifestyle. But lately, more and more of my clients were hinting that I was a little too isolated; that it was a little too hard to place orders, so the day would probably come when I would have one or two or all of the above.

Dewey was still talking: ''. . . I wasn't absolutely certain that my Captiva house was going to be open in December, so by that time I—''

''By that time, you decided to ignore the messages I left.''

''I know, I know. Dependable, punctual Ford.''

There was something wrong with that? If I was in the country, near a phone, I tried to call Dewey every Sunday night.

Dewey said, ''That's not the point. What I was telling you was, Bets did exhibition matches in Madrid and Lisbon, and I went along at the last minute. By then I figured, why not surprise him?''

"Ah," I said, picturing Dewey and Bets together. "Oh."

Dewey gave me an affectionate shake. "We're wasting time. I've got three whole weeks to do nothing but work out and lie in the sun. Then I'm off to Phoenix for the Amateur Classic." She was pulling me up the steps, toward the house; let me stop just long enough to fit the Styrofoam cover onto the tank. Said, "So the fun starts as of now. We run five, lift light, then we come back here and swim out to the island and back."

I said, "In the bay?" My house is built over the water on stilts. The lower level is all dock. The upper level is wooden platform. Two small cottages sit at the center under one tin roof. The platform extends out on all sides, creating a broad porch. Standing on the porch by the screen door, I could feel the first gusting chill of the coming nor'wester. I said, "An hour from now, the bay might be a little cold for swimming."

"Are you kidding? It's got to be, what? Eighty? Eighty-five degrees? Get your ass in gear, champ. Quit stalling. You're the one who told me whatever doesn't kill you makes you stronger."

She followed me into the cottage and futzed around with the stereo and shortwave radio while I changed. She chatted about her flight down. Told me a little bit about the crummy golf courses outside Lisbon. When I asked how Bets was doing, Dewey said, "Fine, fine. She's one busy lady," in a vague, evasive way that suggested that Bets wasn't fine and Dewey didn't want to discuss it. There was something on her mind; something she needed to talk about, and I wondered how long it would take for her to finally get around to it. There are false extroverts who use bluster to hide their shyness and sensitivity. Dewey is one of them. At the core, Dewey is an outsider: the gifted kid who never quite meshed with the crowd. She was different, was always different, and so the shy child within was never eroded away by conformity. The child hides in there, way down deep, and when you are a friend of the child—which is the only way you can be Dewey's friend—you can say any dumb thing you want, any egoless inanity, and the child never challenges or criticizes. But the acceptance must be reciprocal. And maybe that kind of acceptance is the core of all true friendship. When Dewey does let the screen drop, she is still funny. Still irreverent. But she is also without guile, and delicate, delicate. Now, for a moment, she let the screen drop. It was in her tone. "Doc?"

"Yeah?"

"It crossed my mind that it might be a tad awkward . . . hell, a lot awkward, if I breezed in here and you had a . . . you know, a houseguest. For Christmas. Someone staying with you."

"You mean a woman?"

"Sure, what else? Maybe it wouldn't have been such a good surprise."

"I don't know why not."

"I just thought that they, the woman, I mean, might get ticked off. You know, jealous."

I finished tying my running shoes and stepped out from behind the bed screen. "Why would a woman be jealous of you?" The words were out of my mouth before I realized what a stupid and cruel thing it was to say.

Some insist that the human eye cannot register emotion. Those who believe it have not met Dewey Nye. She was staring at me, a wry expression fixed in place to hide the wound. "Thanks, partner. You do wonders for my ego."

"I'm sorry. I didn't mean it that way."

"Bullshit. That's exactly what you meant."

No way out of it, so I said, "Besides, I don't have any women. Nothing sexual, anyway. Just a couple of friends around the island."

Dewey said, "No kidding?," still pinning me with her gaze. She knew it wasn't true. In our frequent phone conversations, I didn't leave much out.

I said, "Well, sometimes it's sexual. Sure. But nothing permanent. Occasionally I meet a tourist lady who seems interesting, who likes to talk about more than which brand of tanning oil is best. But they never stay for more than a day or two."

"But you'd like them to stay. That's the kind of house-guest I meant. The kind you'd like to stay longer?"

Even to Tomlinson I would have probably hedged, but Dewey's intuition is too good. You hedge, you lie, and her screens lock instantly into place. I braced myself against the west wall and began to stretch hamstrings and calves as I said, "Nope, I haven't met one yet who I wanted to stay longer. Not in a while, anyway."

Actually, it had been just short of a year.

Dewey's laughter was only slightly mocking. "Jesus Christ, I can see you're undecided."

"I like women—as people. As roommates, it's another story. Same with men."

"And you get so many offers. I noticed the line outside, all those girls with suitcases, waiting patiently."

"Go ahead and joke, but I'm trying to explain something. The way it is with women these days. They begin by saying they don't want a serious relationship. They always do. They say they're not interested in marriage. They always are. They say they have no desire to impose on my solitude or my work. Inevitably, they impose on both. They leave hair in the sink. They wear my T-shirts. They get pissy when I do the cooking. And they always, always end up asking to borrow my boat—if I'll just take a few minutes and teach them how to run it. Nope, two days is plenty. Three, tops." I finished stretching and looked at her. "I sound cynical?"

"You sound like a prissy old jerk."

"Yeah, well . . . this place is too small for two people. On a full-time basis, I mean. Besides, I like my routine. My work keeps me busy enough. It may be contrary to all acceptable social behavior, but I like living alone."

She still wore the bemused smile. "So let me summarize: No woman wants you, no woman will have you. You're lonely as hell, horny as a goat, and as full of shit as ever."

I grabbed her and wrestled her around until we stood face-to-face. "If you're asking to borrow my boat, the answer's no."

Dewey held me with her eyes, still amused, but then the

intensity and focus seemed to change. Suddenly she hugged me hard, then pushed me toward the door. "You men," she said, nudging me along, "you bastards. It's always the same: First you steal our hearts, then you destroy our dreams."

A workout with Dewey is not a social occasion. When she runs she runs much too fast for conversation. For a guy of my size and of my construction, anyway. The lungs and capillaries of a 220-pound adult male can only distribute so much oxygen. Same when she lifts weights. God help the person who interrupts her concentration with idle chatter. Prior to her flying off to New York to live with Bets, Dewey had been my regular training partner. I dreaded those workouts because of her drill sergeant mentality, but also loved them because we pushed each other to the very edge each and every day . . . and that is the only way to return to the lighter-than-gravity, animal-quick, skin-ribs-and-muscle creature that lies within each and every one of us at the outer boundaries of personal fitness.

Dewey had stripped down to orange Spandex running shorts and matching Spandex running bra. With her blue visor cap turned backwards, blond hair swinging, she might have been modeling high-tech running gear. As we jogged along the shell lane that leads from Dinkin's Bay Marina to Sanibel's main road, I said, "I'll try to keep track of how many cars honk at us. What's the old record—seven?"

"Those bastards, I hate it when cars honk. Geeze-oh-Katy, it makes me jump every time."

Geeze-oh-Katy—a new expression she was using. Sounded girlish and homey. I said, "So try wearing a baggy T-shirt and shorts."

"It'll be a snowy day in hell before I start dressing to please assholes in passing cars." She glanced over at me. "You don't like the way I dress? What's wrong with the way I dress?"

I said, "You look great. You always look great, Dewey."

She was nodding, not buying it. "Flattery. What you'd better do is save your breath. You'll need it."

The hour or more of hell I was about to endure required some psychological preparation. I tried my best. . . . Felt the ache of old wounds and the familiar grating pain of damaged knees . . . and reminded myself that the pain would soon fade into numbness. Felt the thoracic burn that forewarns oxygen debt . . . and comforted myself with the knowledge that the human body can abide a hell of a lot more discomfort than the brain's little warning mechanisms would have us believe. Also reminded myself that this was Friday. Every Friday, all the marina regulars get together after work for a traditional weekend party. By the time Dewey and I finished our workout, Mack would have food out on platters beneath the sea grape tree and Igloo coolers packed tight with crushed ice and bottles of beer. It was a nice thing to imagine, a tough workout then all that ice and beer.

When we reached the bike path that traces the interior of Sanibel, Dewey turned toward Captiva Island and lengthened her stride, running what, for her, was a comfortable six-minute-thirty-second-mile pace. She had a floating kind of stride. I huffed and puffed and thudded along beside. The wind had freshened—a chilled and gusting high-pressure wind—and we ran right into the teeth of it. It was like trying to run through cotton. Chilly or not, I was sweating before we finished the first mile.

"How you feeling?"

Her question surprised me. I had allowed consciousness to blur; was concentrating solely on putting one foot in front of the other. "Good," I gasped. "Pretty good."

"Bullshit. I own golf balls with better color."

"Nope. Feel fine."

"You always say that. And you're always lying."

After that, we ran in silence. Ran Captiva Road way past the elementary school, then cut inland through Ding Darling Sanctuary: a shell road that tunneled through mangroves and wove its way between brackish lakes. The mangroves were hunched up on their prop-root toes, showing the wind. Water in the lakes was the color of strong sassafras tea. White wading birds flushed before us. A bull gator lay wide-bodied on the mud, mouth open, soaking in the last of the fading heat. Biologists once believed that gators and crocs used their open mouths as a sort of thermostat, perhaps to facilitate digestion. Now they're not so sure. Where the shell road curved beneath the wind there were dense pockets of musk . . . iodine, ozone, and sulfur—the smell of primal life: the smell of backcountry Florida. When I crossed to the lee side of Dewey, hers was a more delicate odor but similarly primal: shampoo, miracle fabric, the acidic smell of woman-sweat.

"You get tired, want to stop, just tell me."

It wasn't easy for me to find oxygen enough to form words. "In all the times . . . we've run together . . . you've never asked how I felt . . . or told me it was okay to stop."

She glanced over her shoulder at me. "So? I'm a year older. Maybe I'm a year nicer."

I was shaking my head. "Um-huh. There's something on your mind. You want to talk, let's talk."

"You always think you know so much. A guy your age, I'm just trying to be careful, that's all. Save the paramedics a trip. They've got better things to do."

"I don't need any favors. I feel fine." I did, too. Well . . . I felt *fair*. I'd spent the last couple of months getting into pretty good shape. Running, swimming, a hundred pull-ups a day. No food after 8 p.m., beer only on the weekend.

"It's just that I don't want you to blow a rod. Or have a stroke."

Chuckling, I grabbed her elbow and pulled her to a stop. She looked at me; looked away. I touched my finger to her chin and turned her face, forcing eye contact. Her cheeks were flushed the color of strawberries. Ringlets of blond hair, saturated with sweat, were now a tumid brown. "What's the problem, Dewey?"

"Problem? I don't know what you're talking about. There's no problem."

"You sure?"

"Look, I just told you. . . . Hey, buddy, I just traveled thirteen hundred miles to give you one of the all-time great Christmas surprises, and you're already badgering me." There was a warning tone to her voice—she was kidding, but I'd better watch my step.

Protocol said I should let it go. But there was something in her demeanor . . . a curiously intense reserve that made me want to push it. She reminded me of some troubled adolescent who, driven by self-consciousness, was fronting stratagems to deflect entrance into her private, unhappy world.

I tapped her chin to emphasize my concern. "Let's have it. You come in here full of bluster, determined to make me believe that you're happy as hell, not a care in the world. But you've got raccoon eyes, and you don't get jet lag flying from New York to Florida. Plus your voice is a little shaky and your attention keeps wandering, and you're trying way, way too hard to imitate the Old Dewey. There's something troubling you and you want to talk about it, but maybe you figure the time's not right . . . or maybe we're not the buddies we both pretend to be . . . or maybe you just don't have the courage."

I was looking into her gray eyes and I watched them gauge her deep softness, her pain, and then saw them glow with anger. She slapped my hand away from her chin and turned her back to me. "Knock it off. Sometimes, Doc, you push a little too hard. It's not funny and I don't appreciate it so . . . yeah, maybe you're not the friend I thought you were."

I said, "Then let's finish our run and we can both go our separate ways. We'll each have our own very merry Christmas."

She swung around, fists on hips. "What the hell's with you? Being articulate doesn't give you license to act like a pious dick! All I want to do is run! Just fucking run and you're turning it into some kind of shrink session. Do I pry into your private life?"

"Yeah. All the time. You're one of the very few people I discuss my private life with."

"As if you've told me everything. Don't give me that crap, buster!"

"Never said I did."

She was folded over, stretching her hamstrings, letting me know I was wasting her time; standing there talking, muscles getting tight when we should be running. "Gee, tell me everything, Doc. Make my life complete."

"No need. You're already so happy, why risk being honest?"

"To say that to me . . . it's just so damn offensive—"

"Honesty is offensive?"

She was standing upright again, fists clenched. "Quit it! I'm serious—stop it right now! Nobody pries into my private life. You hear me? Nobody!"

Because she shouted the last of it, the silence that followed resonated. Wind in mangroves made a riverine sound like a distant reach of white water. High aloft, an osprey drifted, whistling frantic, ascending notes. Looking into her face, I waited several beats before saying, "Then run, Dewey. Just keep on running. Sorry I tried to interfere." I turned and jogged away; left her standing. Had run several hundred yards and was beginning to wonder if I had levered too hard; was already condemning myself for being unnecessarily pointed when I heard her deer-light stride behind me, getting closer, coming fast . . . entertained the unpleasant possibility that she might slug me in the back of the head as she ran past. I'd never seen Dewey so mad.

But instead I felt her grab my elbow and I let her swing me around. "Goddamn you!" she said. "Goddamn it . . . what right do you have to speak to me that way?" She was crying. It was the first time that I had ever seen jock-hard, tour-tested Dewey Nye cry. "I don't need to be interrogated and I don't need that kind of cruelty. I don't need that in my life right now!"

I made an effort to say something sharp and clever in reply . . . but found myself taking her into my arms, holding her, feeling her ribs spasm beneath my fingers, feeling her face hot and wet against my cheek as she sobbed, squeezing her tightly to me as if that were the way to both protect her and to apologize.

"I was a jerk," I whispered. "It's the new me. Lately . . . more and more . . . I've been acting like a jerk."

"No, you were a prick. There's a difference."

"It's been a rough year."

Dewey was nodding, her chin hard on my shoulder. "I'm so sorry about what happened, Doc. Losing that girl. How many nights did we talk and you hardly mentioned it? But I could tell. "

Holding Dewey, I suffered a brief cerebral replay of once holding a woman of the same comfortable size and shape, but who had Navaho hair and Cracker sensibilities. I would never hold that woman again. I whispered, "Old news. Water under the bridge."

"It really gets to be like that? The hurt goes away?"

"If you need to know . . . maybe there's a reason."

"There is."

"Someone died?"

"Not that bad."

Anticipating what had happened, I cupped my hand to the back of her head and patted softly. "Maybe worse, huh? In ways, probably worse. I'm sorry."

Dewey pushed herself away from me, wiping her face. "I lied to you. I didn't come down here just for something to do over Christmas."

"No kidding?" I said dryly. "You were so convincing.

So . . . are we going to run, or are we going to talk?''

She managed a smile before jogging off—but now at a much slower pace. "What an asshole," she said. "We'll do both."

What happened was, Dewey hadn't flown to Spain with her lover, Bets Bzantovski. She'd flown over on the red-eye a couple of days later as a last-minute birthday gift to Bets. Dewey had charmed the desk clerk at Madrid's Hotel Barcelona out of a key to Bets's room and carried her own luggage up. Her arrival was a surprise and Dewey didn't want a bellboy around when she flicked on the lights and saw Bets's face.

But the surprise was on Dewey. She opened the door to hear muffled laughter, then an eerie silence. Then she hit the lights . . . and there was Bets, naked, in bed with a woman named Elaine Wengo, one of the young French stars on the circuit. The next part was harder for me to picture because I know Bets and like her very much. "I just stood there like a dope," Dewey said. "It was like one of those god-awful nightmares where something's chasing you but you can't make your legs move. I had a big duffel bag in my hand and I didn't even put it down, and the whole time she's screaming at me to get the hell out, that she hadn't invited me, and what right did I have to walk in on her like that."

"Bets was screaming at you?"

"Who do you think I'm talking about—"

"Well, the French girl—"

"No, I'm telling you. Bets was saying that stuff to me. I'd flown all that way, changed my whole schedule, and she's treating me like some stranger, some uninvited guest. Like she *hated* me . . ."

I pictured Bets: a string-bean woman with muscles; long arms and longer legs; brown hair cropped short and brushed back; lean, European face with dark eyes that lived beneath heavy brows; eyes that knew a lot, that had seen a lot. Bets's face was familiar to anyone who subscribed to sports magazines. Bets was the one with the controversial lifestyle; the one who once told a reporter: "Your average reader and I probably have a lot in common. We both love beautiful women." Bets was the one who had become the darling of the news magazines because, as a Romanian, she had taken a hiatus from tennis to fight as a rebel leader against Ceausescu and the Securitate, his brutal secret police. I knew from friends, people in the intelligence community, that she had been implicated in the assassination of at least three of Ceausescu's people. Used her celebrity to open doors, then popped them. It was not public information. Bets did not know that I knew.

I told Dewey, "I'm surprised she behaved that way. She's an extraordinary woman."

Dewey said, "Yeah, well . . . Bets can also be an extraordinary bitch."

The story didn't come pouring out. It wasn't easy for Dewey. She kept approaching the subject, then dodging away. I plodded along and listened, pretending to look at the scenery. There were pepper bushes and webs of Spanish moss on oaks and stilt-legged egrets high-stepping along the ditches as tourist traffic filed by . . . rental cars and midwestern license plates as pale as the winters they'd left behind; visitors viewing the tropics through windshields, as removed from the biota as if they were peering through television screens.

I didn't say much. Friends aren't supposed to press friends for details, nor do friends leave friends waiting for answers. Both of us were chastened by our obligations. A further complication was that Dewey had never spoken openly to me about her homosexuality. We had a strange friendship. There were things I could not talk about and things she would not talk about, but everything else was on the table. Bets was always referred to as "my roommate" or "my housemate," as if their relationship was based on economic considerations. That I knew and understood was implicit—just as it was also understood that I must never, ever approach the subject openly.

But now, that's just what Dewey had to do.

"You're in love with Bets?" I asked.

We were back on the shell road that led to Dinkin's Bay. It was nearly dark and a high wind sailed scudding clouds across a plum-colored sky. In a very small voice, she said, "I guess so . . . hell, I don't know. Are you surprised? I mean, that it's that way between Bets and me."

Apparently, it was easier for her to pretend that I didn't know—as if that were the only reason she had never discussed it before.

"I knew that you two were close," I said.

"You think any less of me now that I've told you? It seems so . . . weird."

"Offended, you mean? Outraged? Not likely."

"If it bothers you, I'd understand."

Nope, it didn't bother me. The biological truth is that homosexual behavior is almost certainly genetically mandated.

I said, "Why? Does it seem weird to you?"

She shrugged. "At first it did . . . then it didn't seem weird at all. Like the most natural thing in the world. I'd tried it with men"—she paused to look at me—"but it never seemed to work out."

I already knew that because Dewey and I had once tried. It was sweet and tender but utterly without passion. Rather than feeling closer to her, I'd finished feeling as if we'd been distanced and, worse, as if our friendship had been jeopardized.

"So you caught Bets screwing around. You're not the first couple to have to weather an affair. Maybe she was lonesome. Maybe she was drunk. Maybe she just had to get it out of her system. But one thing we both know is that Bets is a good person and has a hell of a lot of character. So, when we get back to the house, you call her on the phone and start sorting it out. Madrid? It's about midnight there, I think."

Dewey said, "No. Nope, we're done. What happened hurts like hell; catching them like that, but we were done before I ever flew to Spain. Before Bets left, we spent the whole time fighting."

"About wanting to see other people?"

She hemmed and hawed and avoided the subject. Dewey is one of the private ones. Talking too much about herself makes her uncomfortable. She needed a break; no more pushing.

It was later, when we were back at my stilthouse that she told me, no, what she and Bets had been fighting about was me.

We had showered and changed. Because Dewey said she wasn't in a party mood, we decided not to go to the marina. How long had it been since I'd missed a Friday night with the fishing guides? I made a light dinner: grilled snapper with mango chutney and salad. We did the dishes exchanging the kind of polite conversation that is really silence. Finally, as I was putting the last dish away, she said, "Are you still in the mood to listen? There're a couple of things I left out."

I told her, "No kidding," then listened to her tell me that, for some reason, it would be a lot easier to talk about if she didn't have to look at me. I suggested we sit out on the deck, lights off, and look at the winter sky. Dewey said no, what she wouldn't mind doing was maybe lie on the bed, her face in a pillow, with only the reading light on. Then she added, "And you might as well rub my back while I'm down there," giving it a tone of indifference—why not do two jobs at once? "I pulled a latissimus the other day when I was lifting. My whole back feels out of whack."

I thought: Why does she want to try this again? Then I thought: Because she's trying to rebound from Bets.

But I did what she said. She was trying to orchestrate so carefully that it seemed needlessly cruel not to go along with it. Sometimes I try hard to believe my own lies. . . .

So I switched the reading light on, switched the other lights off. Heard her fiddling with the stereo and then heard Marianne Faithfull come on, soft, haunting, ephemeral—one of Tomlinson's albums from his flower child days. Then came around the clothes locker into shadows to see Dewey lying there in nothing but her heavy bra and bikini panties. Anticipating me, she was up on one elbow, face looking soft and serious. Before I could speak, she said, "Just shut the hell up and let me get this out of my system. All I want you to do is work on my back."

I said, "Your call."

She buried her face in the pillow and said, "Don't say a word."

"If that's what you want."

" 'Cause what I need to do is, I'm going to pretend like you're not here. . . ."

Sitting on the bed, hip-to-hip; Dewey sprawled belly-down, talking softly about this and that, nothing serious, until she said: "I guess this thing with Bets's been on my mind. So, yeah, maybe I need to talk with somebody about it. Lucky you, huh?"

Long silence.

Then: "What'd you ask me—am I in love with Bets? I answered you, but I didn't answer you. Bets told me for nearly a year—'I love you, Dewey'—before I could even make myself say the words."

I waited through another long pause. Heard, "So . . . I finally said them and . . . Christ, it was like *freedom*. Like I could finally admit, yeah, this is what I am. All the time I spent worrying—hey, why'm I the only one who doesn't fit in? God . . . and the guilt. Gone, just like that. 'I love you, Bets.' Said those words and it was the greatest feeling. Like letting go. You know?"

No, I didn't know. But I didn't say it. Kept working on her back, using my thumbs to knead the lean muscle cordage beneath soft skin. I wanted to tell her something Tomlinson had once said: Guilt is the curse of those who care. It wasn't often, but the man's unrestrained spiritualism sometimes made sense even to me. But this was her time to talk . . . and it was sounding more and more like a catharsis. . . .

"So I moved in with Bets. It wasn't just because I wanted a roommate, like I told you. All I wanted to do was be with her. Be with Bets. Man—we laughed so much together. Something else, first time in my life, I enjoyed . . . sex. First time anyone ever touched me that I wasn't tense or worried or felt like I had to fake it. You know Bets—those long fingers of hers?—but they're soft, too. The way she uses them. And kissing—"

I felt Dewey's body shudder beneath me.

Could feel my own pulse as I listened to her say, "The kissing was so nice. You know that feeling? You're kissing someone so lost in it all, like you're breathing for each other. Then we'd giggle like little girls." She said, "Whatever happens, I've got Bets to thank for that," as she pushed herself up on an elbow, fished around beneath her . . . heard the sound of contracting elastic . . . and she slipped her bra off. Got a brief look at the pendulous weight of her left breast as she turned to toss the bra on the floor. "You mind? This thing's choking me plus it's getting in your way."

I cleared my throat; looked at her clothes in a pile by my feet. Stood and folded them neatly over my telescope, more to put some distance between us than anything. My body was reacting to her story in a way that I could not control. I needed a break.

Heard Dewey say, "Get back here, Ford." Heard her say, "Hey—while you're up? You got any oil? Body lotion, I mean?"

I did. Knew I shouldn't get it . . . but I found it in the medicine locker anyway. Then, when I was settled, pouring oil on her back, she said, "Now . . . where were we?"

• • •

I kept telling myself that I was listening with the careful ear of an objective observer . . . but, more likely, I was forcing an interest to keep my mind off what my hands were doing; off what my hands wanted to do. This was a Dewey that I'd never met and didn't know: the secret Dewey giving me a tour of her secret world.

"They're mostly nice people," she said, "just like anybody else. Not kinky or weird; not perverts. Just women living their lives. Our friends were mostly jocks—it's what we call each other. 'She's a dike.' Or 'she's a jock.' There's a difference, understand. Doesn't mean she has to play sports—it's a *look*—but she probably plays sports.

"I was always what they considered a jock, but then that started to change. It's what I'm telling you about; the trouble between Bets and me. See, the third type's a 'lipstick': a girl who's pretty and feminine. A lipstick is gay, but she can probably go both ways and enjoy it." She hesitated a moment before she said, "I ever strike you as feminine?"

"Of course."

"Well, Bets really got mad when I started *thinking* that way. Before she and I became lovers, she wanted me to be absolutely certain how I felt. I give her credit, she did her best to help me find out." I felt Dewey's hand slide back, feel around, and finally find my thigh. Gave me a gentle pat. "That time you and I tried to sleep together? Bets knew about it. In fact—and this is something I never told you—it was mostly her idea."

She didn't have to tell me because I already knew.

Now I was more aware of what Dewey's hand was doing than of what my hands were doing . . . her fingers exploring around on my thigh . . . stopping here, pressing there . . . maybe searching for something.

"Don't get a big head."

That startled me. I said, "Huh?"

Her voice had gotten softer, sleepier. "Because I said you're the man I was thinking about. Let's face it, Ford—you're not what anybody would call handsome. Kind of interesting-looking, yeah. Big and solid and safe-looking. And maybe that's it. You're a nice guy."

I thought: You don't *know*. . . .

She said, "Some of those guys used to come sniffing around our group were such jerks. Know what this one said to Bets? This dude—he's a little drunk; got the jive attitude—he comes swaggering up and he says, 'Ma' lady, the only reason you're the way you is 'cause you never been with a real man.' I mean, Bets, all of us, just cracked up laughing. Four or five of us standing there, laughing in this idiot's face. Didn't even have a clue what we were all about."

"Apparently not," I said.

"So that's what happened. I finally told Bets: 'Hey, I think I'm a lipstick.' Some of the other girls had already been saying it—they can pretty much always tell. Even if a woman doesn't realize it herself. Like we're on the street and they see some woman, has a couple of kids, hubby there guiding her around. They make eye contact with the woman, nothing more, and we walk away and one of our group would say, 'She's a jock, doesn't even know it.' Or 'She's borderline lipstick, probably never even tried.' They know. They really do."

"And now you want to find out if they're right."

"Yeah, but another thing was . . . pretty much the main thing, really"—Dewey removed her hand from my thigh, getting serious—"I told Bets something that really pissed her off."

I said, "Oh?"

"I told her that I was thinking about kids. That I was thinking about having a child, I mean."

I almost stopped rubbing her back but caught myself.

"I told Bets that I'd thought about it and it was something I wanted to do."

"I can see why that would surprise her."

"Because I'm gay, you mean? No, that's not the way it is. A lot of gay women have the urge, but I think it was the combination of the two: I'm feeling attracted to men and women, *and* I want to have a baby." Felt Dewey's hand return to my thigh, feeling around as she settled herself on the bed; heard her say, "No, there was a third thing, too. When Bets told me she had to go to Madrid, I told her then maybe I'd fly down to Florida and see you."

I felt her hand slide up higher on my thigh; felt her fingers fumbling with my zipper. "We had a big fight about that one. But after she left I started to feel guilty, so I decided to fly to Madrid and apologize. After that, I wasn't in the mood to apologize anymore."

Heard my zipper open—the sound of silk tearing—felt her fingers patting around, not finding anything.

Heard her say, "Oops, wrong side," then laughter. Told myself I should pull her hand away as she said, "My oh my, you really *are* a right-hander."

Which is when the phone rang.

Tomlinson calling from Havana . . .

The way Tomlinson's voice faded in and out, it was as if my house, elevated on stilts off Sanibel Island, was connected to Havana by a piece of string that was being battered by a Gulf Stream squall. On a crow-flies course, the only landfall between Sanibel and Cuba is Key West. Couple of hundred miles of water stood between us; all that dark ocean out there . . . Tomlinson's voice straining to get across it.

"This is serious, Doc. I shit you not. They took my damn boat!"

Talking about the Cuban military.

"You've got to get down here with some money. Cash. They won't take credit cards, they won't take checks, and my good character wouldn't get me a cup of their damn sugar on loan. I'm talking about *No Más!*"

No Más, his 35-Morgan sailboat. It's one of the curious things about water-people: Sailors love their boats—or pretend to; power-cruisers almost always hate their boats—but pretend as if they don't.

Tomlinson said, "When I got here, I had close to two grand stashed away. You know where I kept it—in that little hidey hole forward the bilge? I was damn lucky to get it out before the bulls took my boat."

Dewey was up off the bed now, giving me her "You-were-a-jerk-to-answer-the-phone" look; a little brazen, a little shy. She'd seemed comfortable touching me; comfortable with my hands on her. Not tense, not working at it too hard . . . not at all like the first time we'd tried.

Tomlinson said, "So now I'm down to five hundred bucks or so 'cause they're charging us on a day-to-day basis. You know what they're hoping—"

Yes, I knew what they were hoping. 'They' was the *Guardia Frontera,* the harbor-tasked body of the island's largest governmental agency—MINFAR, which stood for Ministry of the Revolutionary Armed Forces. Largest and also the most corrupt branch of a very, very corrupt government. All under the control of Raul Castro, Fidel's younger jockey-sized brother.

I said, "They want you to spend every cent you have so you have to abandon your boat. Put you on some government flight out."

"Exactly! That's just what I've been thinking." The flavor of panic was beginning to fade from Tomlinson's voice; he was sounding more and more like the old laid-back hipster and sociology guru that he had once been. "So how long before you get here, Doc?"

There was something I had to communicate to him, but I couldn't come right out and say it. I knew from newspaper reports, and also friends who are paid to know, that the Cuban government had gotten sloppy and desperate and meaner than ever, but there were probably still a few good people around doing their jobs, manning the Lourdes eavesdropping systems that the Soviets had left behind.

The call probably was being monitored.

I said, "Look, buddy, how's an American go about getting into Cuba?" Gave it a hick-hard inflection. Said, "It's illegal, right? I mean it's not like I've been there before."

Tomlinson said, "Huh?"

I watched Dewey cross to the telescope; watched her stretch the bra around, sliding the cups down over her breasts, then snapped it tight as I said, "What am I supposed to do, call my travel agent? Or maybe run down there by boat? But I do that, hell, they'd probably just take my boat, too."

I was rewarded with Tomlinson's guarded tone—he understood. "Yeah . . . well, I was thinking maybe you could take a plane. Fly in here. I've heard they've got flights from Nassau and Mexico City. Americans fly in, the Cubans don't ask any questions, give them a temporary visa right at the airport. They need the tourist money."

"That's why you sailed there? As a tourist?" Changing the subject, like I wanted a little time to think about it.

"Hell, no. Why do you think they took my damn boat?"

"That's what I'm asking," I said. "I get there, carrying all that money, what makes you think they won't try to keep me, too?"

Tomlinson said, what had happened was, he'd met a woman in Key West, the night of Fantasy Fest, and she'd talked him into taking her on an extended cruise.

"Julia DeGlorio," Tomlinson told me. "That's her name. I'd let you talk to her but she's up in the room right now. Very handsome woman; Cuban-American. Her family came over January second, 1959, and she was born nine, ten years later. In New Jersey. That was the day after Fidel came to power. January second, I mean."

I was thinking: Julia DeGlorio—a feminized Spanish version of July of Glory. It was in July 1953 that Fidel Castro and his followers made their failed attack on the Moncada Garrison in Santiago de Cuba, thus beginning the revolution. A very important month in Cuban history and a very, very strange name for the daughter of Cuban exiles.

Into the phone I said, "Nineteen fifty-nine? No kidding. It's really been that long?"

"Fidel, you mean? Yeah. . . ." Said it like: "Who *else?*" Then he said, "So Julia's in her twenties. Pretty little young thing. The way I met her, I was sitting at a table at Louie's Backyard—I'm talking about Key West now—and I was talking to a bunch of people. Not the freaks like I was hanging out with but Key West straights. Sitting there thinking, 'How the hell did I end up with these people?' as I was telling them about myself. What my life was about, some of the places I'd. . . ." Tomlinson's voice faded, became garbled. Then I heard him say, "You remember Jimmy Gardenas?"

"Jimmy? Sure—"

"Top Key West guide; an old buddy of yours. Now he runs Saltwater Anglers, the fly shop? Jimmy's there and he tells me, 'Tomlinson, you're too drunk to deal with human beings. You're going to wear yourself out trying. Go back to Duval Street. Better yet, go back to the boat. The strain's beginning to show.' "

"That sounds like Jimmy."

"Um-huh; pretty good advice. I mean I had seriously over-served myself. Rum and some really first-rate Jamaican Blue."

Drugs. Tomlinson was doing drugs again, not even attempting to pretend he wasn't. I could hear his doctor telling me, "Sometimes they regress; go back to the way they were when they were kids. Or teenagers. Sometimes they have to revisit what they were to re-establish who they are."

Into the phone, I said, "Really drunk, yeah. I'm with you," as Dewey, in bra and panties, caught my attention and mouthed the question, *Tomlinson?*

I nodded, covered the receiver, said: "He's in trouble."

Watched her expression change, becoming serious, and she began to dress, listening to me talk—playtime over.

Tomlinson said, "So there's this woman at the table and she leads me out. It's Julia. Says she was getting tired of that group, too, but she loved what I'd been saying."

I asked, "What was it you were saying?"

"How the hell am I supposed to remember, man? I was screwed-up; doing some serious vision-seeking. I remember telling them a bit of my life history . . . you know, most of the high points. Dual doctorate, divinity and sociology. My mail says The Reverend Sighurdhr Tomlinson for a reason, right? Asked if anyone at the table needed any spiritual guidance. That much I remember. Then the nuts 'n bolts stuff like being struck by lightning and raised from the dead. That the doctors wanted the respirator off, so God had to take things into His own hands. Waited for the third day and—ZAP!—turned on the juice. Nothing outrageous—not like I was knocking over chairs and offending people. I pretty much gave them the straight scoop: that I am an alien being who is in spiritual contact with distant galaxies, and that I was sent to earth on a mission I have yet to understand."

"You told the girl that?"

"Julia and the others at the table, yeah. What? You want me to lie?"

"No . . . no, I certainly wouldn't want you to lie. You mention anything about cutting cane in Cuba?"

"Goddamn, Doc, who cares? I'm talking about my boat."

"Or your support for the revolution? There's a reason I'm curious—"

Tomlinson said, "Christ, arguing with you is like arguing with the multiplication table."

"I'm trying to figure out how you ended up in Cuba, that's all."

Heard a groan of exasperation. "Good grass and cheap rum, that's how. Times I've been in Key West, almost everything I ever did, the story always starts the same. . . ."

The way Tomlinson got to Cuba was that Julia DeGlorio had moved aboard his boat and talked him into sailing for Cay Sal, a cluster of uninhabited islands about eighty miles east-southeast of Hawks Channel marker, and only about thirty miles off the northern shore of Cuba. She wanted to go to Cay Sal, Tomlinson said, because she had heard that no one else went there.

"Julia was sure right about that," he added.

Controlled by the Bahamian government, Cay Sal is a cluster of sandbanks with a lone shack built for the customs official who kept a watch on the islands and who, upon their arrival, refused to allow Tomlinson and his girl to land. "I asked him if it was because I was an American," Tomlinson told me, "and he said, 'No, mon, it 'cause you a damn hippie!' The man didn't even know me and he's passing judgment. Jeesh! And it wasn't like I was holding any drugs. All used up by then, I'm sorry to say."

So they had spent a week gunkholing around the islands—lots of drinking, lots of nude sunbathing—before setting sail back to Key West. "That's when the trouble started," Tomlinson said. "We left Cay Sal Bank about dusk. By then I knew Julia well enough to trust her to stand watch. Understand, we'd spent a couple weeks bumming around the Keys, then a couple more weeks on the boat before we headed for Cay Sal. The woman knew her way around *No Más* and I felt comfortable leaving her at the wheel.

"So that evening I got us into deep water and set the autovane for 305 degrees—Key West, right? Then I went below to get some sleep because I was going to stand the twelve-to-two and the dog watch. Julia was going to handle it until midnight. Next thing I know, I wake up and my boat's dolphining in what feels like heavy sea and we're luffing. A norther's blown up and I go topside to find we're in some serious shit. Waves are crashing over a reef directly astern and there's a gunboat off our bow with people shouting at us in Spanish. It's pitch dark, near midnight, and I have the hangover from hell, but I'm still alert enough to realize that we have suffered a terrible navigational error. We're in fucking Cuba, man.

"The gunboat takes us in tow—gad! What a nightmare that was!—and they haul us into Havana Harbor where these Cuban bulls search my boat, steal some of my best equipment, then try to shake me down for a five-thousand-dollar towing fee. I don't have it. Hell, I'd just barely had time to get into my hidey-hole and sneak the two grand into my shorts. They search my boat again, then move us downtown to a hotel where they're charging me two hundred bucks a night for a room against the worth of my boat. That's why we're thinking about moving up the street to the Havana Libre. A little cheaper hotel—if they'll let us."

"Did you offer them a bribe?"

"Sure. Told them I had a couple hundred bucks they could have if they'd turn me loose, forget the whole thing. This Comandante guy—the crew chief; whatever he was—he tells me, yeah, it's a deal. Only he can't let me go until tomorrow. Like *mañana*. Everything's *mañana* down here. So I slip him the dough and that's the last we've seen of the *comandante*."

I had to keep reminding myself that the authorities might be listening. "Geeze," I said, "like some kind of deal out of the movies. So they question you or anything? Or did they believe your story right off?"

"Took me in a room and slapped me in the face a couple times—"

I winced, hearing that. Tomlinson's brain had been banged around too much already.

"—asked me if I knew anything about Alpha Sixty-Six or maybe Brothers to the Rescue. Like I was some kind of Cuban-American spook come back to help overthrow Fidel. You know, one of those right-wing Miami groups? I told them, talk to Fidel. Maybe he'd remember meeting me and my comrades back in seventy-one. Came down here in a gesture of solidarity; shook the man's hand and had our pictures taken. Huey Newton, man! He was there. Now they're treating me like some kind of bourgeois stiff. I say, 'Ask Fidel,' and it really gets a big laugh. I'm telling you, Doc—the old days, they're gone forever!"

I thought: Goodbye, good riddance. "And you with a hangover," I said.

"The hangover from Planet Zoltare."

"Drinking that heavy before sailing the Florida Straits. You should have known better."

The groan again. "I'm really not in any mood for lectures right now. You hear what I'm saying? They're taking my money, they've taken my boat, so this little excursion, frankly, is beginning to lose its vacation feel. Besides, I didn't drink that much. Just a couple of beers. Six-pack maybe? So maybe it was food poisoning. Like some bad guacamole." Tomlinson paused, then sounded as serious as he can sound: "You want me to ask for it? I will. I need help, Doc. I need you to get down here with some money and spring me. That's what I'm asking."

I wanted to explain why I was so reluctant; why it would be so dangerous for me to return to Havana. Instead, I said, "Isn't there an American Embassy or something there? I could wire you the money."

"No embassy, just an American Interest Section. I already checked. A couple of people who work out of the Swiss Embassy; acted like they could care less. Said I ought to be arrested, an American breaking the law by coming to Cuba."

I had attended a reception once at the Swiss Embassy, out east of Havana near Miramar; could picture it: big colonial house with wrought-iron gates, banyan trees dropping red berries on the shaded sidewalks; part of Embassy Row.

I said, "I'll get the money to you, Tomlinson."

"When? When can you get here?"

Today was Friday. I did so little banking I wasn't certain if banks were open or not on Saturday. I said, "Soon as I can. Friday next week at the latest."

"Shit! That long?"

"I'll do my best—but I want you to answer this: Does the girl know where you keep your money?"

"Julia? Sure. We're staying in the same room. Not that she's around much. Every day she disappears, comes back late."

"Does she say where she goes?"

"Nope, and I'm not the type to press."

"Do me a favor and move your money. Don't tell her where."

"But why, man?"

I said, "Because I think it's the smart thing to do. Think back: Once you got to Cay Sal, did she begin to act strange; maybe a little distant?"

"Well . . . matter of fact, she did. Actually canceled bedroom privileges. Not that she'd given me bedroom privileges to begin with, man, but I had high hopes. I don't have to tell you that out there on the high seas, what a downer it is to have your crew tell you the nookie lamp is not gonna be lit. How'd you know?"

I repeated, "Move your money."

Tomlinson said, "Okay, okay—but you're not helping this damn paranoia I've been fighting." Then in a frailer voice, he said, "I mean it, Doc. I'm scared and I keep getting these absolutely killer headaches. Get down here 'cause I can't take much more."

I said, "I can tell."

Dewey said, "Did you hear what I said?"

I looked up and said, "Huh?"

She was sitting beside me on the armrest of the reading chair, arms folded, studying me. "For the last few minutes, it's like you were in a coma. Didn't hear a word I was saying."

"Yeah . . . well . . ."

"You want me to leave?"

I looked up again and said, "Huh?"

She put her hands on my shoulders, gave me a little shake and pressed her face nose-to-nose with mine: gray-blue eyes becoming huge. "What the hell's the problem? Tomlinson's in trouble, that's all you told me. What kind of trouble?"

I stood and went to the little ship's refrigerator; rummaged around until I found a beer. Popped it open and began to pace slowly around the room. Then I spent the next few minutes telling her what had happened, sorting it out in my own mind.

When I had finished, she said, "If he's that scared, why doesn't he leave his boat and fly home? What's the big deal?"

"It's his *boat*. The only home he's had for fifteen, maybe twenty years."

"But if he's that scared—"

"I know what you're saying. If Tomlinson were rational, yeah, maybe that's exactly what he'd do. Cut his losses.

But he's never been rational. And on the phone just now, he sounded . . . lost. Like some misguided teenager who's close to being out of control."

"You need to help him, Doc."

"I know. That's what I've been thinking about—how?"

"If it's the money you're worried about. I've made some pretty good investments—"

"No, I've got it. I'll have to wait until the bank opens."

"Why can't you send it down? Or have somebody take it for you?"

"We're not allowed to take or spend money there. Americans, I mean. We can go to Cuba—that's legal. But you have to go penniless and come back penniless. It's part of the embargo. Department of Treasury."

"You have any Canadian friends?"

"Yeah, but none who know how to deal with Tomlinson. If we pay the money and they still refuse to hand over his boat—that's a real possibility—then Tomlinson may well slip over the edge."

"It's got to be you, then."

"That's what I keep coming back to."

Dewey said, "So let's hop the next plane to Havana," giving it a let's-turn-it-into-an-adventure inflection. "My calendar's open, buddy."

"If I go, I'm going alone."

"Bullshit. My life's in what you'd call a transitional period. A little adventure is just what I need."

"No way, Dewey. You're very good at what you do, but going down there, carrying money to a place like that, it's serious. You don't know anything about it."

"You do? The hermit biologist talking. Like you're an expert."

I let it pass; said nothing.

She said, "What you're forgetting is that Tomlinson's a friend of mine, too. You book a seat, I'll book a seat on the same flight. I don't need your permission."

What I wanted to tell her I couldn't tell her. So I said, "I'm going to bed. I need to think about it."

5

By most definitions it was a nightmare, but to me it was simply a sleeping revisitation of a thing I had done, a thing that I loathed—accurate in terms of its sounds, its terror—but it had been so long since I had suffered the dream that I awoke sweating, fighting the urge to cry out, desperate to fling a nonexistent weapon from my hand. . . .

Over too many nights past, before the dream began to fade with the weight of years, I'd learned to handle it more stoically.

Now it was two a.m. and I couldn't make my brain shut down.

I lay upon the foam-rubber mattress of the sleeper couch tossing and turning, aware that Dewey was just on the other side of the clothes locker, a few yards away, in my bed.

Tried to take my mind off the dream by replaying bits and pieces of our conversation, chastising myself for being so damn firm about it:

"You sleep there, Dewey, I'm sleeping here."

"What? There's something wrong with just holding each other?"

"There's more to it than that. Don't play games."

"I'm done playing games. That's what this is about."

"I know, I know, you're looking for a man to father your child. That's a lot to take for granted."

"Think back, buster. I never asked you."

"Fine. We can talk about it in the morning."

"Fine!"

Now I checked the phosphorescent numerals of my watch again. Only seven minutes since I'd last checked it . . .

Threw back the soft wool Navy blanket, pulled on a pair of running shorts, and tippy-toed out the door.

Blustery night with winter stars. Not quite cold enough for breath to condense, but cold enough to shock the skin and maybe help quiet my brain. I stood on the porch looking out across the bay. Watched mullet stir green arcs through the water; heard a night heron squawk. Listened to waves slap at the pilings of my house—a boat-hull sound without rhythm, without order.

Down shore, through the mangroves, the marina was still. I could see the bait tank illuminated by mercury lights . . . a wedge of yard with coconut palms . . . the broad window of the marina office and the silhouettes of boats. On the guardrails of one boat, Japanese lanterns were swinging in the wind. They painted the black harbor with yellow streaks. I could hear the fast metronome gonging of a halyard slapping against an aluminum mast. A hollow, hollow winter sound . . .

Something about the rhythm of that sound—the cadence of careful gunshots?—brought to my mind's eye the Kodalith vision of a person's head materializing through a rain forest gloom, the head becoming larger, more distinct, as I hunted quietly through the trees, moving nearer; my right hand raising, coming up into firing position when I was close enough . . . then of the head vanishing in a cloud of iridescent mist—

The damn dream again . . .

I had to get my mind on other things, so I forced my thoughts to consider Tomlinson and his situation.

Southward beyond the marina, beyond the high palms and rolling surf, lay Cuba. I wondered if Tomlinson was awake, standing out on the balcony of the Hotel Nacional, looking up at the same sky, the same stars, too worried to sleep.

I checked my watch again and reconsidered calling Jimmy Gardenas despite the hour. No . . . Even retired Key West fishing guides are the early-to-bed types.

I'd call Jimmy at his shop in the morning. Try to catch him first thing.

But I couldn't sleep. No way. So I stood there looking at the sky, thinking about what I would ask Jimmy.

There were elements of Tomlinson's story about Julia DeGlorio that troubled me. A twenty-something-year-old woman—good-looking, by Tomlinson's description—picks him up at a restaurant and talks him into taking her to Cay Sal. She, the daughter of Cuban exiles with a very, very unusual name.

Tomlinson has his charms; women love the man, there was no arguing that. Women of all sizes and ages and of varying sensibilities were drawn to him and trusted him—with good reason. Tomlinson exudes a kind of serene and nonjudgmental acceptance that women treasure. It is not an exaggeration to say that if Tomlinson said yes to all the women who wanted to mother him and coddle him and also share his bed, the man would never have to spend a night alone aboard his boat.

Still . . . this wasn't a normal Tomlinson. He had been drunk and drugged and ranting—again, by his own description. Also, this wasn't just any woman. She was Cuban-American; came, presumably, from the more strictly moraled society that the hyphenated prefix implies. Yet she convinced him—a stranger—to sail her to a bank of lonely uninhabited islands just off the Cuban coast?

It was an unlikely scenario. That's why it bothered me.

I could hear Tomlinson saying, "I had the hangover from Planet Zoltare."

Yes, he had regressed; had returned to some of his old destructive ways. But the man was a sailor in the same way that others are commercial pilots or physicians. He took his craft very seriously. Would he really allow himself to drink heavily before attempting a night crossing of the Florida Straits?

It is a quality of mine that is not attractive. There was a time in my life when I was suspicious by profession. Now I am suspicious by nature. When data does not fit comfortably into a likely chain of events, I reassemble the data into a worst-case scenario. It is my way of establishing the parameters of possibility.

Here was one possibility: The woman used all the means at her disposal to lure Tomlinson close to Cuba. Once in Cay Sal, she withdrew those favors, then drugged him so she could sail his boat into Cuban waters.

Could she have a reason for doing so? There were numerous plausible reasons. Was it possible that she did it? Yes, it was possible. But was it likely?

No.

In all probability, Julia DeGlorio was just one more casualty of the Florida Keys; a woman who'd gone to Key West looking for adventure and found, in Tomlinson, a man who happened to have a boat and was willing to take her along as crew.

But I wanted to call Jimmy; talk about it. There were other people I wanted to contact, too, and not just to discuss Julia DeGlorio. The way I saw it, there were only two ways to get Tomlinson out of Cuba. I could contact my local congressmen, contact the media, and make a political issue out of it, or I could go there myself and try to buy him out.

No getting around it—the second option was the most practical option.

If Tomlinson's predicament was approached through public channels, the Cuban government would do what it had done before—claim their people had caught Tomlinson with drugs aboard, then ransom him to our own government while wringing him dry of political juice.

That would mean months in Cuba . . . and he wouldn't spend them in the Hotel Nacional, either. It would mean prison. Maybe at the State Security Villa Marista complex in Havana, but more likely the much larger, dirtier, and more dangerous Combinado del Este—the gray-walled fortress where they kept the death-row people; the dangerous dissidents who had made the mistake of voicing their disapproval of Castro.

The thought of that turned my stomach. Tomlinson locked away in some crypt-sized cell . . . as frail as he was, as sick and confused as he had become . . . he wouldn't last a month.

So I would have to go. . . .

It was a stunning thing to acknowledge: *Yeah, I'm going to do it; I'm going back to Cuba. . . .*

Just making the decision, though, stirred an old energy in me. It awakened all the night-raider cognitive patterns that I had packed and put away long ago. A kind of attack mentality that I found both galvanizing and disturbing because it stirred in me an unsettling doubt about the life I had so carefully built.

If I'm living the way I want, why is it I miss elements of the life I had?

I looked at the stars, looked deep into the dark water and allowed the question to dissipate. I had more important things to think about . . . many things to do and information that needed to be assembled before I left for Cuba in, what, three days? Maybe four.

It was possible that the exchange would be easy to make. I'd fly down, give the man in charge ten thousand cash, put Julia DeGlorio on a plane, then sail back with Tomlinson.

Nothing to it . . .

But it was also possible that things wouldn't go smoothly. What would I do if they took the money and refused to release *No Más?* How should I react if some bureaucrat with a long memory connected me with my past work in Cuba?

The potential for trouble was very real. There were contingencies that I had to anticipate.

When setting out to attack a mountain, smart climbers do their homework first; set up the safety lines and establish all possible means of escape.

I had a lot to do in a very short time. . . .

On the phone, Jimmy Gardenas, former flats guide and now owner of Key West's top fly tackle shop, said to me, "Julia DeGlorio? The night I saw Tomlinson, there was nobody by that name at our table."

It was Saturday, nearly five p.m. On the desk in front of me was a pad of paper on which I had written, in a vertical line, the words:

BANK
SKIFF
HOUSE
FLIGHT
HORSESHOE
JIMMY
ARMANDO
GEN. RIVERA (PILAR?)

All brief memory goads relating to things I wanted to get done before Monday.

Already, I had placed neat little checks beside every word except for the last three names.

Now I picked up a pencil and placed another checkmark

as I said to Jimmy, "You sure? Tomlinson said he was at your table when he met her. I got the impression you were all—"

"Nope, I would'a remembered," Jimmy said. "No woman by that name. But Tomlinson was really drunk. He could have imagined it. I think he was imagining a lot of things that night. I doubt if he remembers much of what went on."

"He sailed to Cay Sal with her, now they're in Cuba. He's not imagining that."

"But where he met her," Jimmy said. "That's what I'm saying. You probably don't want to hear this, but I think he was more than drunk that night. I think he was on something. The way he was talking—saying crazy biblical stuff—I think maybe he was doing some kind of hallucinogenic."

"It's possible."

"I tried to get him to go home with me. You know, look after him till he settled down. I don't know him very well, but he never seemed like the self-destructive type. Until the restaurant that night."

I said, "A Cuban-American woman, probably late twenties. Attractive . . ." I tried to remember what Tomlinson had said about her; made some plausible deductions from that. "She would be unmarried, articulate, well-read, not much money, and probably not from the Keys. Maybe down there trying to meet people."

Jimmy said, "*Cubano* in her twenties?"

"That's right."

"Why didn't you say so? There was somebody like that. I know who you're talking about—"

"Yeah, Julia—"

"No, her name's not Julia whatever-you-said. Her name's Rita Santoya. 'Least, that's what she told me. She came into the tackle shop that afternoon—during Fantasy Fest?—and said she'd been given my name, maybe I could help her. What she wanted was the names of boat people who might be headed for Cuba, willing to let her go along as crew."

I said, "That's the one."

• • •

Jimmy Gardenas said, "In the Cuban-American community, that name still carries a lot of weight—Santoya. The Santoya family controlled most of the sugar production in La Habana Province. Unbelievable wealth, like royalty down there. And damn good people, too, from what I've heard. Of course, they lost it all when Castro took over. So I told her to come by the restaurant that night and I'd introduce her to some guys who might be able to help. I've been so Americanized," Jimmy added, "it's hard for people to believe that I'm Cuban, too. I try to keep up on things; help when I can."

"Maybe she used the name Santoya to impress you," I said.

"I don't think so. She knew the family history too well. It's quite a family. Back in the forties and fifties, when things were about as corrupt as they could get, there were these two rich brothers. Ask any Cuban, they'll know the story. There was Eduardo Santoya and Angel Santoya. Eduardo . . . this girl we're talking about said Eduardo was her grandfather . . . well, Eduardo, he was the one who spent a ton of the family's money to help found a political party . . . I can't remember the name of it . . . but this party was devoted to administrative honesty, that kind of thing. Doing good stuff . . . national reforms."

"Ortodoxo," I said.

"Hey!, that's it. Ortodoxo. This rich guy, Eduardo, with nothing to gain, doing it because it was right. His brother, Angel, was involved, too, but he was more into the power part of it. You know how some rich kids are just total shits? That was Angel Santoya. So young Fidel Castro comes along and Angel wants him in the party but Eduardo sees the guy as the clown he is and says no way.

"The brothers have a hell of a fight; splits the whole family. In fifty-nine, when Fidel comes marching down out of the mountains, guess who's right there patting him on the back, telling him what a genius he is? Angel Santoya, by then a working informant. Same day, Eduardo is packing the one bag he's allowed and hustling his wife and teenage son to the airport to escape Fidel's firing squads. They left a couple of mansions behind, a couple thousand acres of prime sugar, I don't know how many yachts and cars. That's the kind of wealth we're talking about."

"This girl, Rita, she claimed to be the daughter of the teenage son?"

"Right. Eduardo the second, Eduardo Senior's only child. Senior, he started out in Miami, then moved up to Trenton, I think—somewhere in New Jersey—where he started from scratch and built a new fortune. I think it was car sales; something like that. But then he went bust. Lost it all. Less then a year later, Eduardo-two—married and a daddy by that time—gets caught by Castro's people back in Havana. They decide he's there to assassinate Fidel, so they march him down to Mariel Harbor, stand junior on a cliff in front of a firing squad, and shoot him."

When Jimmy Gardenas said the word "junior," the name suddenly clicked in my memory: Junior Santoya. I thought, Jesus, I *knew* the guy.

I said, "That was in seventy-three, right?"

Heard mild laughter through the phone. "A gringo who knows the history better and speaks the language better than me." Like: Why do I bother telling you?

"I remember reading about it," I said.

Jimmy said, "Sure, Doc. Sure. That's not what my friends with Alpha tell me, but, fine. If it's what you want me to believe."

Meaning Alpha Sixty-six, the Cuban Exile Brigade that trained privately and secretly in the Everglades, readying to invade the homeland. With willing intelligence sources in Nicaragua, Masagua, Cuba's Interior Ministry, and Panama's G-2, it was not surprising that certain members knew about me . . . at least knew what I had once been.

I said, "After the son died, what happened? Rita told you all this?"

"Some of it; some of it I'd already heard. What happens is, Eduardo Senior gets the news about his son being executed and he dies within the month. They said it was a heart attack, but it was more like a broken heart. You know how *Cubanos* love their kids. Which leaves the grandmother, the mother, and the new daughter all orphaned, penniless. So yeah, a girl comes in here saying she's Rita Santoya, you bet I tried to help her. The Cuban community, we take care of our own."

"Did she say why she wanted to go back to Cuba?"

"She told me she wanted to go back, see where her roots are. Said her grandmother had just died and she'd been reading her grandmother's letters, going through her things, and got the urge. I got the impression her mother was somehow out of the picture. Remarried or something like that; left the girl on her own."

"She's in her twenties?"

"Late twenties, yeah. Not beautiful but handsome-looking. You know the look—outdoorsy, into climbing maybe; like that. She struck me as intelligent; pretty well educated. When I told her it might not be too smart, someone named Santoya poking around Cuba, she didn't seem surprised. Like she'd already thought about it. I figured that's why she wanted to go as crew on a boat. If she flew, she'd have to use a passport."

"That's why she gave Tomlinson a fake name."

"Maybe," Jimmy said. "Thing is, I never saw her talking to Tomlinson. I'm not even sure she was at the table when he came in. 'Fact, I'm pretty sure she wasn't. That's why it didn't click right away."

"Any of the people you introduced her to offer to put her on a boat?"

"They said they'd check around, but I got the feeling they weren't going to risk it. She probably read it the same way."

We spent the next few minutes talking about what Cuban-Americans love to talk about: What happens to Cuba when Castro falls? Talked about how it would be; the fast changes that would take place on the island the exiles were forced to leave but where, in their hearts, they still lived. Just before we hung up, Jimmy said, "I'll tell you one thing—they find out Tomlinson's with Rita Santoya, the daughter of the man who wanted to kill Fidel, he's apt to lose a lot more than his boat."

Dewey had gone off mysteriously; disappeared in her rental car—which really wasn't much of a mystery. Four days before Christmas, people are prone to disappear. She'd probably driven to the mainland; was shouldering her way through the Edison Mall circus, doing her shopping. So I worked around the lab, alternately trying to telephone my friend Armando Azcona—kept getting his recorder—and finishing up unfinished business. Because I had already left a message with the secretary of General Juan Rivera, down there in the small Central American country of Masagua, I didn't want to stray far from the phone. The general would call me back; he always had. I was less certain of contacting Armando.

Armando Azcona was an old associate and now a Miami businessman who was involved with the Cuban American National Foundation, a politically powerful Cuban exile group that lobbied effectively in D.C., had worked closely with the Reagan and Bush administrations, and was the organization most likely to provide political infrastructure once Castro was out of the picture. Known as CANF, the group had set up a government in exile and, presumably, had knowledge of and perhaps supported anti-Castro ranks living in Cuba. Not that there could be many—anyone Fidel's people suspected of being a dissident was imprisoned or shot.

In Cuba, it was a fact of life not mentioned in Castro's famous "History Will Absolve Me!" speech.

If such a fifth-column group existed in Cuba, I wanted to know about it. If I got into trouble, real trouble, an underground network would be the only place to hide.

So I futzed around the house and the lab, waiting for the phone to ring, waiting for Dewey to return, occasionally hitting the redial button, getting Armando's recording again and again. To leave a message, I'd have to leave a name, and I didn't want my name on tape.

It was nearly dark. Through the west window, I could see that the guides were in, hosing down their skiffs. Watched Felix, from his skiff, toss Jeth a can of beer. Watched Jeth bobble it and drop it off the dock. Smiled at his can't-I-do-anything-right? expression. Watched him jog to get his landing net so he could fish the can out. Saw Mack standing by the bait tanks taking it all in, enjoying it. He was wearing a Santa Claus hat at a jaunty angle. Even so, Mack did not look elfin.

Another day of charters off the calendar . . . another Christmas Saturday done at Dinkin's Bay.

I sat at the table, thinking about my conversation with Jimmy Gardenas—the what'll-happen-when-Castro-falls? discussion that all Cubans enjoy.

Like most Cuban-Americans, Jimmy knows that it will not go as smoothly as he likes to pretend. By air and boat and inner tube, more than a million Cubans have immigrated to the United States and, when Castro falls, the return migration will not be as peaceful, nor as massive, as some believe. The Cubans are one of the great American success stories. They are a brilliant people: smart, industrious, family-oriented, goal oriented. In the space of less than two generations, they have accumulated extraordinary wealth and power in the wealthiest and most powerful nation on earth. Were they really going to abandon that?

A few years ago, the *Miami Herald* ran the results of a poll which indicated that, even with Castro gone, only one in five Cuban-Americans would return to their native island. Although the poll did not supply demographics, it is not unreasonable to assume that, of that number, most would go expecting to recover their old properties and resume their old lives.

It's a pipe dream. It will never happen.

Even organizations such as CANF agree that an attempt to regain expropriated properties will result in chaos. If the Cuban-Americans are smart, which they are, they will settle for a compensation program in which properties are sold to the highest bidder and the revenue prorated.

The life they knew, in homes and on the island they loved, is gone forever. . . .

Another fallacy is that, after the fall, Cuban-Americans will receive a warm welcome from their long-suffering countrymen. Despite the lengthy political separation, weren't they still brothers?

Nope. They are not brothers . . . and never were.

It is a ticklish problem; one seldom discussed, but the fact is that ninety-five percent of the Cubans who fled the island were white. With their exodus, blacks became the racial majority in Cuba . . . and it was Cuba's black population—historically used as little more than slave labor—who rushed to take over the homes and properties abandoned by the exiles.

On the day that Castro came to power, Havana's Miramar and Vedado neighborhoods were made up of tasteful mansions and estates. Now most of those mansions are black tenements and slums.

On the day that Castro took control, Catholicism was the national religion. Today the most widely practiced religion is Santería, an Afro-Cuban belief very similar to Haiti's voodoo. Santería plays prominently in Castro's political decisions. The predictions of Santería priests are even reported in state newspapers.

Is this new Cuban majority eager for the return of the Miami exiles? Absolutely not. Indeed, they are terrified at the prospect. In Castro's essentially all-white puppet government, blacks have very little input. But they had absolutely no influence at all when the people who fled Cuba were in control.

That's why they don't want change. And that's why they will probably fight it when change comes knocking on their door.

The what-will-happen-when-Castro-falls is an enjoyable conversational game, but the reality is much darker. It will be a difficult and painful transition . . . and it also may be very bloody indeed. . . .

• • •

The first words out of my mouth in Spanish when I picked up the phone and heard the voice of Gen. Juan Rivera, prime minister to the sovereign Republic of Masagua, were, "How is your arm, General?"

Meaning his throwing arm. Rivera has lived an interesting and varied life: cane-cutter, guerrilla leader, army general, and now politician, but he has always viewed himself first and foremost as a gifted pitcher who, because of politics, was slighted by the American major leagues.

"My arm—what a coincidence you should ask, Marion. My arm is wonderful! I threw a hundred pitches this morning as a demonstration for the president of Nicaragua who happens to be visiting on state business. Never have I had better control or velocity!"

Sitting at the desk, phone wedged between shoulder and ear, I could picture Rivera—six two, grizzly-sized with black and gray beard, cigar in the mouth, probably still dressing in fatigues—as his voice boomed through the receiver. Could also picture him out on the mound: big leg-kick, loosey-goosey slingshot release, his expression predatory, taking it dead-serious even though he is nearly fifty years old.

Rivera said, "I allowed the president to attempt to hit against me three times—as a kindness. The results were expected: three strikeouts!"

Enjoying the formality of Spanish, I said, "I am not surprised, General. Not at all surprised."

"True, the president of Nicaragua is not a gifted player. Madame President told me that she had never played the game before."

I cleared my throat, took a sip of iced tea before I said, "That's very difficult to believe. In Nicaragua, where everyone plays—"

"Exactly! Perhaps it is what we call 'political dissimulation.' " Gave it a sly touch—we both know she's lying—before he added, "A woman of her age has certainly had a few at-bats. Even so, I did not pitch as I would pitch to a quality player. No breaking pitches; all fastballs. And yet, the results were expected."

"General," I said, "I still believe that you should be pitching in the major leagues."

"As do I!" Said it with conviction and a touch of anger. "When a catcher of your abilities—my very favorite catcher—says this, then I can only wonder why the Dodgers of Los Angeles do not return my calls."

I had caught Rivera six or seven times when I was living and working in Central America. In those days, collecting information about people like Rivera was part of my job. More than once, I had joined a team or joined in a game to do just that. It was astonishingly effective.

I said, "But Pittsburgh contacted you—"

"Yes, yes, your friend, the Pittsburgh Pirates manager . . . Mr. Gene Lamont? Mr. Lamont suggested I play a season in a place called . . . Birmingham. In your minor leagues. A thing he called 'single-A.' A very attractive offer, but I have so many duties as prime minister . . . always some meeting to attend or some dignitary to meet." Said it like he would much prefer to be in Birmingham. "For the good of my people, I decided that I could not run the affairs of our country while pitching in Alabama."

I said, "Baseball's loss, Masagua's gain. You did what you had to do." Then I said, "General—may I ask how your connection is?" Meaning: was he speaking on a secure telephone line?

Rivera said, "Very good. Excellent, in fact." Meaning I could speak as freely as I wanted to.

I told him, "I am not so sure of my own." Meaning that he should follow along, read between the lines.

I said, "Some years ago—it was nineteen seventy-three—I caught another pitcher; a pitcher you once admired, though his fastball was very poor compared to yours. It was in an exhibition game before the start of an amateur world series."

Rivera said, "Yes! This man—he was once drafted by the Giants of New York?"

It was a lie that Rivera and many others chose to accept

as truth—that Fidel Castro had been courted to play in the major leagues.

I said, "That is the pitcher. On Monday, I am flying to this pitcher's homeland because a friend of mine is there and in trouble."

"Is he in prison?"

"No. It is a matter of money." Without using Tomlinson's name, I explained what had happened, then I said, "It should be an easy thing for me to do. I have the money; I give it to them. But what if they take the money but refuse to release my friend's boat? Or refuse to release my friend? It is a worry."

Rivera said, "Marion, hear what I am saying to you: that is the least of your worries. Please remember I know why you were there for that baseball series—just as I knew why you played baseball with me . . . and just as I know the thing that happened when you visited that place in nineteen eighty. What happened that time is what you should remember most."

I thought: How did Rivera find out? Was he bluffing? No . . . the tone of his voice, the way he emphasized it—the *thing* that happened—he really did know. Listened to him say, "Take my advice, old friend, stay away from this weak-armed pitcher."

I said, "I have no choice. My friend is in trouble." Let that hang there, because it was something Rivera understood—the Latinos, some of them, still believed in a code of honor—then I said, "I seem to remember that you have a house at this place." Meaning the Masaguan Embassy. It, too, was in Miramar, west of Havana; a small house among bigger estates on Embassy Row.

"Yes," he said. "I have a house there." Said it carefully, not volunteering anything. We were getting into politics now, something he took very seriously.

"I think you know what I am asking, Juan." Used his name for the first time, making it personal.

In the long silence that followed, I knew that he was calculating the political fallout while also reminding himself that he still owed me one very, very big favor. Finally, he said, "The answer is yes—but only if things become extremely difficult."

"Of course," I said. "No other reason." Then I added, "To avoid having to impose, it would also be useful for me to know the names of anyone—local people, I'm talking about—who might be willing to help outsiders in a time of need."

Still guarded, Rivera asked, "People who are friends of this pitcher?"

"No. People who are not his friends."

Another long pause. "It is possible. But let me ask you again, on the honor of our friendship—do you go only to help your friend?"

"I swear to you. It's the only reason. In fact, you know him. The last time we played baseball together? He nearly hit a home run off you."

Heard Rivera hoot. "The hippie!"

"Yes, he's the one."

Sitting in a staff tent in the jungles of Masagua, Tomlinson and Rivera had spent evenings exchanging baseball trivia, drinking rum, arguing political theory.

"Marion, why didn't you say so? Of course, for him—the great DiMaggio, remember?—I will check on these names. A man of such abilities deserves to be helped."

I hadn't planned to ask, but Rivera's enthusiasm seemed to invite it: "Perhaps, General, you could help our friend by telephoning this pitcher? Asking for his release?" Cuba had only one sovereign friend left in Central America—Masagua. There was no doubt that Masagua's ruler had enough political clout to get small favors done quickly.

But Rivera said, "No, no . . . that is asking too much, Marion." Now being very open; no more diplomatic sparring. "You know how these things work."

Yes, I knew. If the nation of Masagua asked Cuba for a favor, Cuba would politicize it, use it, demand a far more costly favor in return.

There was something else I wanted to ask but was reluctant to, because the answer, any answer, would bring back uncomfortable memories, unwanted emotions. I heard myself say, "You have been a tremendous help, General. Please pass along my compliments to your people . . . and also to Her Majesty," meaning the sovereign of her country, Pilar Fuentes Balserio. Then I heard myself ask the question anyway: "How is she doing, Juan?"

Knowing, sympathetic laughter. "Her Highness is doing very well, Marion." He said it with the empathetic tone that men use when discussing another man's lost girl. "She is busy, always busy."

Busy indeed. Under Pilar's guidance, the banana-republic economy of Masagua had been jump-started, social reforms were being implemented, the largely Mayan citizenry was already benefiting from more schools and better health care, and the government—for the first time in Masaguan history—was stable.

I said, "I have read about her. The people still love her?"

"They worship her. Who would not?"

Imagining Pilar—the silk-black hair, her face, the coolness of her skin—I said, "But I have heard very little about her husband, the former president."

"Tevo? Hah!" A name spoken with contempt. "Who knows or cares where that worm is. In Spain, I heard. She says that she is no longer married to him, she is now married to her people. And of course . . ." I waited through his indecision—should he bring it up? ". . . Her Highness is absolutely dedicated to her son. Marion, he has grown so large so quickly! Such a brilliant boy, already reading books while others his age are just starting school. But an athlete, too—the way he charges around the palace, always with a baseball or a bat in his hands. I am teaching him to pitch!"

I said, "He couldn't have a better coach, General."

"It is what I tell him! But already he contradicts me. This child, Marion, he forgets nothing and is very precise about everything!"

Increasingly, I regretted that I had asked; I held the phone slightly away from my ear as he said, "Can you imagine? This blond boy with glasses, correcting me? *Me*—the greatest general in Masaguan history? It makes me angry but it also makes me laugh . . ."

I was shaking my head very slowly; it was impossible not to listen.

". . . do you know that feeling, Marion? A feeling that squeezes the heart but also causes one to smile?"

I said, "Yes. I know the feeling."

"That is how this child affects me. Offended and happy, both at once."

Imagining the way it had been with Pilar: the clean muscularity of her legs and Indio hips . . . the way glossy hair swung when her head tilted in thought . . . the way her face softened when I surprised her, as if her aloofness was a wall to all but me, I said, "I am very happy for her."

Rivera said, "I will tell Her Highness that you asked."

"Thanks, Juan."

"And one more thing? If you go to this place, do not make the mistake of trying to go quietly. Go as all American tourists go. Wear a colorful hat, a bright smile. Carry a camera around your neck. Ask for directions in very loud English!"

"Very good advice, General."

It was, too.

7

That night, Dewey stayed up after I went to bed. Restless, I lay awake thinking, listening to the crackle of Christmas paper, the ripping of Scotch tape, feeling the weight of her through the vibrating floor and shifting pilings. The high-pressure system was now stalled squarely over western Florida; the temperature outside had dropped into the forties. The windows of my little house were fogged with condensation.

"You asleep?"

I looked, to see Dewey's head peeking around the clothes locker.

"No."

"Still mad at me?"

While shopping, she had stopped at a travel agency and booked two seats on Bahamas Air, Miami–Nassau, because the agent told her—incorrectly—that Cubana de Aviación flew daily from Nassau to Havana. But I had already checked and the only Monday flight into Havana was out of Panama City, and I had booked it and a Sunday afternoon flight, Miami–Panama. One seat only.

She had insisted that she was going; I had insisted that she was not. We had argued briefly.

I said, "Nope. Not mad."

"You're not exactly talkative."

"It's not you. There's a lot on my mind." What I'd been thinking about was what Juan Rivera had told me about Pilar; the way he described things. That . . . and Dewey's biological clock . . .

She said, "We didn't have our workout today, did we?" Said it like a kindergarten teacher placating a grumpy child.

"I did. I ran. It's too cold to swim."

I watched her unbuttoning her shirt while simultaneously unbuckling the belt of her jeans, as she said, "Well, I didn't, and I've got a lot of energy to burn." A few seconds later, I heard her say, "Scooch over. Geeze-oh-Katy, you're hogging the whole bed."

I reached my hands out to fend her off—it was Dewey's bullheaded independence that I found so compelling but also so maddening. I said, "Do we really have to go through this whole discussion again?"

As she gently pushed my hands away, she answered, "Nope. But we're going to keep doing the other thing till we get right."

I said, "Are you sure?"

Sliding into bed beside me, she said, "For a guy so quiet, you sure do ask a lot of questions."

And just like that, it was done.

An hour or more went by and she was up again, lights on, walking around naked. She had a towel in her hand, toweling off sweat. She was talking to me as I lay in bed watching her—an attractive woman to watch, the way she moved. As she used the towel, she said, "I gotta tell you, it was a whole lot different for me this time. This time it was . . . *fun*. Even with you in one of those Gary Cooper moods, it was a really good time." She reflected for a moment. "Something like that, how many calories you figure?"

How much energy had we burned, as if I were her physical trainer.

"More for you than me. You were all over the court."

"Nope, just exploring the foul lines, that's all." I

watched her disappear into the main room, heard the refrigerator open, heard her say, "I called Bets this afternoon. Talked to her when I was in town."

I listened.

"She wanted to know if you and I'd done the deed yet."

I continued to listen.

"She said I was heading for another disappointment if we did, which is when I told her . . . wait, listen to this—" Dewey came into full view again: skin golden in the light of the reading lamp, hips canted, a quart of milk in her hand, drinking right from the bottle. "I said to her, 'Look, Bets, I already know you're a better kisser, but Doc's a lot better hung. So it's kind of a toss-up.' That's exactly what I said. Didn't even piss her off; actually made her laugh."

I threw the covers back, took the bottle from her and held her; felt her bury her face in my shoulder. "She's back in New York? Maybe you should fly up there, spend Christmas with her."

Dewey pulled away just enough to look into my face. "You got water in your ears or something? Bets and I are no longer a couple. We'll stay friends, but the other thing's done." When I started to speak, she held her palm to my lips, shushing me. "No need to get nervous, Ford. I don't have any mixed-up dream of moving in with you or any other man. It's not all clear in my mind yet, but I'm getting there—figuring out who I am, what I want. What I am and will always be is a gay woman. It's where my friends are; I *like* it." She gave me her bemused and slightly wicked smile before she added, "It's just that I have broader interests. Like tennis and golf. Why can't you enjoy both?"

Laughing, I kissed her, then kissed her again. "So which am I?"

She thought for a moment before she said, "Doc, you're more like arena football."

The next day, Sunday—anticipating that I would still be in Cuba on Christmas Day—I carried a sack of small presents around the docks, handing them out to a few of my marina friends. When I got back to the house, I tried once again to call Armando Azcona. I had listened to his recorder so many times that I was taken aback when I heard him answer the phone in his singsong Ricky Ricardo English.

I said, "Armando, this is an old associate of yours. The bird-watcher, remember? Back when we were both bird-watchers."

I knew the first thing that would come into his mind was sitting in the bushes by a path, at night, on the southwestern shore of Mariel Harbor, Cuba, at the time of the refugee exodus. 1980. A thousand American boats in the harbor—stinking shrimp boats and cruisers; anything that could float and carry human beings—but the two of us interested in only one boat, a sailing vessel named *Peregrine,* and concerned only with the three Cuban Interior Ministry agents, posing as refugees, who had been ordered to sail her to a major U.S. port.

Armando's tone communicated little surprise and less enthusiasm. "Yes," he said, "bird-watching was once a hobby of mine. But no more."

"I've given it up myself."

"I see. Then you haven't called to discuss old times."

"No, I'm calling to ask a favor. Do you remember the place where we went to study falcons?"

I waited while his brain made the quick translation. "Of course I remember. I remember it very clearly."

"I'm going back soon. But not as part of a study group. I was hoping you might know someone there who'd be willing to show me around. If I needed help."

I wondered if that was too cryptic . . . but no, Armando was right with me. I listened to him say, "I'm surprised you're not going there to study. It's such an interesting place."

"As I told you—I gave it up. This is strictly a personal trip."

As Armando asked, "Are you looking for a tour guide?" I could picture him that night in Mariel, standing to stretch his legs at precisely the wrong time . . . could hear the stunned thoracic noise that he made when he realized we were not alone . . . could see the smoky red disc of a gunsight laser beam on Armando's forehead . . .

I replied, "I don't need a tour guide. Just the name of someone who might help if I get lost."

Knew that Armando had to be remembering it, too . . . hearing me charging through the bushes from behind; feeling the impact of my body hitting him behind the legs, knee-high, knocking him to the ground. I wondered if that night had scarred him with the same dream I suffered.

I listened to him say, "Lost? You really think it's possible you might get lost. You once knew the place so well."

"It's unlikely. But it's been a long time. The name of someone who can come to the rescue"—I laughed when I said that, as if it were a joke—"like in the movies? That's the favor I'm asking."

I thought that he would want some time; tell me that he would call me back, give himself some wiggle room and an opportunity to check with other members of his group. Armando was a respected businessman now. He could be expected to take things through proper channels.

But after a very long silence, he said, "I think I may know the names of one or two people. But these are very, very busy people—"

"Only if I really have trouble finding my way around," I told him. "That's the only reason I would impose on them."

"I'm not certain how much they could help you."

Meaning the lives of these people were already in danger and they probably had very little authority.

I said, "I realize that, too."

Another very long silence. I could hear a sound, like a file drawer being opened, then the sound of papers being moved. Knew that, in his businessman's mind, this was final payment on a very old debt. "In that case," Armando said—and he gave me a name.

An hour later, General Juan Rivera's secretary—not that he identified himself—supplied me with another.

• • •

That night at dinner, I tried to explain to Dewey why she couldn't leave with me in the morning for Cuba.

"I'll be down there and back," I said. "A couple of days—unless I sail to Key West with Tomlinson. It's not like you're missing anything."

"Bullshit, Ford. You'll have to do better than that."

"Let me put it this way: I don't want you to go."

I was rewarded with a coy mock-smile. "I can see you're undecided, sweetie. Perhaps we should sleep on it." As if she might get me in bed, use sex as leverage.

"I don't know how else to put it."

"Well," she said, not kidding now, "you might try telling me the truth."

We had driven my twenty-foot Hewes Light Tackle flats boat north through Pine Island Sound to the restaurant on Cabbage Key. It was a cold and blustery night for boating, but Dewey had insisted. So now we sat by candlelight on the back porch of the old inn looking out at the heavy foliage of banyan trees, air roots twisting down. Every few minutes, Kim, the blond bartender, would come cruising by—"Need another beer? How's the grouper?"—and we could hear Jerry Shell on the keyboard playing Jimmy Buffett in the bar.

I said, "What do you mean tell the truth? What makes you think I'm lying?"

"Because you keep saying no and can't give me a good reason. You're the logical one. You always have a reason for everything you do." She didn't say that very kindly.

I looked across the table at her—handsome face suspended above candle flame, blond hair bright as platinum spilling onto the black turtleneck sweater she wore. I said, "It bothers you that I try to be logical?"

She folded her fingers together and rested chin on hands. "Sometimes it bothers me that you let it run your life . . . but I'm just realizing it bothers me a hell of a lot more when you aren't. Logical, I mean. That's what I'm saying: Give me one logical reason. You're going to go off, leave me here all alone for Christmas? You can be a shit, Doc, but you're usually not this big a shit."

I picked up my can of beer, sighed, settled back. "Okay . . . I'll tell you."

"Then there is a reason." Nodding like, See, I was *right.*

"Because it could be dangerous. I mean it. It's because I might be a dangerous traveling companion." When I saw that she was unconvinced, I added, "This won't be my first trip down there. Cuba, I'm talking about."

"I know that. You mentioned it once before. Some reference—'The time when I was in Cuba.' A long time ago. So?"

I cleared my throat. "The first time was in nineteen seventy-three—"

"Jesus," she said, "you were practically a kid—"

"Close to it. The United States sent a baseball team to Havana—actually, two baseball teams to play in an amateur world series. I was a bullpen catcher. The only time I played was in this exhibition game. Only got a couple of at-bats, didn't even get a hit."

"Cubans don't like Americans who are bad hitters? That's why it's too dangerous—?"

"Give me a chance to explain it. It's involved. See"—I wanted to word it carefully—communicate details without communicating the truth—"during the exhibition game. The one I played in? As a goodwill gesture, the teams switched pitchers. It was a meaningless game. The coaches played; one of their military people, a guy named Ochoa, was at second base. A very gifted officer and a first-rate man . . ." I caught myself. She didn't need to know about Arnaldo Ochoa . . . now the late Gen. Arnaldo Ochoa. I said, "The point is, Castro pitched two innings for our team."

I watched her eyes widen. "Fidel Castro? You were Castro's catcher? Damn, Doc, you never told me this before." Like I had been holding out on her. She leaned forward on her elbows. "How was he? Any good?"

"He was terrible. Worse than terrible. At the time, he was like forty-four, forty-five years old. Even so, I could tell the man had never been any good. Zero velocity, no control, clumsy motion. If a guy really played, he can pick up a ball twenty years later and you can tell, right? Just the way he handles himself."

Dewey was taking it in—she understood sports. She said, "The same with tennis. Exactly the same."

I said, "So there I am catching Fidel Castro and I'm calling pitches—nothing but fastballs, because he can't throw anything else, but he keeps shaking me off. He wants to throw the curve. Understand, he's pitching against his own guys who, of course, keep striking out. A ball over their head, they swing. Two feet outside, they swing. Like they're praying they won't hit the ball by accident and offend the Maximum Leader—which is what he likes to be called.

"Finally, he waves me to the mound. Castro with the beard, wearing this floppy uniform that says *Sugar Kings* on the front. In the stands—this was the main stadium in Havana—there are at least thirty thousand people and he's trying to act like he's not pissed off, but he's fuming. When I get close enough, he grabs my shoulder and whispers, 'I think you are calling a terrible game; a shitty game—' "

"He said that?"

"In English, too. Pretty good English. He says, 'I think I will call my own pitches. No more signals from you!' "

"Yeah? What did you say?"

I had to smile, remembering it. "I said what a catcher is supposed to say in that situation. I said, 'Pitchers aren't supposed to think. First time you cross me up, I'll make you look like the rag arm you are.' "

Dewey's expression described shock and delight. "You really said that?"

Had I? Something similar—"Be quiet or I'll make you look worse than you are." Pretty close. Nodding, I said, "He was so mad he was shaking. But what could he do? All those people in the stands, watching us. So he pitches the rest of the inning, never says another word."

"And you didn't call a single curveball."

"No, I called three. Just to make him happy."

"You're telling me that's it? That's why you're dangerous; why you can't go back to Havana again?"

I had to say the next part very carefully. Could I tell her about Mariel? No . . . there was no way to disguise what had occurred in Mariel. I said, "That and something else that happened. When Castro called me out to the mound, turns out some guy in the stands chose that moment to drop a gun he'd been hiding. Dropped it right in front of one of the security people. Bad timing."

"Yeah, but what's that have to do with you?"

I said, "This guy, the one with the gun, was a Cuban-American in the country illegally. Somehow he'd slipped in, like he was a member of the team or something." Trying to remember what Junior Santoya had looked like—I'd met him only once—I said, "Later, some people claimed they'd seen me talking to the guy. That's why the State Department made me and a couple of other players take a special plane home. That the guy and I had been seen together the night before, drinking beer at a hotel called the Havana Libre."

"Were you?"

I said, "Maybe. It's a busy bar. What matters is, they believed I was. Plus, their president wasn't a fan of mine after our conference on the mound."

"Like this guy was planning to shoot Castro."

"That's what they apparently thought."

"And you think they're still after you . . . what? Twenty-some years later." Her tone said: I don't buy it.

"They'd still have my name on file. You can be sure of it." Not my real name. I'd never used my real name in Cuba, but I didn't tell her that. In 'seventy-three, I'd gone as . . . ? It took me a moment to recall the last name I'd used—an absurdly ironic choice, as it turned out.

Dewey said, "What's so funny?"

I said, "Nothing, just something I remembered. So you see why you can't go."

She had a little bit of wine left—becoming quite the cosmopolitan drinker. She tilted the last of it down, showing me her pale throat, shaking her head at the same time. "What'd that friend tell you? Go as a tourist?"

I hadn't mentioned Juan Rivera's name, but I'd told her that was what I planned to do.

She said, "Who looks more like a tourist? A big blond nerdy gringo traveling alone, or a guy and his girlfriend—his mistress, maybe—who want some private time in the tropics?"

She had a point.

Dewey placed the wineglass back on the table; picked up the napkin and dabbed at her mouth. Said, "Doc, for once in your life, try to be logical."

As the sun-bleached old Soviet-built Tupolev jetliner strained to free itself of the smudge, the frenzy, the diesel and mango stink of Panama City, Panama, Dewey looked down upon the toy cars and the horizon of rooftops and she said, "I could see you were right at home; knew your way around that place, but I've got to tell you, buddy, I'm glad to be in the air again."

We'd arrived the day before, Sunday, and I'd spent the evening showing her the sights; took a couple of private hours to renew one or two old contacts. Then it was dinner at the Continental Hotel on Via España Avenue which, prior to the fall of Noriega, had been run by Panama's Defense Forces. I liked the irony of that—sitting beneath crystal chandeliers, among tuxedoed waiters, in a restaurant that had been the late-night meeting place for Noriega and his Cuban advisors . . . lots of cigar smoke and nervous Spanish as they coordinated weapons shipments in advance of the U.S. invasion.

Now Dewey fidgeted in her seat and said, "You give a pretty good tour, but I feel a lot more comfortable up here than I did down there."

The veteran of an international tennis tour that focused

myopically on the world's big-money glamour cities, Dewey had been unprepared for the slums and the noisy poverty of what, in comparison, was one of Central America's wealthiest, healthiest cities. That she was glad to be in the air also told me that she didn't know a damn thing about Tupolev jets.

We were side by side on threadbare seats, sitting port side, forward of the engines, in a fuselage not much wider than a commuter bus. Two broad-shouldered Americanos among forty, maybe forty-five Latinos—business types and embassy types wearing suits or guayabera shirts—in an aluminum tube crammed with seats for more than a hundred.

The door of the forward bulkhead was open and I looked through into the cockpit. Saw the co-pilot—maybe the pilot—standing there, smoking a cigarette, laughing with a stocky, busty flight attendant whose body was too pudgy for her gray Cubana Airlines uniform. Watched him pull out the pack—Marlboros—and offer her one. Watched her lean to his lighter.

"Holy shit!" Dewey had grabbed my arm. "What's happening?"

White vapor was pouring out of the overhead vents like steam from a fire hose, filling the cabin with a haze dense as sea fog.

I patted her hand. "Relax—it's because they just turned on the air conditioning. It's the way these planes are built; the way the system works."

"You sure? Geeze-oh-Katy!"

"Notice anyone else getting nervous? They've flown Cubana before."

She was beginning to relax her grip on my arm. "Hell, I can't even *see* anyone else."

I smiled. The fog wasn't that bad. No one else even seemed to notice. People settling back with magazines . . . a man sitting to our right shaking open *Granma*, the national newspaper of Cuba . . . a couple of women forward of us peering into a sack, pulling out bananas and an atamoya. Even so, there was no vacation giddiness; none of the we're-headed-for-paradise cheer that is the hallmark of other island flights.

Dewey said, "Long as the plane's safe, I don't care."

How was I going to reply to that? Cuba, like all former Soviet bloc countries, was suffering the gradual breakdown of its mechanical infrastructure. The Tupolev, its replacement parts, and its technicians all came from a place that no longer existed. The same was true of Cuba's bulldozers, harvesting machines, power plants, buses, medical hardware, oil refineries, radios, televisions, and windup toys—the entire metal-electrical scaffolding upon which modern civilization is built. A couple of years ago, a friend of mine, who happens to be a National Security Agency research analyst, explained it to me. "By the late eighties, there were nearly thirty thousand Soviets living and working in Cuba," she said. "They kept the machines going, kept the systems working. The Russians didn't mix much with the Cubans; they never learned the language. They had their own clubs, their own restaurants, schools, and sports facilities. There wasn't a lot of knowledge exchanged. Why bother? The Soviet Union and its satellite countries were going to last a thousand years, right?

"But then the U.S. came up with the Strategic Defense Initiative," she said. "Remember how the press called it Star Wars?"

Yes, I remembered. I remembered that time all too well.

She said, "Our people laughed at it, but the Soviets weren't laughing. They believed SDI would work and all but went bankrupt trying to come up with their own version. Perestroika was a result. The Soviets began to withdraw financial support from Cuba. Then the collapse came and all the technicians were called back to Mother Russia. Left the Cubans high and dry." She chose an interesting metaphor to illustrate the predicament. "Years back, when VCRs first came out? A few people, a very few, chose Beta—and ended up on a dead-end street. Well, Castro chose Beta."

I decided that, with Dewey, evasion was the kindest course. I patted her knee and said, "I've flown these jets before, never had a problem.'' I had, too. Out of Saigon, out of Hanoi, out of Shanghai—always tight-sphincter flights filled with dread; the kind of flights that dissolve our public personae, forcing us to reassess as we peer over the tippy-toe edge of the black abyss, wondering: Has my life been of value? Have I contributed some tiny piece to the puzzle . . . ?

Dewey relaxed a little; shifted in the cramped seat. Said, ''Well, if you're not scared, I'm not scared.''

Pretending to ignore the creaking wings, the hydraulic whine of frayed cables, I told her, ''Know what might help? When that flight attendant finishes her cigarette, maybe she'll bring us a couple of beers.''

Through the starred Plexiglas, from 21,000 feet, I watched the mosquito coast of Central America slide by: sea as luminous blue as a country club swimming pool; jungle a green so dark that it implied the gloom of caverns, the silence of a great void.

''I don't get it. Is that Jamaica or what?'' Dewey had a little map open on her lap—''Might as well make it a learning experience,'' she had told me—and she was looking from the map's coastline to the coastline outside the window.

I told her, ''It's the northern border of Nicaragua. Where it humps out?'' I touched the map. ''A couple of more minutes, we'll be right over the capitol of Masagua—'' I had to stop mid-sentence, realizing where we were . . . that I'd be only—what?—four miles above Pilar and her young blond son. It was the closest I'd been to her in slightly more than six years; the closest I'd ever been to him. I wondered if the Christmas present I had sent anonymously, always anonymously, was down there under the palace tree. A Rawlings Heart of the Hide catcher's glove, Gold Glove series. More likely, Masaguan security had piled it with the public's other gifts to the royal heir. Probably distributed them to the poor kids on Christmas Day, which would be just like Pilar. And besides . . . that damn Juan Rivera was teaching him to pitch anyway. . . .

"Then what I don't understand," Dewey said, "is why we're flying up the coast first when it'd be a hell of a lot closer to fly straight north across the ocean."

"Nope, it's about the same distance," I said. I didn't want to tell her the truth: Aware that the Tupolev was a bad risk, the Cuban pilot probably didn't want to stray far from an emergency runway. I said, "This way, you get a look at Central America. See? That's Masagua City down there."

She was looking, shaking her head—it was a how-do-you-know-so-much mannerism with which I was growing familiar. "You've been there, too, I suppose."

"A couple of times. You'd like the parks and there's a palace tour. Some pretty spectacular Mayan ruins, too." As if I'd visited as a tourist. Even so, I could feel the question coming; the same question she'd asked me in Panama City.

"A marine biologist who spent all his free time traveling." She said it quizzically, thinking it over. Yesterday, my reply—"I used to travel a lot"—hadn't put the subject to rest. I could see her wondering: Why is he being evasive?

So I decided to stop it before it went any further. "Traveling in my free time? I never said that. I went to these places, Panama, Masagua, some others because it was part of my work."

Dewey nodded, listening. Finally, it was all going to start making sense.

I said, "See, what happened was, when I got out of school, I was recruited by a company to do research—"

"This was after you played baseball."

"Yeah, just after I played ball, but pretty close to that time, though." Already lying to her. "This company, they'd pick a research area then provide funding so I could set up a research station. Usually a small house or shack, and money for a boat and a lab. Or the host country would provide me with a place, like a kind of educational exchange. I'd be there a few months or sometimes as much as a year or more."

All true.

She said, "We'd send them our people, they'd send us theirs?" Not doubting it, just asking.

"Right. But usually it was just this company, the one I worked for, setting me up, paying the bills, while I did my work. For a biologist, it was a great opportunity." Also true. I said, "I was able to spend time in places, do the kind of serious work that most people in my field only dream about. Like Masagua—" It was gone from the window now; once again I was leaving Pilar behind. "—I spent more than a year in Masagua. I had this great beach shack and lab on a deserted stretch of shore about fifty kilometers from the city. The fishermen there—same as the fishermen in Honduras—had a legend about a place off the coast. They called it the Magic Mountain—"

"Underwater, you mean."

"Yes. An underwater mountain. Not that you could tell it was there, but the fishermen, they knew. They claimed that every year sea turtles and manta rays came there by the thousands. They could see them on the surface, understand. And they weren't making it up. I confirmed it. Biologists are still researching it, but the .fact that the mountain contains large deposits of iron ore probably has something to do with the migration. Turtles and rays both have great navigational abilities; fragments of iron in the mastoid area, like a built-in compass. Some people think it has to do with that."

Dewey said, "Man, I've got to pull things out of you." Like: Why didn't you ever tell this story before?

I was enjoying talking about it; pleased that I could neutralize the subject so easily. That, plus it was nice being honest for a change. "I spent nearly a year in Africa," I said, "studying freshwater sharks on the Zambezi River. Later, I studied the same shark—bull sharks, we call them—on Lake Nicaragua, more than a hundred miles from the sea. Only now the Japanese fin industry has all but exterminated them."

"And this company paid you to do this. Like one of the really big conglomerates."

"The parent company, yeah. But the group that hired me

was very small. You've never heard the name. No one has."

"Hoping you might discover something and they could make a lot of money off it."

"Or contribute to their overall knowledge. The sea products industry is a huge global business. It had to do with that."

Dewey had finished her beer. Hatuey, in a can. She crushed the can with one hand—her jock side showing—and thought about it before saying, "I can see why you liked it, but I can see why you quit, too. All those places you mentioned, wasn't there always a lot of fighting going on? Like revolutions and stuff? Panama, Nicaragua, Masagua, that's all you ever read about."

I didn't like the direction the conversation was headed. I said, "That was the great thing about being a marine biologist. A credentialed researcher. The world's scientific community takes pains to be nonpolitical. No one much notices us. I could come and go as I pleased."

"Still," she said, "you'd think the company would have sent you to places that were safer. Africa? Wasn't there fighting there?"

I was nodding, eager to be done with it. "Yeah, it started getting dangerous. You're right. That's why I quit."

She said, "I don't blame you. Jesus, Ubangis with guns. You're lucky to be alive."

That was true, too.

After the jungles of Central America, after the space and light of the Caribbean, western Cuba looked barren, untended—like some massive ranch that had been worked too hard then abandoned. Treeless hills on a treeless windscape etched with dirt roads that seemed to originate from the sea and traveled architect-straight to nowhere. No cars, no movement, no people. The jetliner's pressurized silence assumed the silence of the land beneath us. Then we were descending and Cuba accumulated life—but not much light—as we neared Havana. I looked away when I saw the bluffs and basin of Mariel Harbor . . . looked again and saw the blanketing gray suburbs and high rise hotels along the beach and lichen black Morro Castle bonded to rock above Havana and the sea . . . then we touched down fast and heavy on the tarmac, but contrary to Latino custom, no one applauded upon landing, and I wondered if my fellow passengers were subdued by our destination or simply exhausted with gratitude at having survived the flight.

As we waited in line at immigration, Dewey said, "Christ-o-mighty, it's hot, huh?" She thought about that for a few seconds before smiling. "Hey, it *is* hot. Two days before Christmas, they're freezing up in Florida but it must be like eighty-five down here in Havana town. And Bets is stuck in New York!" Very pleased with herself; she had talked herself into a vacation in the tropics and was already enjoying it.

Good. Dewey was no actress. For me to be convincing as a tourist, Dewey had to be convincing. It had to be real.

"Doc, know what I think I'll do? We find Tomlinson, get checked into our hotel, I think I'll go down to the beach and bake a little bit. I haven't been really warm in about a month. Maybe send Bets a post card and rub it in."

Her mind still in New York, up there with snow and smoking chimneys . . . and her lover.

"Wait and call her when you get back. That would be faster. A card out of here would take a couple of weeks. Maybe a month."

"I don't care. I want her to get it and picture me down here on the beach. Up there freezing her ass off and she goes to the mailbox and there it is."

I smiled. "Because you're friends."

Received a catty smile in return. "Yeah, because we're friends."

I was less aware of the heat than of the three men watching us—a customs officer in naval blue and two soldiers in khakis. Baby shit brown, Tomlinson had described it. Not shy about staring at us, either. Ruddy faces, short black hair and with eyes you expect to find behind mirrored sunglasses. Looking right at us and not looking away when my eyes briefly met theirs. Forty-some people in line—still outside on the tarmac beneath a sign that read "Welcome to José Martí International"—and they had singled us out.

I touched Dewey's arm. "Give me a kiss."

She said, "Huh?"

"Give me a kiss. Like you mean it."

Privately, our relationship had changed. But publicly, Dewey was still Dewey. She was a nudger and a rough-houser, not a hugger or toucher. Public displays of affection were as out of character for her as they were for me. She said, "Knock off the mush, Ford. Not in front of all these people."

I gave her a tender smile, turned my back to the men and formed the words: "We-are-being-watched."

Received a quizzical expression—she'd missed it. Listened to her whisper, "Truthfully, 'bout the only time I like to kiss is when we're screwing. No offense," as I touched my lips to her ear and said, "Don't look. Those guys in uniform are staring at us."

She pulled away . . . stole a peripheral glance . . . grinned at me and said in a much louder voice, "Darling, when we get to the hotel, I'm going to give you a Christmas present you won't *ever* forget," then smothered me with a passionate stage kiss.

Well, maybe she was an actress. Just not a very good one . . .

Out of the corner of my eye, though, I could see the soldiers were laughing—See the Yankee couple? I heard one of them say, "Mother of God, her body! You think he'll know which end to use when he gets her in bed?" He said it loud enough that I knew he assumed I didn't understand Spanish. I listened to the other soldier say, "Men with money. They get all the beautiful women," which gave me pause—did they know I was wearing a belt loaded with carefully folded hundred dollar bills? But then heard him add, "If he was rich, of course, he would have come by yacht. Not on *Cubana!*" Which got a laugh.

I relaxed a little. They had been staring at Dewey, not at me. Couldn't blame them. She was wearing what she called her Lipstick outfit: sandals, small shoulder pack rather than a purse, and a burnt orange sundress that showed her legs, that turned her skin to copper, and made her blue eyes glow. Back in Panama, when she'd asked, "How do I look?" she'd blushed a little when I replied, "Healthy and fertile."

Now she wrapped her arm around my waist—part of her act—and said, "You're paranoid. They're just hanging out."

"Maybe so. We'll find out pretty soon." Meaning the two checkpoints we had to pass through.

At the immigration window, a dour woman checked a computer screen, caught my eyes for a second—a sharp, officious appraisal—before slipping a green visa card into my passport. No stamp for Americans. Then signaled for Dewey to come next. Customs gave us the same fast treatment. No search, no questions. We were gringos bringing money into the country. The official position seemed to be leave the tourists alone.

Outside, after Dewey had collected her luggage—I had only my carry-on—we walked across the street to a rental car stand: a tiny block house in a dusty yard beneath mango trees. Havanauto. I expected to find Soviet-made Ladas or Moskvitches. Instead there was a line of beat-up Nissan subcompacts that were not much bigger than golf carts. I went through them pretty carefully. Found a brown one that had a good emergency brake and a decent spare tire. There was no negotiating. Prices were fixed; it would be the same at the rental car agencies downtown. So I paid way too much in cash for the car; way, way too much for a liter of gas. A couple of teenage prostitutes with ripped skirts and dirty ankles watched the attendant pour the gas into the empty tank. Their reverence added a ceremonial flair. Cuba was out of petroleum. Something as valuable as a bottle of gas demanded their attention.

As we pulled out onto the boulevard, headed north, Dewey said, "See? All that worrying for no reason." I was looking in the rearview mirror . . . saw the customs officer who had been watching us step out into the street . . . saw him pause to look after us . . . saw him take a notebook from his shirt pocket and jot something down . . . watched him disappear in the direction of the Havanauto building.

I thought: *Damn.*

Dewey was still talking, telling me with her tone that she'd been right all along. "Know what your problem is, Doc? You think too much. Most people, I'd say it was their imagination. But not you. With you, it's your brain. The whole package." Her knees were jammed up against the dashboard and she was trying to find a comfortable position. It was an absurdly small car. She said, "What we're going to do is treat this like a vacation. Get some food in you, a couple of cold beers. Everything's going to be a lot simpler than you think. Find Tomlinson, that'll make you feel better."

But it wasn't simple finding Tomlinson. At the Hotel Nacional—marble floors, El Greco paintings, marble columns—a uniformed desk clerk told me he'd checked out two days before. We walked up the crowded street, as all the Cuban girls we saw, age twelve to maybe thirty, ignored Dewey and tried to sell themselves to me with their pointed looks.

"They're either crazy or they're desperate," Dewey fumed. "Don't they have any self-respect?"

I said, "To be with a gringo who has money?" She was shaking her head, just couldn't understand it when I told her, "It's not because they're crazy."

We found the Havana Libre. It looked just as I remembered it. And discovered that a man fitting Tomlinson's description had been at the bar the last couple of nights but that he had never checked in.

9

The Havana Libre was located downtown on Calles L and 23rd, a few blocks south of the sea and just to the west of Havana Harbor—one of the few tourist strongholds in a city that was imploding beneath the pressure of its own withering poverty.

The hotel was a beige domino stood on end, five hundred-and-some rooms, balconies, outdoor pool with private dressing cabanas on the mezzanine, conference facilities, a two-story domed lobby in which there was a garden bar and outdoor patio, plus two restaurants—though only one was occasionally open. "Closed for repairs," a sign on the door read. More likely, food rationing dictated limited hours.

A bottle of beer, Hatuey or Cristal, cost more than the bartender made in two weeks. A gristly hamburger was equal to the average Cuban's monthly salary. Not that Cubans could have purchased either even if they had the money. They were banned from entering hotels or the few restaurants. Castro didn't want his people's ideology polluted by outsiders.

I booked a room, then decided to splurge and get a suite. Dewey is a big woman. The prospect of our stepping over each other, banging into things, didn't appeal to me.

Pretty nice suite: fourteenth floor with ocean view, tile floors, bedroom, kitchenette with stove and refrigerator, neither of which worked, and furnished in fifties deco, like the suite in a Bogart movie, or as if time had stopped when Castro marched into Havana.

"I'll be go to hell," Dewey said. "A Russian television." She was fiddling with the thing, exploring the suite while I unpacked. "It's like something from the *I Love Lucy* days, man. Old black-and-white tube . . . Hey, check this out, Doc."

On the screen, a bottle-nosed dolphin was tail-walking; clicking and squeaking.

"It's Flipper. They get Flipper down here! See—he's trying to tell Chip and Ranger Rick something."

I watched for a moment. The Ranger and his son were speaking Russian to the dolphin over Spanish subtitles. American broadcasts that featured animals were once a favorite of Soviet media pirates. Less translation, less work.

"I've seen this one. Flipper's trying to lead them to a torpedo, I think." She seemed delighted by something that was both strange and familiar—yep, she was in Cuba, no doubt about it. She said, "You ever see anything so weird? Those boy actors, Chip and Sandy. They must be what, now? Probably forty-some years old? Down here, though, they're still kids. Teenagers in cutoffs, never aged a bit while the rest of the world got older." Then as she changed channels: "What're the chances we get ESPN? There's a Virginia Slims tournament on later I wouldn't mind seeing."

No doubt. Probably because Bets was playing.

I said, "I don't think the chances are good."

"Guess not . . . Christ, only three stations. Everything in goddamn Spanish."

Dewey with her sweet, sweet face and locker-room mouth.

I watched her plop down on the couch, then stand again and suddenly strip the orange sundress over her head. She stood there in translucent bra and bikini panties, thinking about something, scratching absently at belly and corn-silk pubic hair. Sensed me looking at her, turned, and said, "I'm not in the mood right now, big boy. Let's do it later; help us get loosened up before we run."

I was smiling.

She said, "Is that okay?"

"First thing I have to do is go from hotel to hotel and track down Tomlinson. Even if you were in the mood."

"Always trying to trick me into bed—you're so good for the ego, Ford."

"Yeah, well . . . He couldn't have gone far. He was low on money. I'll check the cheaper places."

"He should have left a message."

"He would have. That's what bothers me."

"There's a phone book. Why don't you use the phone?"

"Have you tried it?"

"You mean it doesn't work?"

"That's right."

"Nothing in this whole damn place works." She stretched, yawned, showing me she was tired. "You want me to come along?" Not wanting to, but offering.

No, I didn't want her along. Even before I tried to find Tomlinson, I needed to make a stop at the Masaguan Embassy. Dewey couldn't be a part of that.

I pulled her forehead to me, kissed it. "Take a nap. Or watch Flipper. I won't be gone for more than a couple of hours."

She was digging into one of her suitcases. "I show you this? What I think I'll do is go down to the pool"—she was now holding up what appeared to be two tiny pieces of red silk—"and get some sun."

"That's a bathing suit?" I'd seen her in many swimsuits, always competition Speedos or triathlon latex.

"The tiniest little bikini I could find." She was holding it in front of her, modeling it. "I got it in Madrid, the next morning after finding Bets. This, and I got a pair of these lacy little panties, the kind I always used to hate. They're jade colored, kind of shiny. Only I'm not going to show you. I'm going to wear them tonight, let you do some exploring for a change.'' She looked up. ''Like my suit? It's the new me.''

I almost said, ''I liked the old you just fine.'' Instead, I kissed her again and said, ''Just don't catch cold. And Dewey?''

''Yeah?''

''If someone knocks on the door, keep the chain on until you're sure who it is. Ask for identification. The word is *identificación*. Easy to remember.''

Her expression said you're-being-paranoid-again. When I didn't react, she said, ''You're serious?''

''Yeah. Humor me, okay?''

She was unsnapping her bra, her mind already down there at the pool. ''If you want.'' Then she said, ''I mean, this place seems so dangerous and all,'' as I locked the door behind me.

I'd been on the streets for less than twenty minutes before I was absolutely certain that I was being followed.

I hadn't had any problems driving to or from the Masaguan Embassy, so it took me by surprise.

But comforting, in its way. The good ones, the professionals—the small and elite group I was really worried about—are not so easily spotted. If they were tailing me, they would have worked in a kind of wolf pack; a lot of complicated switches and handoffs so that it was unlikely I would have seen the same person, or car, twice. Which is why I had looped and backtracked my way to Embassy Row. Even had to stop and fill up with black-market gas to finish the long trip.

But no, these were amateurs. Not very good amateurs at that. Two of them: a man and a woman, early twenties, dressed a little better than other Cubans on the busy streets, both black—the man onyx colored; the woman cinnamon skinned—and both trying way too hard to appear disinterested, as they tracked me down 23rd to Paseo where I checked at the desk of the Caribbean—no Tomlinson or Julia DeGlorio listed—then stepped back out into the December heat.

Now they were on the other side of the street, pretending to read a billboard: a rough painting of a devilish Uncle Sam being taunted by a Cuban soldier. The caption read: *Imperialistas! We Have No Fear of You.*

Standing there as if they'd never noticed it before—this old Cold War billboard that had been there in '80 during Mariel. I'd seen it.

I watched them in window glass and from the corner of my eye as I made the rounds—the shabby Inglaterra and the Kohly—calculating their motive as I did. Made a wide detour from the hotel area, past the sports center, the Ciudad Deportiva. Looked at the empty baseball diamond, picturing Fidel out there in his baggy Sugar Kings uniform; pictured myself in catcher's gear twenty years younger, harder, certainly colder, but never naive.

The couple was still with me. I looked at the knee-high grass in the outfield and thought about the situation. Probably careful scam artists who wanted to get a sense of my habits before they tried to set me up. Figure out why I was on the streets before they made their pitch. Maybe I was looking for black-market cigars . . . or young girls. Less likely was that they knew that I had come to Havana carrying ten thousand or more American dollars to bail out a friend's boat. The problem was, I wanted to find out. I could have lost them easily enough—established a pattern of entering and exiting hotels by the front, then left by the back—but I would have learned nothing. If Tomlinson's story had spread, if I'd already been singled out, I needed to know.

I slowed my pace. Walked down to the Malecón—Havana's busiest street, the old promenade that ribbons along the sea. Did some rubbernecking: big gringo tourist taking in the sights, looking at the lovers petting on the seawall, seeing waves break over the stone foundation of a city four hundred years old, watching the riverine flow of loafers and whores and thousands of Chinese bicycles—*Flying Pigeons*—that were the Maximum Leader's answer to the gas crisis. It reminded me of Asia: Cambodia and Vietnam.

Straw hats hunched over handlebars. Why was it that people with nowhere to go were always on the move?

Behind me, the couple stopped, waited. I thought: If they don't make a move it's because they know about the money. I wanted them to think—hey, here's our chance. So stood looking out at the Gulf Stream . . .

Land, sea, or air, ninety miles is ninety miles, except when describing the waterspace between Havana and Key West. It is a distance protracted by a generation of despair. I thought about men and women who had taken to launching inner tubes beyond the landfall beacon off Morro Castle and paddling north. Crossing the Florida Straits in a luxury liner is one thing, but attempting it in a rubber donut, one's legs fluttering through the bright skin of the abyss, is a whole different proposition. In Cuba, desperation framed crazy optimism, or there was no optimism at all.

I wondered about the couple tailing me. How desperate were they?

Beyond the flow of bicycles, the sea was inflated with gray light. I could smell the sea and the heated asphalt and there was the odor of sargasso weed on wet rock. A streak of indigo marked the Gulf Stream's edge—it swept in close to Havana Harbor—and there were men in inner tubes fishing the rim of the Stream as if fishing the bank of a river. There was no fuel for boats, so they floated out in inner tubes. More and more of them just kept going.

I turned and stared at the couple full faced for the first time. The woman—she looked more like a girl now that they were closer—averted her eyes, then seemed to gather courage. She gave me a bawdy wink, then puckered her lips as if kissing. It was the standard come-on of the *jinetera,* a street prostitute, but I got the impression she hadn't had much practice at it. I smiled, looked around, then pointed to my own chest: Me?

She winked again and I signaled her over. Watched the man give her a little nudge to get her going.

In Spanish, she said, "If you are looking for a good time, mister, perhaps I can be of help." A very formal approach for a whore.

I said, "Huh?" looking down at her. She was pretty in the way that parochial school girls are pretty. The uniform was in her face, her eyes, even though she wore tight jeans, a ruffled blue blouse. Her black hair was pulled back in a ponytail.

She said, "I will be very nice for you."

I shrugged, grinning foolishly. "I don't hab-la the Es-pan-yol, Sen-yor-rita," I said.

The girl turned helplessly to the man. Concerned, but trying to appear friendly, he came up, clapped me on the shoulder and said in Spanish, "I attend university with this lady. She likes you very much. But she is badly in need of money. Perhaps you and she could step into that private place"—he motioned toward the shadows of a nearby park—"and get to know each other better."

I said, "Huh? *Parque?* Sorry, buddy, I don't com-pren-dough."

Listened to the girl say, "Carlos, he doesn't understand a word you're saying. Must we do this?"

Carlos was nodding—relax; everything was going to be okay—as he said, "We've talked about it; it's what we've decided. We know he's a Yankee, just as I said. What does he care about the price?"

That gave me pause. He could have meant a couple of things by that. I decided I had to see it through. I touched the girl's shoulder. Felt her cringe before reconsidering and then she leaned heavily against me. "Carlos, I'm not certain I can do this."

Carlos said, "Do we have a choice?"

"Perhaps we should find someone else. He's so big, maybe he's dangerous."

"That's why we followed him, to make certain. He's a tourist. He seems respectable and clean. Lena, it's what we have to do."

Lena. The girl had a name.

Carlos smiled at me as he created a circle with thumb and index finger, then poked a finger through the hole. International sign language. Then he flipped his fingers at me twice: twenty bucks.

I let Carlos watch me think about it before reaching into my pocket and handing him the money. Then I took Lena by the hand and led her off to a little private hollow created by frangipani trees and hibiscus. When I turned to face her, she moistened her lips then got up on tippy-toes and tried to kiss me. Got a faint whiff of cornstarch before I stopped her by holding up my palm.

She said, "Is something wrong?" Started to say, "What do you want—?" before she remembered that I didn't understand.

I was listening; I wanted to see if Carlos and maybe friends were going to come through the bushes and jump me. If he or they had, I would have run. I would have assumed there was a possibility he knew about the money and that's all I needed to know. But there was only the sound of bike traffic on the Malecón and parrots in the trees. It was just Lena and me; Carlos out there waiting for us to be done.

The girl misinterpreted my reticence. She began to unbutton her blouse. Maybe I wanted to watch. I got a quick glimpse of pinecone breasts and belly scar before I touched her shoulder and said in Spanish, "Señora, I will not help you do this to yourself." I left her standing there as I walked out of the bushes and found Carlos sitting on a bench. He had his face buried in his hands. Again in Spanish, I asked, "How old is the child, friend?"

First there was the cornstarch, then her scarred stomach.

Carlos was talking before he realized who had spoken to him. "Two years old and she is very sick—" Then he stopped, looking up at me. I watched him teeter between fear and anger—maybe I was some kind of undercover cop. He thought about it before he asked, "Why did you pretend? You understood everything we said."

I didn't reply.

His tone took on a pleading quality. "The only reason we did it is to get money for the child. The things she needs, we can get them only on the black market, but we have no—"

I was shaking my head. I didn't want to hear his sad

story. If you allow it, the private tragedies of the Third World will worm their way into the cerebral core and drag you into a vacuum of that world's own despair. Tomlinson doesn't agree, but most emotional entanglements are pointless. It pleases me when he says that I am unfeeling—just as it irritates me when he says that I often lie to myself, implying that I am more empathetic than I really am.

I took four more bills from my pocket and stuffed them into Carlos's shirt. "I didn't touch her. With that, maybe no one will have to." I took him by the arm and steered him toward the bushes. I remembered the little shove he'd given Lena, now did the same to him. Told him, "Go get your wife."

It was sunset by the time I got back to the Havana Libre.

No one I'd spoken with had ever heard of Tomlinson. Same with Rita Santoya, a.k.a. Julia DeGlorio.

Dewey was still out by the pool, sitting in a lounge chair positioned to catch the sun's last rays. She had a bottle of Hatuey beer in her hand and was speaking animatedly with a squat, bearish man. The man had pale red hair and an incongruously dark mustache. He had a thoughtful, professorial style of nodding. Probably his way of showing that she had his full attention.

Dewey's corner of the deck was the only busy corner in the pool area. A small but intense coterie of men sat or stood or moved around her, apparently waiting for the red-haired man to finish so they could have a turn. Spaniards, mostly. A couple of Germans and maybe a wealthy African. Same with the white-shirted waiters. Each man demonstrated his interest by being pointedly indifferent as he peeked at Dewey, taking her in with his eyes, probably sending the red-haired guy telepathic messages to get the hell away from her.

I thought: Good-bye closet, hello world.

Not that I was surprised that Dewey had drawn a crowd. Her wet hair was darker, combed back. She had a copper-colored scarf wrapped around her waist, sarong-fashion. Very stylish. The two silk swatches of bikini top hung on her as if held by a mild breeze. She looked stunning, but that's not why I wasn't surprised. Undressed, or in any partial stage, Dewey's body and her mannerisms would awaken in men what therapists might refer to as the Tarzan Syndrome. Because there was no hint of self-consciousness in the way she moved—yawning, scratching, knees thrown wide apart as she leaned to grab her beer—her physical language communicated a primal acceptance of all body functions . . . a primitive, welcoming sexuality to any male strong enough . . . a form of muscle-and-marrow primal challenge.

It made me smile, watching men compete for her; a very old and intricate drama indeed. But it also made me a tad uneasy. I knew they'd never understand or appreciate why they were among the very few men who had seen her undressed the way she now was. Doubted if they would accept or sanction the inner conflict that had prompted her to buy and wear a tissue-sized swimsuit. Mostly I thought: God help the guy who actually tries to make a move on her.

I stood there for a couple of minutes, but she was way too involved for me to get her attention. So I took the elevator to our room, showered, changed into T-shirt and running shorts, and went back down for a swim. This time she saw me and waved me over, still listening to the red-haired guy but looking at me as I approached. I watched her mouth speak a private message to me: "He knows . . ." somebody. Couldn't decipher it. Then, when I was close enough, heard her say to the man, "Here's Doc." Then to me: "Doc, this is Lenny Geis."

The man was standing, extending his hand as she added, "Lenny was just telling me that he knows Tomlinson."

Geis was a couple of inches under six feet, probably weighed a little over two hundred pounds. Had one of those pulling-guard bodies, a layer of fat over pounds of muscle. Heavy chest and shoulders covered by a pelt of Viking hair and balanced on a set of spindly bronc-buster legs. He looked a little like a grown-up version of Mayberry's Opie: the jaw, the hair, the perceptive collie eyes. Probably in his mid to late thirties, but already had the handshake and the poise of the successful businessman. Not self-important, but city-smart, easy to talk to. A difficult impression to communicate without the executive's tailored-suit uniform, but Geis—wearing only green trunks and thongs—pulled it off without much effort.

"Doc, I was telling this beautiful lady. My week here? I went from the outhouse to the penthouse, just like that." He was smiling, being familiar as if we were old friends, as he repositioned chairs at a nearby table—"You guys be more comfortable here?"—and signaled the waiter. "Didn't I say that, Dewey? A place like this, meet one gringo a month, you're lucky. Especially around the holidays. Who'd want to spend Christmas in Havana? But first I meet Tomlinson and Julia, now you two. Man, I'm telling you, it's like being in jail and getting visitors. Just to hear someone speak English, you know?"

Dewey said, "Lenny's Canadian. He works in Havana a month on, a month off. He's got an important meeting tomorrow or he'd be up north and we'd'a missed him."

Geis said, "The Cubans do stuff like that on purpose." Set up meetings on Christmas Eve, that's what he apparently meant.

Dewey said, "So we're lucky I ran into him." She was standing behind me, massaging my shoulders, being affectionate—maybe her tourist act, maybe not—letting the men watching know that the game was over, her guy was here. I took an absurd and adolescent pleasure in their disappointment. Thought to myself, *You're as bad as they are,* aware that Lenny Geis appeared unaffected, like he was just as happy to see me.

I said, "Where in Canada?"

"Montreal," he said. "I've got an office there and my backers have offices in Toronto. Poor Dewey, she had to sit here and listen to the whole story." He looked at her so Dewey could smile and shake her head—she didn't mind. He said, "At first, it sounded like a great assignment. Spend every other month in Havana making contacts, setting up joint ventureships. That's my specialty. You know, laying the groundwork for when the Cuban economy switches to the free market. It *has* to happen, right? That's when Havana's gonna boom. The first people in, the ones who've done their homework, we're going to make a mountain of money." His tone was confident but his expression was boyish, vulnerable, as if he'd just about reached the end of his endurance but couldn't let himself quit. He said, "I believed that eighteen months ago and I still think it's true. But, man, my time in Havana goes slower and slower and the months I spend at home just fly by. I've got a fiancée up home." He looked at Dewey again—he'd already told her about his girl. "We're supposed to get married in June. Big wedding, catered with an orchestra, the whole works. So I about go nuts missing her, but with this shitty phone system we only talk maybe once a week and most of the time the phone patch doesn't work. Nothing against Cubans, ay? I like the Cubans a lot. But living in Havana is like living on another planet."

I listened to the rounded French vowels and the way he said, "ay?" as if it were an automatic question mark. I said, "You're the one who helped Tomlinson telephone me."

He was nodding. "He needed to call somebody, yeah. I met him out in front of the Hotel Nacional. Took one look at him and knew he was either Canadian or American—the difference might mean a lot in Quebec or Detroit, but not a darn thing down here. I liked him right away. He's an . . . unusual kind of guy, but nice. He told me about his trouble with the boat and I tried to do what I could." Geis's tone was fraternal—we North Americans have to stick together, right?

Noted the way he said "Quebec"—K-beck. Noted the nearly new Rolex Submariner watch on his left wrist. No rings but a necklace with a thin gold cross around his neck. Religious, perhaps; he was drinking pineapple juice while we sipped beers. I said, "Do you know where Tomlinson is?"

"Wish I did but I don't, sorry. He went somewhere but wouldn't tell me."

"Left Havana, you mean."

"That's what I couldn't figure out. Not many other places in Cuba for an outsider to go. Varadero Beach, maybe. They've got hotels there but very expensive. Pinar del Rio or maybe the Isle of Pines. Anyplace but a tourist area, Tomlinson and his girl wouldn't even be able to get food, because it's all rationed. There's not enough beans and rice for the Cubans. I told him that, but he still wouldn't say."

"Didn't tell you, or wouldn't?"

Geis said, "He wouldn't, so I didn't press it. Truth is, it was none of my business."

"Maybe he took the girl and went and stayed on his boat."

"No-o-o-o, I doubt that. The boats they impound, they keep them under guard out west of the city; this big harbor where they can keep an eye on them. No . . . he went somewhere, but it wasn't to his boat. Like I said, I tried to talk him out of it."

"But he went anyway, knowing you thought it was a mistake."

Geis smiled, trying to lighten things up. "I'm beginning to think it's a mistake for anyone to come to this island."

He was joking, but his eyes—weary and a little frantic—said he meant it.

Geis told me he was surprised that Tomlinson had left because he and the girl had planned to check in at the Havana Libre. I sat at the table knee-to-knee with Dewey and listened to him say, "Two days ago—yeah, it was Saturday—he came around asking if I could talk to the manager, maybe get him a special rate. Spaniards run this place"—he was talking about the hotel—"so at least it's clean even if the restaurant can't offer much of a menu. The manager works a monthly deal for me; he's become a buddy of mine, so he gave Tomlinson a pretty good discount and I thought everything was set. But early yesterday morning I was in the bar eating breakfast and your friend shows up looking very nervous, like he hadn't slept and maybe was a little hungover. He told me that he had to split. That's what he said, 'split.' And that he needed some money. In the way he talks, like a hippie. I gave him a couple hundred U.S. Figured sooner or later he was good for it."

I asked, "Was the girl with him?"

Geis said, "Julia? No. But I got the impression she had something to do with it. The thing that was upsetting him, why he had to go."

"Tomlinson told you that?"

"Uh-uh." Geis was thinking about it, apparently not sure himself. "When I asked what'd happened—I asked a couple of times—he put me off. Finally, he said, 'Turns out God has assigned me to help Rita,' which didn't make sense to me. Still doesn't, unless Rita's a nickname for Julia." He looked at Dewey. "Is it?"

I told Lenny Geis, "We've never met Julia," wondering what had motivated the woman to tell Tomlinson her real name, Rita Santoya. Watched Geis lift an eyebrow, cock his head—a visual comment: he'd met her but would remain noncommittal unless asked. So I asked.

"She seemed . . . okay, fairly nice," Geis said. Being diplomatic about it. "Much younger than him and attractive in an . . . in a plain sort of way. No makeup, very short hair. That type. Always stayed in the background, didn't say much. Was always on the go; didn't hang around with your friend much. I only saw her twice."

"I get the feeling you didn't like her, Lenny."

His smile was an attempt at deflection. "After a month in Havana, I like *anybody* who's from the States."

"Okay, you liked her but didn't trust her much."

Geis shrugged.

I said, "Lenny . . . Tomlinson's one of my oldest friends. Maybe you couldn't tell but he's not in the best of health. I'm not asking you to judge the woman, I'm just trying to get a sense of what's going on."

Geis thought about that for a little bit before he said, "Like I mentioned, I didn't talk to her much. I know what it is you're after . . . yeah, worried about an old friend, but . . ." He was wrestling with it. Finally, he put his elbows on the table and leaned toward me. "Know what it was? They didn't seem to fit together. Simple as that. You know how certain couples fit? Like my fiancée and me. We fit. You and Dewey, you two fit. But they didn't. It wasn't just her age. It was, well . . . Tomlinson is so open and outgoing, and she was so . . . silent. But she didn't miss anything. Always very alert, but it was more than that. Like she was always on her guard. I got the impression that she let Tomlinson do all the talking but, when they got back to the room, she's the one who made the decisions."

Dewey said, "Like she was using him."

Geis said quickly, "I wouldn't say that. I really wouldn't. It's just an impression I had, and I'm probably making too much of it. But you asked, and I really would like to cooperate—" He finished his pineapple juice; noticed our empty bottles, and began to search the pool area for a waiter. "—and I think Tomlinson would have said something if the girl was giving him a hard time. But he didn't. He described you, Doc. Told me to keep an eye out for you and to tell you he'd be in touch. 'A day or two,' he said. Not more than a couple of days."

"That's all?"

Geis was looking at Dewey, shaking his head slowly and starting to smile. "Well . . . there was something else. But I don't think he knew that you were bringing her along." Meaning Dewey.

"He wanted you to fix Doc up with a woman?" I couldn't tell if Dewey disapproved of the idea or just had a hard time believing it.

"No, what he said was, 'Tell Doc not to worry because—' " Geis stopped. "It's going to sound pretty weird."

"He's an old friend. I'm used to it."

"Okay—" He'd warned me. "—what he said was, 'Tell Doc not to worry because I've assigned an angel to protect him.' Something like that. 'He'll be traveling with an angel?' " Geis was trying to remember, amused by it. "It's hard to tell when he's joking, but he had this way of speaking like he was some kind of holy man. Or even God."

With that cross around his neck, Geis might be offended. So I didn't tell him that, lately, Tomlinson had been talking more and more like both.

Geis came by our room at seven to take us to dinner. To join us, really, since I'd insisted on paying Tomlinson's loan and using the interest to pay the tab. I decided a night on the town wouldn't hurt. As Dewey had said, "Why sit around on our butts waiting?" Besides, I had the names that Armando Azcona and Juan Rivera had provided—Juan's secretary had offered a couple of other bits of information—and I wanted to look around Havana, see if I could decipher where and how to get in touch with the anti-Castro underground. Something to do, like an old hobby.

I opened the door to find Geis dressed in white dinner jacket and tropic worsted slacks, red hair brushed, mustache trimmed, shoes with a plastic shine. Smoking a cigar, too. One of the big ones wrapped hard with black leaves.

"Cohiba," he told me, moving it back and forth under his nose. "Couple of weeks ago, Fidel gave me one of his Trinidads to try. Next to that, this's the best cigar in the world."

Jesus, put a dinner jacket on the guy and he became a name-dropper. Having meetings with Fidel?

An hour earlier, I'd made it a point to strike up conversations with some of the hotel staff and managed to slip in questions about Lenny Geis. Yes, they said, he was a businessman from Canada. Yes, he'd spent every other month at Havana Libre for more than a year. Certainly—he was a nice man! And very important, judging from the government officials who sometimes came to dine with him.

Now, from across the room, Dewey took one look at Geis, hooted, and said, "Shit, Lenny, you didn't tell me we were going formal!" and hurried back to the bedroom to change. She came out a few minutes later wearing a gauzy, form-fitting black dress with silver buttons down the front that I'd not only never seen before but couldn't imagine her wearing. She saw the question forming in my eyes and answered in advance. Leaned to my ear to whisper: "Madrid, you big dufuss. Think I order all my clothes from Cabela's, like you? And I've got on those little jade underwear I told you about."

Finding Bets in bed with the French tennis star had been good for the Spanish fashion industry.

We walked seaward, then east along the Malecón. The evening had weight to it, warm and saturated with Gulf Stream air. A tropic night with stars above the silhouettes of stone garrisons and palms, while salsa music—it always sounded like an accordion player on a galloping horse—drifted through the streets.

Havana seemed healthier, more alive after dark . . . probably because decay is best revealed by sunlight.

The promenade was busy: bicycles, strollers, black-market hucksters, a few cars. Mostly Detroit's big-finned classics coming out of the shadows and showing themselves in the streetlights. Fifty-seven Chevys and Studebakers, a '49 Ford cruising beetle-like with its lavender taillights. They were something for Geis to talk about. Issue one of his nonstop monologues that seemed designed to purge loneliness rather than demonstrate what an expert he was on Cuba. At least the cars got him off the subject of prostitutes, who were hounding him, he said, making his life more difficult than it needed to be—he was so committed to the fiancée waiting for him in Montreal that he resented the temptation. "A lot of them, you can't help but notice are just plain gorgeous," he had said, "particularly some of the young mulattos. But I've got a good solid routine; I'm *working*. You won't catch me paying ten bucks to bring one up to my room!"

Now, walking beneath ficus trees, studying the traffic, he said, "These cars would be worth a mint back in the states. A forty-two Packard, you kidding? That old Buick? What'a you think *that'd* be worth? But they're just transportation to the *habaneros*. The only machines in the whole damn country that still work . . . use baling wire and Jeep tires to keep them running. Their gas ration is like ten gallons a month so they trade chickens, fish—you name it; their *sisters*—for a little extra gas so they can cruise the Malecón at night."

Dewey, who'd missed her run and wasn't in the best of moods, said, "I've got a new Corvette back home. Candy apple red." Not particularly interested. She was walking between Geis and me. Geis, with his short legs, was having a tough time keeping up.

Maybe to slow her, he said, "But your 'vette's not worth half what these cars are worth. Believe it. Couple years ago, the Cuban government was so tight for money they offered new Russian Ladas to the owners in trade. You know, polish up the classics and sell them for tens of thousands on the international collectors' market. But the *habaneros* didn't want that Russian garbage, so they started hiding their cars. The one Castro's people really want is a fifty-five Chrysler convertible." He looked at Dewey, then at me. Did we know why? I waited it out until he said, "Because it was Ernest Hemingway's car. White Chrysler two-door, red-leather upholstery. He lived just south of Havana, drove it to *Cojímar* every day to fish. Remember *The Old Man and the Sea?* Hemingway would drive around with the top down, figuring out the story in his head. But Castro's people never found the thing, so it's probably long gone. What'a you think a car like that'd be worth?" He was serious now, talking to me man to man. I waited until he said, "I figure the bidding would start at a couple hundred thousand, go up pretty quick to a million-five, maybe an even two. Remember what someone paid for Elvis's car a while back? Get some rich Japanese involved, yeah, I could see it happening."

When I said, "That's a lot to pay for a Chrysler," Geis's slow chuckle told Dewey that I didn't know anything about it. But when Dewey said, "Shit, with Hemingway alive and still *in* it, that's too much to pay," he let it go.

That showed me Dewey was having an impact on him, too.

He liked doing that. Liked pointing out bits and pieces of Havana, then calculating what they would be worth in Canada or the U.S. "Back in the world," he would say. Eating pork with lime and drinking mint mojitos at La Bodeguita—a cramped little restaurant where graffiti covered the walls—he said, "Frame some of the signatures, box up all the little signs and mementos, they'd bring thousands at an auction in New York. It's history," he said. "This little restaurant is so famous. Jane *Fonda's* name's on that far wall. She came to visit Fidel after sitting on that ack-ack gun in Hanoi, pretending to shoot down American planes. Hell, she'd of done it if she'd had the chance."

This Canadian talking like some pissed-off vet, showing me he empathized. Why else?

I had already studied the walls, not looking for famous names but searching for a bit of graffito that Rivera's secretary had told me about. Didn't find it.

Geis behaved the same way while he and Dewey drank daiquiris at Floridita. "That painting of Morro Castle behind the bar? That bronze bust of Ernest? Man, the *stools*. All priceless."

Geis toured us around Old Havana. Stone streets just wide enough for an oxcart, stone buildings with verandas hanging over the sidewalks. "Like New Orleans," he said, "only not that fake, touristy bullshit. People *live* in these places. Sometimes two families to an apartment." Every block, pointed out a statue or a museum . . . Lenin, Marx, Guevara . . . the Rosenbergs, too—"They're heroes here, the American traitors who sold A-bomb plans to the Soviets.'' He whispered it, as though it were a dangerous thing to say. When Dewey told him, "The whole place's like one big museum,'' he said, "Yeah, the museum of a failed system. I keep telling my fiancée that Havana gets to me. Like living in a city that's dead but has survivors walking around. But believe me, one day there'll be a ton of money to be made here.''

Now we were in the oldest part of Havana, the Plaza de la Catedral, a cobblestone courtyard fronted by ornate block buildings. The opening to each building was set deep behind stone pillars so the courtyard seemed enclosed by a catacomb of caves. I'd been standing in the background listening to Geis talk about it, working hard at charming Dewey, fiancée or no fiancée. I drifted off by myself when he started talking about the priests, the bishops—"I have a strong interest in the church,'' he explained—and the conquistadors who once frequented the place. Then I stopped at the entrance of what appeared to be an open cathedral. I stood peering in as if looking at Gothic windows, the coral rock floors, and the Nativity scene near the gold-and-onyx altar—first sign of Christmas I'd seen in Havana. But what had really caught my attention was a number and a letter that had recently, very recently, been scraped into a stone archway: *8A*.

Juan Rivera's secretary had told me that *8A* was what I should look for. It was the newest of the ever-changing code words that Havana's anti-Castro people used to communicate. Find that symbol and I might be able to connect with someone named Molinas or Valdes, the contact Armando Azcona had given me.

I didn't have to ask why dissidents went by single names and kept changing their codes.

I gave it a few seconds before turning toward the garden at the center of the courtyard. There were a few people sitting on stone benches in the darkness. I thought about strolling over and making a polite tourist inquiry: "Did my tour guides Mr. Molinas or Mr. Valdes pass by here?'' but decided it would be a stupid thing to do unless I really needed help. Besides, Geis was coming toward me now . . . taking Dewey's arm as if they were on a Sunday walk.

"Got to say, you've got taste, Doc. Wanna know what you're looking at?" I thought he meant the graffito but, no, he was talking about the open room of the cathedral. He leaned up against one of the limestone pillars, pointed, and said, "This is one of my favorite places in Havana, the Cathedral of the Conception. It was built more than four hundred years ago"—he looked at Dewey to see if she was impressed—"to be like the Vatican of the New World. See that little niche in the wall? This place was so holy, Columbus himself used to be buried right there. Well, not buried but . . . interred. Like in a vault?"

I was trying to read the marble slab beside the niche. Difficult because it was in archaic Spanish . . . something about remains that were to be preserved for a thousand years in remembrance of a nation. I wondered which nation, Cuba or Spain?

Geis was still talking to Dewey. "Columbus, his bones I mean—the actual explorer, I'm talking about—he lay right there for more than a hundred years until he disappeared like in nineteen-hundred. Him and his little solid lead box."

Dewey said, "You're telling us somebody came in and stole Christopher Columbus?"

"Not really, but some of the religious Cubans—there're more religious people here than you'd think—they'd like to believe Columbus never left. Not because of what he did. Jesus, the Indios *hate* him for what he did. It's because of the medals he supposedly wore around his neck. You've seen the paintings I'm talking about?"

Dewey turned to me and said, "In a place that doesn't get ESPN, I guess you have to get interested in history or go nuts, huh?" Geis chuckled, showing that he really liked her style. "I know what you're saying, yeah, it seems kind'a dry, right . . . ? Anyway, what probably happened was, the Spaniards shipped his remains back to Spain. Columbus I'm saying. Him and the medals—one given to him by Queen Isabella and blessed by the pope, the other some kind of sacred medallion the Spaniards took from this rebel Indian before they burned him at the stake. The beer you were drinking, Hatuey?'' With his good Spanish, Geis pronounced it correctly: AH-tu-way. He said, ''It's named after him, Yara Hatuey. That's why it has a picture of an Indian on the label. Hatuey supposedly gave the conquistadors fits before they finally caught him, and Columbus was given the medallion. Like to show they had control of the island and prove that Hatuey was dead. Before they burned him, know what this Indian asked when they offered to baptize him? He asked if there were any conquistador Christians in heaven. When they told him yes, plenty, he said he'd rather go to hell, so go ahead and light the fire.''

I was looking at the *8A* carved into the arch as Dewey said, ''So what would Columbus and his medals be worth back in the states?'' joking, but giving it a soft touch. Maybe Geis would get it, maybe he wouldn't.

I realized Geis was looking from me to the arch, then back to me. It had finally dawned on him what had really drawn me to the cathedral; I could tell by his sudden nervousness. I listened to him tell Dewey, ''It's like all this waterfront property. A fortune. Whatever the international money guys will pay for it,'' before he touched my shoulder and said, ''We better be moving along, ay?''

Geis waited until Dewey had crossed the lobby, headed for our room before he said, ''I notice you've got an interest in street art, shit like that. A guy like you—kind of bookish, like a college professor—that's kind'a unusual, huh?''

No longer in the presence of a lady, Lenny Geis had an earthier vocabulary.

We were sitting in the patio bar of the Havana Libre. I could have chosen to watch Dewey walking to the elevator—swing of hips, bounce of soft hair; full of herself, confident in the person she perceived herself to be and secure in her view of the world.

I could have watched her, but didn't. Later . . . later, I would deeply regret that small indifference. . . .

Instead, I looked through the palms into the street where

young girls in tight dresses stood staring back at us. Their restlessness, standing out there wanting something to happen, put me in mind of behavior that was familiar. Stray dogs?

I took off my glasses and used a napkin to clean them, as I said, "We've got an audience, Lenny."

He didn't have to look. "The *jineteras?* They're always out there. The manager won't let them in unless they're with a guest. Hey . . ." Now he did take a peek. ". . . you see a tall mulatto in a white dress? She's usually there; always wears the same white dress, but clean. I mean, *spotless*. No-o-o-pe . . . must be two dozen or so and . . . but she's not around. . . ." He sat back in his chair. "She'll show up. Always does. Believe me, once you see her you'll remember. No older than nineteen with legs that go clear up to her tits. My God, and her *face*. I've never said a word to her. I've got no reason, right? But sometimes I think she comes to the Havana Libre just to see me. The way she looks at me, you know? Stares right into my eyes. God *damn!* A girl like that, back in the states, what'd she be worth? She'd be grabbed by some rich doctor. A rock star maybe? Anything she wanted. The kind of woman you see at the best dinner parties. What a buddy of mine calls a Gold Card woman—kind of like Dewey . . . no offense."

I smiled—none taken.

Geis said, "The mulatto shows up, you'll understand. That's the thing. In Havana? She's just another ten-buck whore." He paused for a moment, his mind on the girl, before he added, "Not that I care. Because it's like I told you: I stick to my routine. Watch my health, never have more than a couple of drinks a night. For me, Havana's strictly business. That's what I told my fiancée—an investment of time that's going to pay off big."

I was still smiling at him. Not that I found him funny, but many times I'd seen Westernized men and women struggle against what they perceived to be that dark side of the Third World. I had done my share of struggling as well. I said, "They can really put the hook in you, Lenny."

"*Hook?* You know why God gave women pubic hair?

To *hide* the hook. But don't get the wrong idea, Doc. I'm not *interested*. You know what it's like . . . bored and alone in a place like this. I'd never do anything about it. But no—" He finished his daiquiri and motioned for the waiter to bring another round. His fourth tonight. "—what I was asking you about was the graffiti." Changing the subject, putting the ball back in my court.

When I didn't answer right away, he said, "I noticed you studying it at the restaurant, then at . . . other places around town."

Geis knew what the symbol over the cathedral door meant. I was certain of it. I said, "You seemed pretty interested yourself. A number and a letter over a church door. Why would somebody put that there?"

I could see that he wanted to finesse it . . . then I watched him change his mind. Finally, he said, "You came down to help your friend, right? That's the only reason?"

"The one and only reason."

"I've got to ask for your word of honor on that. Seriously. I'm seen with the wrong person in this town, they'd put me on the next plane out."

I was tempted to say "Scout's honor." Instead, I said, "Pay off Tomlinson's bill and get him back on his boat. That's why I came."

He cleared his throat and scooched his chair closer to the table so he didn't have to speak so loud. "Okay, then let me give you some advice. Things go on in this country you don't want to know about or even hear about. The way to deal with it is see no evil, hear no evil. Do that—which is *exactly* what I do—you won't have any problem."

"It's that bad? Eight A?" I said it in Spanish: *Ocho A*.

It got me a long look of appraisal before Geis said, "Let's drop the bullshit, Doc. You mind? The way you were looking at it, I could tell it meant something. You're from Florida. A smart guy and educated. Maybe you've got friends in the Cuban community. Maybe they told you one or two things." He held up his palm to silence me. "Don't tell me. I don't want to know. I'm just saying the smart thing to do is ignore shit like that. A place like this, you're being watched even if you don't think you're being watched.'' He swirled the ice in his glass, began talking in a normal tone of voice. ''It's good advice and I hope you take it. No offense, but you don't know how things work down here.''

I waited until the waiter had placed his drink on the table and left us before I said, ''Just looking at something carved over a church entrance could get me in trouble?''

He nodded. ''In this country, people have had their dicks bobbed for less than that.'' I watched him wait for me to reply—a guy who liked to talk, but not sure he should. Finally, he asked, ''You really don't know what it means?''

''No, but I'm getting curious. And what you said about the way Cuba works. Politics? I'd like to hear about it.'' I gave it an articulate touch: the professorial type eager to learn.

Geis took a look over both shoulders; lowered his head to look through the palms at the prostitutes. He said, ''You want to take a walk?''

''*Ocho A* is street language,'' Geis said, ''for a guy who was executed, a Cuban general named Ochoa.''

Arnaldo Ochoa—he'd played second base in the exhibition game with Castro; a man I had met briefly and liked immediately. I'd guessed what the symbol meant, but wanted to hear Geis tell it.

''People are so afraid to speak, everything down here is in code or sign language. Someone's pissed at Fidel? Even talking to a family member, they scratch their chin—you know, meaning a beard?—to signal who they're talking about. It's because they're afraid to say his name. For his brother Raul, they touch their mouth because he's gay. Hangs out with the beanie-weanie packers a few blocks from here, down Twenty-third at the Casa de las Infusiones. No one comes right out and says anything that can get them into trouble, so they invent these signs and signals. *Ocho A*. That stands for Ochoa, the dead general.''

I said, ''Because they're afraid to write it out.''

Geis said, "Yeah, but it's a lot more complicated than that."

We had walked south on Twenty-third past the University of Havana campus, then beneath seventeenth-century stone warehouses with wash hanging from the windows, old men and women sitting in doorways.

Lots of restless, wakeful people in Havana. It was a few minutes after ten p.m.

Several of the prostitutes had tagged along after us but finally gave up. Looking back at them had given me an opportunity to see if we were being followed. It seemed as if we were on our own. Streets were nearly empty. Even so, Geis kept his voice low.

"Ochoa was Cuba's most popular military leader. He fought with Fidel against Batista, then led troops in Venezuela, Angola, Ethiopia, you name it. Even the Russians considered him a military genius. Placed their own troops *under* him, and he was probably Fidel's best friend. But Ochoa really screwed up."

"Something he did, you mean."

"Arnaldo Ochoa? No way. He was an absolute straight shooter. Didn't take bribes, followed orders, lived like the rest of these people live; crummy little house in a neighborhood. No, what he did was became too popular with his troops and with the Cuban people. The whole country knew his name. Which is why a few years ago—eighty-nine, maybe?—Raul marched him out in front of a firing squad and had him shot. No more Ochoa, no more threat to Fidel. You know what his last words were? 'I'm no traitor.' That's the kind of man he was."

I said, "So that's how Cuba works."

"Abso-fucking-lutely right and don't you forget it. When it comes to Fidel, don't believe a thing you read about him in America. Canadian press? Same bullshit. The American media, man, they've always loved the guy. You see that thing with Barbara Walters? Dan Rather? Closest thing to blow jobs Fidel ever got with his pants zipped." Geis leaned forward, getting into it. "Back in the Batista days, nobody in Cuba even knew who the fucking guy *was* until the *New York Times* runs a series about him being a national hero. Some left-wing reporter interviews this pathological liar—Fidel, I'm talking about—and comes out with stories that make Fidel seem like Sir Lancelot. Reports everything Fidel says as the gospel truth.

"Batista, the idiot, tried to have his people destroy all the copies of the story as they came off the boat, which made every Cuban on the island want to read the fucking thing. Said Castro'd killed a lot of Batista's troops, all bullshit. The only skirmish Fidel was in, he ran off and left his men. But this thing, this story said he was like a God living up there in the mountains, idolized by thousands. So what happens? Everybody who reads it, millions of Cubans, they start to idolize this guy they know absolutely nothing about. It was in the *New York Times,* so it had to be true, right? The men instantly admired him, every woman on the island wanted to screw him, have his illegitimate child—and, buddy, there are *plenty* of those floating around. The other revolutionaries, hey! it didn't matter that they thought Fidel was a weirdo, a joke. Called him *El Loco,* and they *meant* it. They laughed at him. But Castro had the people on his side. That's all that mattered."

Geis said, "So when Ochoa, Fidel's most dedicated friend, got too popular, they used AK-47s on him. But see"—Geis touched my arm to emphasize his point—"Ochoa wasn't pure Castilian like Fidel's other top guys. He had some Indio in him. Fidel called him *El Negro,* like it was a pet name, but I think the man has a thing about race . . ." Geis hesitated. "You with me so far?"

I said, "I'm learning a lot, Lenny."

Listening to him, putting it all together—Geis's background, this right-wing Canadian knowing the whole Castro story—it was true.

Geis liked compliments. They seemed to make him stand a little taller. I listened to him say, "So . . . let's say there are certain people in this country who aren't pure Castilian and who think Cuba needs a change of leadership. Like there's this Afro-Cuban group, the *Abakua,* an all-male secret society—a guy told me they drink blood from human skulls. Not just blacks either; lots of whites have joined up. They are a very violent people, heavy into crime and Santería, so Castro deals with them a couple of ways. One, he pays them public respect. Population wise, they're the majority, see? The Santeros, I'm talking about, not the *Abakua*. But two, he liquidates any *Abakua* who gets out of line. His Gestapo shows up in the night, and the troublemaker *disappears*.

"To the *Abakuas*—and I'm not saying it's just them—but to those *kind* of people, Arnaldo Ochoa is a hero. Which is why they use his name in code. Other than that, we are talking about a group so far underground you never hear a thing about them. Just *Ocho A*, like a reminder they're there."

I said, "So that's why it made you nervous, my looking at it."

"Fuckingaye right. Let's face facts: I don't know you from Adam, you don't know me, but in a place like this, us gringos have to hang together. That's why I'm telling you. If I hadn't met up with Tomlinson . . . I *liked* the guy. He says you're friends, so that's why I'm trusting you. Tomlinson, there's no doubt he's exactly what he seems to be. But you . . . for all I know, you could be one of those holdover Soviet spooks that Fidel keeps on his private staff. His *Rojo Seis*—that's what they supposedly call themselves. Only six of them, right? Red Six. Sends these Russians out to do his personal dirty work, the intricate stuff, espionage or setting up foreigners. Speak their language, then arrest them or shoot them in the back of the head. Just telling you, I'm taking a risk."

Castro's elite special operations team of Russian mercenaries, Red Six, had been active in 1980 at the time of the refugee boat lift. Still listening to Geis, I had a fast memory flash of our long-ago escape from the harbor in an IBS—Inflatable Boat, Small. All that Gulf wind and black water. Remembered Armando Azcona leaning against me, bleeding, but conscious enough to say to me, "You think now they'll change the name to *Rojo Cuatro*?'' Meaning Red Four.

To Geis, I said, ''You're serious about this.''

''Aren't you listening to what I'm saying? Of course I'm serious.''

''About the Russians, I mean.''

''That they'd set me up?'' Geis shrugged, palms turned upward. ''Havana was built on Indian corpses and Spanish rumors. That's an expression here. I don't know if they'd set me up. Shit, I don't really know if Fidel has Russians on his intelligence staff anymore. It's just one of those things you *hear*. These spooky guys, experts in just about everything, and Fidel sends them out like falcons. It's a *rumor*. Like Raul wears dresses, Fidel's got inoperable throat cancer. You know the kind of thing I'm talking about? Fidel and Santería, there's another one. That he actually believes in that shit—he's the one that got Noriega painting himself with chicken blood, making sacrifices.

''What else the Cubans got besides rumors? You don't get any news here. The media's a promotional branch of the government. Nobody knows anything. You got about a thousand different little government agencies all out for themselves. Raul runs the military and he hates the Interior Ministry and the Interior Ministry hates Castro's people, and Castro's people don't give a shit 'cause everybody's corrupt and that's okay as long as Fidel keeps his job.

''The whole fucking country,'' Geis said, ''is like a hockey brawl. No one winning, just some people losing a little faster than others. It's the way the laws are. Everything's illegal, so everyone has to be a criminal to survive. It's the way Fidel wants it. Keep everyone ignorant *and* guilty, he's in complete control.''

''It's a technique,'' I said.

''Fuckingaye,'' he said. ''The Big Lie, just like Hitler.''

''You know him through meetings. Castro.''

''Well . . . I've been to one. Just because I don't like the guy doesn't mean I can't do business with him.''

Maybe my silence told Geis I thought he was exaggerating because, after a short pause, he added, ''Well . . . actually, the meeting was with him and about ten of his advisors. That's where he gave me the cigars . . . one of his advisors, really, 'cause when Fidel's in the room nobody talks but him. That Trinidad, it's a fine smoke."

The way he said it, I decided he might be lying about the whole thing. "Sounds like you're doing pretty well, Lenny."

"Yeah," he said, "but it's just part of my job." Grinned at me—enough of *that* subject. Said, "Only, I'm off duty now."

We were at the corner of Twenty-third and G. Off to our left, an alleyway cut between buildings. Across the street was a seedy looking bar, the Casa de las Infusiones. Flickering oil lamps and smoke, dark shapes moving inside. A place that would have ceiling fans and curtains of strung beads. I remembered Geis saying it was the bar where Raul Castro sometimes hung out. I was deciding whether I should ask Geis how he knew so much—why would anyone risk telling him what he'd told me?—when I heard a soft mewing sound, then what seemed to be a child's muffled scream.

I looked toward the alley to see a boy standing there. He looked about ten, but probably older. Baggy pants, no shirt. He had an index finger pressed to his lips—be *quiet*—and was motioning to me frantically. Geis was looking by the time I turned and started toward the boy. I felt his hand on my shoulder and heard him say, "Are you nuts? Stay out of it."

There was another scream, this one louder. Definitely a child back there in some kind of trouble. I took off running toward the boy, hearing Geis call after me, "Hey . . . HEY! It's not our business!" Heard him yell, "I'll leave you . . . I *mean* it, man!"

I watched the boy turn into the mouth of the alleyway as if to lead me. At a jog, I followed him into the darkness. Black stone walls on each side closing to form a passage not wide enough for a car. Back doorways blocked by garbage, cobblestones wet, glistening with sewage. One of those big city caverns, walls high above, that stank of uric acid . . . human waste . . . rodents that ambushed from gutters.

When I nearly slipped and fell, I slowed to a walk. My eyes wouldn't adjust. I took my glasses off, cleaned them on my shirt.

Glanced behind me. Narrow rectangle of light at the entrance.

Geis was gone.

Peered ahead. The boy had disappeared, too.

Stopped and listened. Heard a weary call in Spanish—*Help me!* It seemed to come from some far corner of the alley . . . a sound that echoed strangely, as if it originated beneath the cobblestones.

I began to move slowly toward it, fishing in the pocket of my cargo pants for some kind of weapon. I found the hotel key and I wedged it into my left fist, point protruding between my knuckles. I stripped off my leather belt and wrapped it around my right fist, small brass buckle with anchor facing outward. Picked up the pace, running, until I came to the alley's back wall.

I stopped and turned, feeling my heart pound, breathing heavier than I should have needed to.

Off to the left and right were narrow walk spaces between buildings, no light at all.

Which way?

Stood listening again.

Somebody . . . please!

The sound came from my right, way back in and from below. The subterranean sound again. Could the kid be stuck in a drain? I took several fast steps toward the walk space . . . which is when I felt big hands grab me from behind.

Heard: "Be smart, friend. Don't move." The guttural Spanish of a big man.

It scared the hell out of me . . . demolished the careful process of thought and self-perception. I was no longer the person who rushed to the aid of children. Instantly, I was a diminished creature . . . small, panic charged . . . I was prey. The abrupt adrenal fear squeezed at the anus. It buckled my legs and instigated the process of physical shock . . . which, in the microsecond of its happening, I recognized . . . so it vanished.

I turned to free myself . . . but the man got his hands around my chest, holding me. I tried to ram him into the wall, feeling his breath in my ear, smelling him—tobacco smell and sweat and a sweeter odor like cologne or incense—but he swung me around like a big rag doll.

A very powerful guy. Stronger than me. He seemed quicker, too. The combination did not rally my confidence. Even more unsettling, he was still talking to me, very calm. "Why make it difficult, friend? It's nothing personal, why take it so personally? Or perhaps it's true"—His fingers found my windpipe, a sudden, numbing pressure—"that you are a man who enjoys the dance."

Christ, the guy was having fun.

Heard him say, "Dance with me *now?*"

I felt his whole weight on my back, riding me. I stumbled around, fighting to keep my balance. Got my hands under his wrist and pried the thick fingers free long enough to grab a bite of air . . . then his grip was on my throat again. I had enough thoracic pressure remaining to create gagged words: "Stop . . . no more . . ."

The grip relented. I began to breathe again in his deflated silence. "Ah-h-h-h, you learn too quickly, friend. So you agree? It's nothing personal."

I nodded, trying to buy myself some time, willing my brain to work; calculate how to deal with it. I said, "Right, of course. Nothing personal . . ."

"I can do it quickly, or you can make it difficult for both of us."

Do *what* quickly? What the hell was he talking about?

I said, "You want money? Let me go, I'll give you money. I've got a watch, too. A nice one."

He was still behind me, his arms keeping me under control. "Yes, the money. I will take the money. With men like us, it is business. But . . . it's like these whores say: If it's business, why is it so much fun?" Delighted laughter—*tee-hee-hee*—his heavy chest spasming on my back.

With men like us . . . ?

I listened to him say, "As long as you understand."

Panic time again. This wasn't a robbery. He knew who I was, this guy with the freaky laugh, and now he was asking my approval before he murdered me. His tone, what he was implying was: *We're in the same line of work, you and I.*

I stood there trying to lock onto that cold place within me, the bell-hard conduit that was unblemished by emotion. No fear in there, no rage, no peace . . . just clarity. I had a fleeting picture of Dewey back at the hotel, then back in Florida, wondering why I'd never returned. I saw Tomlinson, those haunted eyes of his, meditating my disappearance away. No . . . Tomlinson would feel what had happened; he would *know.*

At least, he would convince himself that he knew. . . .

I stopped struggling for a moment, let the man feel me relax. Gave it two or three seconds—both of us breathing heavily—before I twisted and drove my left elbow back into his abdominal triangle, the solar plexus.

I heard the air woof out of him hot on the back of my neck as I turned and locked his right elbow in the crook of my arm, twisted it abruptly, using my hip as a lever, and drove my fist, shielded by the hard brass buckle, into his throat. I hit him a second time on the bridge of the nose, then three more times in the throat before I released my lock on his elbow.

I heard a metallic gong on the cobblestones—he'd dropped something—as he fell to his knees, making a gagging noise. It was the sound of a dry pump sucking air. I stutter-stepped and kicked him in the ribs . . . positioned myself to kick him again, this time in the face, but caught myself. Stood there feeling a rage as strong as nausea move through me, a predatory fever that I knew to be part of me, but that I loathed. I waited, breathing heavily . . . felt the fever receding, receding, then, finally . . . it grew smaller and vanished back into its dark hole.

The man was on the ground in a fetal position, hands over his windpipe. Still making the gagging noise, but he seemed to be getting some air in.

I searched around on the pavement until I saw a chromium gleam. Stooped and picked up a thin shaft of metal that was spaded on one end, scalpel-sharp. It was something I'd seen before. An embalmer's tool. A trocar? I wasn't sure of the name. Slide it up through the throat and remove the brain.

He'd dropped it when he fell. I could hear him saying, *I can do it quickly*, as if he knew exactly what he was doing. Like he was an old hand who'd done it before.

I thought, Yeah. A guy who loved his work.

I tossed the shaft into the darkness and knelt beside him. I frisked him quickly as I said, "Who sent you? You were going to kill me—*why?*"

He rolled slightly to his back. He was looking up at me,

but it was too dark to look into his eyes. Jesus, the guy was huge—had to be a couple inches taller than me, had to outweigh me by forty, fifty pounds.

"Tell me!" To threaten him, I grabbed his throat but immediately yanked my hand away—the feel of the fibrous esophagus and Adam's apple was all wrong . . . much too flat and soft. I'd done some serious damage.

I said, "Tell me why, I'll go get help," not certain I meant it.

His reply—a whistling *tee-hee-hee*—told me he was sure that I did not . . . and that he didn't much care. No fear at all in his freakish laugh.

I stood and looked toward the walk space from which I'd heard the child calling. Had there been a young boy in trouble? Or had it been a trick to lure me into the alley?

I began to move cautiously toward the walk space, keeping an eye on the big guy. I called toward the darkness, "Hey? Anybody in there?" with a voice that sounded much steadier than I felt. I hoped there would be no reply; no reason to continue on. Stopped at the entrance, listening. Heard a strange slapping noise, coming closer. It took me a long moment, much too long, to realize it was the sound of someone running; someone charging right at me. I was already backing away when a human figure materialized out of the gloom, sprinting as if to run me down . . . which is why it was so surprising to be hit with tremendous impact from behind.

"Blindsided" is the football term. Neck vertebra pop, the optic nerves transmit an explosive burst of white light. I went down in a heap; landed on my stomach in the slime. Immediately got to my knees and turned, crouching.

I heard: "What did you do to him?" in Spanish.

There were two men: dim silhouettes standing above me. One of them had something in his hand, a club maybe. I scampered back a few feet out of range, then got slowly to my feet, palms held outward and high—*I surrender*—as they approached. I said, "He tried to kill me. I had no choice."

I heard one of them say, "Wait . . . this isn't Rosario."

As if they'd mistaken me for someone.

They were approaching me cautiously. I heard the same voice say, "Are you the Yankee? We only want to talk to you."

I thought: *Right.*

As they neared, I tried to make myself look smaller. Tried to sag a little, as if I'd been hurt. Waited until they were in range . . . then dove toward their ankles and rolled, knocking their feet from under them. Came up and tried to run—almost always the best decision in any fight—but was immediately tackled from behind. Got to my knees, then got one foot under me for leverage and used my open palm to smash the nose of the man who had tackled me. Felt the hot-oil explosion of blood . . . then the other one was instantly on me and locked his arm around my throat. Held me there long enough, choking me, for his partner to get to his feet.

"Don't fight us!"

Through the gauzy, dreamy veil of strangulation, I watched the man stagger around until he found the club he'd been carrying.

He came back, still spitting blood, then kicked the soles of my shoe. "Are you an American?"

Ridiculously, I nodded.

"No more fighting! You come with us!" He sounded furious, as if he was the one who'd been wronged.

I watched him turn to stare at the massive figure of the man who had first attacked me. The man was on his hands and knees now; he seemed to be trying to crawl bearlike toward the alley's exit.

In my ear, I heard the man who was strangling me say, "Kill him."

I tried to twist and throw my elbow into his stomach; tried to lever his arm away from my throat so that I could explode away from him and turn—a wrestling move. The last thing I did was try to reach behind me; I wanted to get my hands on his face, my thumbs in his eyes . . . while slowly, slowly, the dreamy veil faded to gray . . . then all awareness vanished into darkness. . . .

• • •

I had several brief flashes of consciousness . . . of being steered, like a drunk, through some dark place, my arms over the shoulders of a big man . . . of silence, silence then a guttural scream, an animal's scream, the horror of that noise instantly absorbed by the slap of my own shoes on wet pavement . . . of sitting heavily in slime, hearing the sound of rock grating against rock while the big man stooped in the shadows . . . of descending a ladder of iron rungs, then of slipping, falling, clawing frantically for a handhold as I spun into blackness, waiting to hit, waiting to hit . . . then of feeling a crushing impact and another explosive burst of white light. . . .

Then . . . then, there were voices; voices fading in and out, blending with dreams. The voices of several men and at least one woman. One of the voices slowly separated itself from the others, became steadily louder and insistent . . . also, very familiar. I listened to the familiar voice say: "Doc? Hey, Doc—wake up!"

I knew that voice; had I been sleeping?

I listened to the voice say, "You die, it's no big deal. I'll just bring you back to life again. Hey . . . you hear me? Put my hands on your head, suck the death right out of you."

Yes . . . I could feel my head being cupped; a light pressure.

I heard, "Don't doubt it, man. I've got the inside track on that mortality bullshit, so you might as well wake up, save us both some energy. . . ."

I opened my eyes to see a man's gaunt face, skin stretched tight over bone, a small, elongated burn scar on the left temple like two circles linked; an infinity symbol that reminded me of something . . . of a friend of mine who had been dead but . . . was connected to electroencephalogram wires? Yeah . . . wires that . . . that were struck by *lightning*. . . .

Yes . . . I was beginning to remember things.

I saw arctic blue eyes, dirty blond hippie hair hanging shoulder length, a wild unkempt beard that I associated with crazed hermits or with certain orthodox religions. I said, "Tomlinson?" my voice sounding froggy, as if I had been sleeping.

I watched the face grin. Saw it turn away and heard, "I told you about this guy. To kill 'im, you'd have to cut his head off and hide it." Then the face turned back to me. It said, "How you feeling, man? I told my comrades you'd be fine, but you think these beaners would believe it?"

I ran my hands through my hair. Big bump on the back of my head, tender to the touch. "I . . . I've got a pretty bad headache. Somebody must've hit me—" Then I sat up quickly. Where the hell was I?

I looked around into a blur of shadows and flickering light. Patted my shirt pockets until Tomlinson pressed my glasses into my hands. Put them on and saw that I was in what seemed to be a cellar: rock walls, water stained, low ceiling, damp floor; large room with corridors leading out from either side. There were candles on rough wood tables, walls and ceiling stained with candle soot.

On one of the walls, someone had used the soot to write *8 A* in huge figures.

Two men, one of them black, a mulatto boy, and a Hispanic woman sat on oil drums, looking at me. The black man had his head back, holding a towel to his face. The towel was blood soaked. I thought: the guy I hit. I recognized the boy—he was the one who'd signaled me from the street.

Tomlinson had his hand on my shoulder. "When Valdes was bringing you down, you slipped and fell off the ladder. Landed right on your noggin—like about a ten-foot fall onto this shit." Meaning the slimy rock floor.

Valdes . . . the name was familiar.

I was on a table that had been cleared. I swung my legs over and stood. Felt a little shaky but not too bad. Turned to Tomlinson—he was wearing a baggy brown smock over his frayed jeans. The clothes hung on him, he was so skinny. He'd lost weight since I'd last seen him—over six feet tall but couldn't weigh more than one forty, one fifty.

All bone, beard, and Buddha eyes. I said, "Down where? Where are we?"

"Underneath Havana, man."

"In a basement, you mean."

Tomlinson's eyes had a familiar glow. "No, we're *underneath Havana.* In an old aqueduct these people found, runs beneath the old part of the city. Dug out of solid rock by Indian slaves then forgotten. Now here it is protecting us." The irony of that pleased him, I could tell.

It was starting to come back to me, what had happened—being lured into the alley, then jumped. I said, "These people are friends of yours?"

"As of Saturday, yeah. Friends, comrades. Partners in crime—you name it." Tomlinson was patting my shoulder as he said, "You know me, man. Couple of days, it's impossible not to do some effective karmic networking."

I was looking at them. The guy with the towel was busy trying to get his nose to stop bleeding, but the other man—tall, fast-twitch muscularity beneath olive-colored skin—gave me a little nod, withdrawn but friendly. I guessed he was Valdes, the one Tomlinson said had helped me down the ladder. The woman just stared at me. Shopping mall jeans, black T-shirt, attractive face, short hair, very dark eyes that didn't miss much. She had to be Rita Santoya. Not pretty but handsome, just as Jimmy Gardenas had described her. Outdoorsy, looked like she maybe did triathlons; this modern Generation X girl sitting with revolutionaries in a rock chamber that had to have been dug three or four hundred years ago.

I said, "So if they're friends, why'd they try to kill me?"

Tomlinson said, "See, that's where you're confused—" before the woman interrupted, "*Them?* You're the one should apologize. They saved you. It wasn't for them, you'd be dead right now. You maybe broke Molina's nose and we *need* him." A little pissed off; a slight Hispanic accent combined with an Atlantic coast accent—New Jersey. Yeah, she was Rita Santoya. Talking about Molinas, the man with the towel. I had to think about it: Valdes and

Molinas; both of them names of anti-Castro leaders given me by Armando Azcona and Juan Rivera.

How had Tomlinson managed to hook up with them?

In Spanish, the tall man, Valdes, said to her, "What's he saying? What are you talking about?"

I spoke to him in Spanish before she could answer. "Up in the alley, you were the one who tried to strangle me. That's what I was asking her—why you attacked me. You really expected me not to fight back?"

Valdes gave me a very dry smile. "No, no I've never tried to strangle anyone." As if he found the idea of himself doing such a thing humorous, it was so unlikely. "That was another man, Juan Pablo. Juan Pablo told me it happened because he believed that you were a man named Rosario. Rosario was trained by the Russians to be very good at killing. He enjoyed it."

He used the Cuban slang for Russian—*Bolas*. *Bolas* meant "balls" and described the basketball appearance of many of the Soviets.

Valdes said, "With a man like Rosario, Molinas and Juan Pablo couldn't take chances. They had to attack first, ask questions later. On this island, among people who know about things, he is a very famous killer."

I said, "The big man who tried to kill me."

"Exactly. That's why our men were there. That's why there was so much confusion. They arrive in the alley—it's very dark—and they see one big man standing over a beaten man . . ." He made a gesture of dismissal—how were *they* supposed to know? "They assumed that Rosario got to you before they did. They assumed it was you who was trying to crawl off like some injured animal. Poor Molinas"—he nudged the man who held the bloody towel—"paid for the confusion with his good looks. See his nose? How crooked it is?"

Molinas removed the towel long enough to say, "You son of a whore, I'll kill you next time." Meaning me. Then he groaned, saying, "I feel like I may vomit."

To Molinas, I said, "I'm sorry. You took me by surprise."

Valdes gave me a very hard look—*don't flatter yourself*—before he said, "It's not what you did to Molinas's face that makes him sick. It's what he and Juan Pablo had to do to Rosario."

There was something else I now remembered—a sudden scream followed by a silence that resonated. Rosario's scream.

Valdes seemed shakier, far more upset about it than Molinas. He sat there looking at me, letting the implication settle, before he added, "Understand, we're not killers. Certainly not trained killers. We are . . . educated people who know something has to be done to save our country. Some of the things that have to be done make us sick to our stomachs, but we care enough to do them. And sometimes we make mistakes."

As I started to reply, he held a hand up, shushing me. "Please let me explain first. Earlier this evening," he said, "we received word that you had arrived in Havana. We were also told—and this came from a very good source—that Rosario had been assigned to kill you—"

"By who?"

The hand again. "Please let me finish—"

"I'm not going to let you finish because I have a friend at the *Havana Libre* who could be in trouble. If they're after me, maybe they'll go after her. I need to know—"

"They're getting Dewey right now, Doc. She's probably already on her way." Tomlinson had moved to the other side of the room and was standing beside the woman. He had his hand on her shoulder, very friendly, very familiar. "They sent a couple of people to get her, nice and quiet. I didn't even know she was coming to Havana, so it was quite a shock, man—not that I mind." To the woman, he said, "You're going to like Dewey. You two, you've got a lot in common."

I started to press for an explanation, then stopped. Valdes and I had been speaking in Spanish. Tomlinson, who could order food in a Cuban restaurant but not much more, had spoken to me in English. How had he understood? The way he was smiling at me now, same thing—like he knew what

I was thinking before I said it. I watched him shrug, still smiling at me; listened to him tell me, "Weird, huh?"

In Spanish, I said to him, "Don't pretend you understand, because I know you don't."

In English, he said, "Like a native, man, a damn native. Since like . . . two days ago when they had me eat a couple of peyote buttons. Can't speak a word, but, hey—they say it, I understand it. Call it intuition, call it cerebral osmosis, but, personally, I like to think it's a lifetime of good drugs finally kicking in. Like the book says: God helps those who help themselves."

Valdes said to me, "This is something we've wondered about. He says he never understood Spanish before."

About himself, Tomlinson had once told me that his whole life was like being asleep, dreaming, except for the two or three times he'd woken up just long enough to scream. To Valdes I said, "What Tomlinson does and doesn't understand has always been a mystery." I looked at Tomlinson—seven years of university, he had to have taken a language. Probably Spanish and now it was coming back to him a decade or two later, like an amnesia victim. I watched his smile broaden as I added, "To the best of my knowledge, though, he neither spoke nor understood. And I've known him for years."

"The crazy wisdom." Rita Santoya reached and placed her index finger on Tomlinson's burn scar, the small elongated infinity symbol. I realized, for the first time, that it could also be a lopsided figure eight, as Rita added, "He's been touched by God. It's what Taino said."

Taino?

Valdes—this articulate, educated man—said, "And Taino has never been wrong." He said it matter-of-factly, either with a hint of sarcasm or a hint of reverence, I couldn't tell. I wondered which it was he felt.

Tomlinson said, "Yeah, Taino. He's *magic,* man."

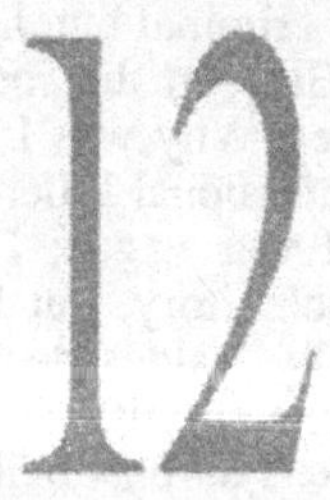

The first chance I got, I took Tomlinson aside; led him off into one of the dark corridors. I said, "You couldn't just send a messenger to the hotel? Or send a note, tell me and Dewey to meet you someplace? Jesus, setting me up like that." They had given me a wet cloth. I was holding it to my head, wishing the pounding would go away.

Tomlinson said, "You okay?"

"No, I'm not okay. When Dewey gets here, I'll be better but, no, I'm not okay."

"What choice did we have, Doc? Rita and I've been on the run since Saturday morning, then like a little bit ago, Molinas comes in and says, 'Hey, one of my contacts just told me your friend Ford is going to get hit tonight . . . or someone wants your friend Ford hit.' Molinas says, 'And I just saw them leave the Havana Libre, headed this way.' So what the hell are we supposed to do?"

"Yeah, lead me here, someplace nice and dark for some assassin to jump me. That makes sense."

"You think we *knew* he was following you? Come on, man."

When I didn't reply, he said, "I . . . felt bad, the way Valdes laid all those heavy questions on you. Like you were the criminal but, hey, these people have to be very careful.''

Back in the room, Valdes had pressed hard for an answer: Why was I so important that someone would send a professional killer like Rosario?

I was vague; I repeatedly said I didn't know. Not the whole story, but I saw no need to confide in Valdes. Finally, Valdes decided it was probably because of my association with Tomlinson and Rita Santoya. Maybe it was true. I sure as hell hoped so.

But acknowledging it seemed to frighten Valdes. I heard him say to Rita, ''There's no use pretending. The wrong people know that you're here. They know why.''

I remembered the story Jimmy Gardenas had told me about the two Cuban brothers, Eduardo and Angel Santoya. Angel would be Rita's great uncle. He was the one who had been an informant; sided with Castro. He was probably pretty high up in the corporation by now. If Rita returned to Cuba, he'd be after her.

Tomlinson was still talking about why he hadn't sent a messenger. ''These people, the *Ochoas,* they know best. Very smart people. No one knows anybody else's real name—they're that careful. They say we can't be seen with you, that's all I need to hear. So we had to wing it. All night long, they said Geis never left your side, so we had to find a way to get you off the street. I said use the boy—Doc's a sap for kids. Like I said, it was last minute.''

''You were so sure Geis wouldn't come into the alley with me.''

''Yeah, pretty sure. I've met a handful of men who'd go charging into a dark alley to help a stranger, but Geis isn't one of them.'' Tomlinson waited a few moments before he said, ''It's really good to see you, man. I appreciate your coming.''

Like he'd invited me to a weekend party or something.

I wasn't in the mood for pleasantries. Standing there telling me how careful these people were when, judging from what I'd seen, they were pretenders, amateurs; worse, their security was terrible. No one knew anyone else's real name? Then how did they know who anyone really was? I felt like slapping that drug-bleary, holier-than-thou smile off Tomlinson's face. I took a deep breath, calming myself before I said, "You don't look like a man who's suffering terrible headaches. Or maybe that was just a line to get me to Havana."

I watched him twisting strands of his long hair, a nervous habit. "No headaches since Taino gave me the peyote, man. Did this truth ceremony thing—you know, see if I could be trusted. My scar"—he touched his temple—"he was very impressed by my scar. He told me it was exactly the omen he'd been waiting for. That name? Taino? He took it from a dream he had when he was a child; turns out it's the name of some lost Caribbean tribe and he's the spiritual heir."

"Quite a coincidence," I said. How could anyone as smart as Tomlinson believe such crap?

"Now he's a *Babalao,* like a very important high priest for the Palo Monte. That's like a branch of the Santería religion. Palo Monte, I'm talking about. But where magic plays a lot bigger part. Magic is Taino's *thing*. Since then, my head's felt healthy as a horse. Real tingly."

I was whispering, trying to control my anger. "No more panic attacks, no more paranoia?"

"Paranoia? Man, that was back when the dark forces of about a hundred solar systems were after me. You thought I was *imagining* that? That wasn't paranoia, it was a rational assessment of my position in the universe. And it sucked, man." He said, "It *really* sucked."

I had to remind myself that this was a troubled version of the Tomlinson who lived aboard a sailboat back in little Dinkin's Bay, Sanibel Island. Reminded myself that the real Tomlinson—the dropout prophet, gentle and wise, whom everyone on the island treasured—was still alive, still healing somewhere deep in his brain, behind those glowing, arctic eyes.

I said, "I was talking about your boat. On the phone you seemed a tad paranoid about the Cubans taking your boat. You still want to get it back, don't you?"

"*No Más?* Damn right I want it back. I know where they got her anchored, too. This customs outpost where they keep the confiscated boats. Saw her yesterday. Me and Taino were out cruising, trying to tune in on the vibes. We drive up this bluff, I look down at the sea, and there she is."

Out cruising around with a leader of an anti-Castro voodoo faction.

Tomlinson said, "She looked pretty, man. Blue on white, like this toy sailboat, but it was like I didn't even have to look because I could feel her at anchor. *Waiting* for me. *No Más,* she knows, man. She knows. At this place called Mariel Harbor, west of Havana."

I winced. *Jesus.*

"Mariel," I said.

"Yeah. Big natural harbor with a narrow mouth, kind of remote. Not much activity. Taino said it's because the Russians pulled out. That's where we're going when Dewey shows up. They got a place there."

I said, "Oh yeah?" wanting to grab Tomlinson by the arms, shake him until his teeth clattered; yell into his face, "You idiot! You're going to get us all killed messing with these two-bit revolutionaries!" Instead, I said, "Mind telling me what happened to your original plan? I bring the ten thousand, pay off your fines, and you sail back to Key West. On the phone, you're like, 'Please help me, Doc. I need help.' So it's kind of surprising to walk into this mess."

"Couldn't be helped, man. God has gotten involved, so who's going to argue? On the phone, when I told you that Rita disappeared every day? I finally found out what she was doing."

"Yeah, but you said 'Julia' 'cause, if you remember, she used a fake name. Or did that slip your mind? She's been lying to you the whole time. What I'd be willing to bet is, she set you up from the moment you met her. Meets this guy who has a record of being pro-Castro . . . so who are the Cubans going to give their full attention if you two show up unexpectedly? The night you're supposed to sail back to Florida, she spikes your drinks so she could hijack your boat, sail it herself twenty-some miles to—"

He was nodding. "Exactly; that's just what happened. But that was before she *trusted* me, man. Before she explained everything. Turns out, where she was disappearing was to see these people. She's connected, man. This hard-ass American chick, using me to sneak back into Cuba—I *love* it. But Saturday, the morning after I talked to you, Rita, she realized she was being followed. I mean, someone completely trashed our room at the Hotel Nacional, so we had to run for it."

"She tell you why?"

"You'll have to ask her, man."

"She say how she plans to help your revolutionary buddies?"

"She wants to tell you, she'll tell you, Doc."

Grab Tomlinson by the arms and shake the hell out of him—maybe it would do us both some good. I said, "Are you aware that I could have been killed tonight? Are you also aware that someone *was* killed? That guy they called Rosario. I think Molinas slit his throat. The blood all over his shoes? It didn't come from a broken nose."

I had a hard time controlling myself when Tomlinson answered, "A bad day for the life insurance people is a good day for the morticians. You've got to look at the big picture."

And it had been difficult for me to imagine him killing a cockroach.

I said, "I hope you're kidding. You'd better be kidding. A man gets his throat cut and you shrug it off with some bullshit aphorism?"

"A *syllogism,* man—two truths and a conclusion. An aphorism is . . . it's like what Chairman Mao said, 'A noble end justifies any ignoble means.' In other words, you name it: terrorism, murder, whatever has to be done to reach a noble goal."

Christ, he was talking to me like some Ivy League teacher now.

"Besides," he said, "the guy was out to murder you. You said it yourself."

"I strike you as the type to walk up to a disabled man and cut him? Because that's just what Molinas did."

That got me a long look of evaluation—a little bit of the old Tomlinson showing through. "No . . . you wouldn't do that. It's *in* you, but you fight it. How many times I said it? Your whole life, that's your karma—fighting your own nature. Remember that line from Flaubert? 'Be regular and orderly in your life so you may be violent and original in your work.' That's you, but you hate it."

More quotes.

He said, "But these people are *revolutionaries,* man. They've got a righteous cause. A week here, *I* could see what Fidel's done to this country and it's about turned my stomach. Every girl over the age of ten trying to sell herself, adults walking around like robots, skulls for faces, standing in line for beans, man. For *beans.*"

Now he was starting to wave his arms around, something Tomlinson always did when he got excited. "It's like those kids you see on the street, the Malecón every night; the ones wearing those cheap-ass rags but trying to look like punk rockers. They got the hair, they got the attitude—" He had to think for a moment. "They call themselves something. . . ."

I thought: *Roqueros.*

He said, "Whatever the hell it is, but . . . these kids, man, they're like me, like my comrades from the sixties—the dropout generation. Probably way too sensitive and smart for their own good, and you know what they're doing now? They're injecting themselves with HIV-infected blood. Giving themselves AIDS! These teenagers, man, these *straight* teenagers because they got no other way to protest; showing what they think of that slogan—shit, I used to *say* it—the slogan you see all over Havana on billboards: Socialism or *Death.* And why?"

I expected him to say because of the U.S. boycott; some political inanity—that would have been the old Tomlinson. Instead he said, "It's because Fidel's too proud to say he was wrong. Like his ego's the only thing that really matters, which is a fucking crime against humanity! No, what I'm saying is . . . here's the way I see it: Back in the states, I was his biggest fan. I *worked* for the guy. Now I feel like a schmuck; 'bout pig stupid and butt ugly."

"You feel responsible for a screwed-up country because you came down here, cut sugar cane for a month? Spare me the guilt rationale. You and your wealthy hipster friends—"

"No, what I'm saying is, I get a chance to help the *Ochoas*, man, I'm going to do it."

I stood staring at him; wished I could look through his eyes clear to the back of his brain, see if there was any hope of reasoning with him. It was like trying to reason with some academician clone; someone whose view of the world was one-dimensional, tunneled and sharpened by his own cloistered antecedents. I was still staring at him when he said, "Man, I bet I know what you're thinking."

I said, "You don't want to hear what I'm thinking."

I got another perceptive look—yeah, the old Tomlinson was still in there. "That's good. Havana, it's a dangerous place to say anything out loud. No matter where you are."

Was he trying to tell me something?

I said, "What I think we ought to do is get Dewey, then find the quickest, safest way possible out of Cuba. That's what I think. I don't know what they did with Rosario's body, but someone's going to miss him and we want to be long gone by that time. If we have to, pay somebody to see that your boat gets cleared and sailed to a neutral place—the Yucatán, maybe. We can pick it up later."

Tomlinson said, "I can't do that, man. The revolution needs me." But he was nodding his head: *Yes*.

Watching him closely, I said, "It may need you, but it doesn't need us. Tell me something—do you trust Rita?"

Emphatic shake of the head. "Of course I trust her. Now that I understand her motives, I trust her completely."

Hell no, he didn't trust her.

I said, "Then maybe you could convince her, Molinas,

and the rest to help us find a way out. I think flying back commercial's out of the question."

He was shaking his head again—*no*. Did that mean we couldn't fly commercial or that he didn't trust any of them? Listened to him say, "You gotta do what's best for you, I gotta do what's best for me. But, yeah, we can bounce it off the *Ochoas*. I know Valdes has something to do with shipping. Or knows somebody involved, because I overheard him talking to Rita about how their cargo ships can only go to Panama. Cuba's cargo ships I'm talking about. Like he's definitely got some juice in that department. Who to pay off, how to do it. So yeah, maybe he could get you guys on one of those boats."

I thought: *Panama?* Colón was the major Caribbean port there, and I knew several people in Colón knowledgeable about shipping.

I said, "Would you go with us if we got it arranged?" expecting him to nod. Instead, he shook his head again—*no*. What the hell did that mean?

"Can't, man. I've got a karmic obligation to Taino. That's in God's hands, not mine."

Damn it, there was no making sense of the man. I took a step, grabbed his shirt, and pulled him to me. Into his ear, I whispered, "Do you mean that?"

Tomlinson pulled away, actually seemed surprised. "What the hell you think I've been talking about?"

Eleven-thirty p.m., still no sign of Dewey.

Four men had arrived earlier—they didn't introduce themselves—and Molinas, with his broken nose already swelling, had left with them.

Now I was pacing around the underground room alternately checking my watch and listening to Tomlinson, Rita, and Valdes talk among themselves.

A strange discussion to monitor. Everything in Spanish except for Tomlinson, who Rita was translating fairly accurately. Didn't take any crap off him, either. In Spanish, heard her say once, "Tomlinson, if it wasn't for the brain damage, I'd say you're full of shit."

So I wasn't the only one who knew that he wasn't well.

But, yeah, it was true—Tomlinson *understood.*

They had a map spread across the table, discussing places, discussing routes. Rita had in her hand notes from what she said was a three-page letter given to her by a trustee after the death of her grandmother, wife of the late Eduardo Santoya, heir to one of the great fortunes in Cuba before Castro came to power.

She'd intentionally left the letter back in the states, Rita said, because she wasn't sure she'd find a boat in Key West, plus she didn't want to risk all the details falling into the wrong hands.

I'd thought: *Right.*

Knowing I was listening, Rita and Valdes took the time to tell me vaguely, very vaguely, the significance of the map and the letter; what they were doing. The letter was a kind of treasure guide; told Rita where grandfather Eduardo had hidden all the valuable things that his family couldn't carry when they fled.

That wasn't uncommon: Even as late as Mariel, the country was still being potholed by desperate Cubans as well as troops under orders, all looking for assets left behind by those who had evacuated.

I'd asked her, Gold? Jewels?

Got a sharp look and an evasive reply. She said she wasn't sure. She said that her grandmother's letter didn't say specifically. Just *valuables.*

"The Eduardo Santoya family left millions," Valdes said. "Had to; things that have never been accounted for. Angel Santoya never found it—of that we are certain. Our revolution needs money. Even a small amount would help. That's what this is all about."

Knowing that he wanted to, I waited for him to drop a hint about the money I'd brought for Tomlinson—why else would they have told me anything?—but he didn't, as if deciding to hold off. I also noted the weary cast to his voice; like he knew what he was up against, had thought it all through thoroughly. Fighting Castro in a country where there was no communication, no freedom to organize, and where only the military was allowed to keep weapons?

More so than the others, Valdes seemed a rational man.

I also got the impression that they were having problems making Rita's notes jibe with the map of Cuba spread across the table. Once heard her say, "What's she mean, 'La Esperanza'? Cuba's got three or four little villages, all the same name, and my family had property near every one." Later heard her say, "Candelaria? No, there's nothing in Candelaria. I already told you, that's the first place I went. I spent, what? Two days looking for a mausoleum that was either torn down or, somehow, Grandma got the directions mixed up."

I thought: Two days? If there was nothing to find in Candelaria, why spend so much time? Pre-Castro mausoleums tended to be large and ornate. Plenty of room to hide lots of stuff, and easy enough to find in a village as small as Candelaria. Was I the only one who suspected that Rita was lying?

At one point, Tomlinson said, "What you people need is a first-rate logical mind. Hey, Doc—you want to step over and take a look at this?"

I told Tomlinson I wasn't going to do anything, didn't want to hear another word until I knew Dewey was safe.

I listened to Tomlinson tell Rita, "The big guy's a little stressed-out right now. Someone tries to murder him, it really screws with his aura. But he'll come in handy, don't you worry your pretty little head about that."

Listened to Rita tell Tomlinson, "One more remark like that—my pretty little head? Just shut up and concentrate on what I'm saying."

She struck me as one of those dilettante ball-breakers, standing there in her muscle T-shirt playing a role, maybe seeing herself on some internal theater screen and getting into it—street-tough American girl hanging out with revolutionaries. Perhaps . . . or running her own private scam . . .

I had to also think: *I met this girl's father. . . .*

I couldn't remember his face well enough to judge if there was much of him in her. Junior Santoya. But then, physical appearance wasn't the key—that was in the delicate synapse junctions, the genetic coding passed from parent to child, parent to child.

Now, as I paced, I noticed that the small mulatto boy they'd used to lure me into the alley was pacing along with me. At first, I thought he was making fun of me—this kid, maybe eleven or twelve years old, his face a synthesis of Africa and Spain and pre-Columbian Cuba. Skin the color of old wheat, long bony arms sticking out, big brown eyes, African nose and lips, but straight brown hair. Wearing slacks that were bunched at the waist like a garbage bag, a ripped T-shirt that read *Que Viva Cuba!*

But no, he wasn't mocking me. He was just up too late, tired and bored. Probably lonely, too. From the moment I took the time to ask his name, he paced when I paced. He sat when I sat. That small bit of attention had won his allegiance.

He'd smiled slightly at my question and barely whispered: *Santiago.*

To pass the time, I began to try to talk to the kid. Where did he live?

Shrug of the shoulders. It maybe meant here, underground, maybe in that alley, maybe from house to house—the kinds of places that constitute nowhere.

I said, "Are these people your friends?"

Smaller shrug. "More or less."

"You hungry?"

No, he said he'd eaten that morning.

I wanted to ask about his parents—what kind of people or person would allow a child to be in this place . . . not that it was uncommon in the Third World . . . or in any other world, for that matter. Poverty spawns indifference, then allows the stepchildren of both to be fed upon in the streets.

I asked, "You have any relatives who should know where you are?"

I realized that Valdes had been listening to us when he walked over and put his hand on the boy's shoulder. He gave me a kind of camp counselor smile as he said, "Everybody in Cuba is related to Santiago. We take care of him, he takes care of us all."

I watched the kid react to that; slightly pained expression—he was too streetwise for that kind of sap. I liked the way he wouldn't be patronized—this twelve-year-old dressed in rags, wide awake at two a.m. I wanted to smile but didn't. Instead, I gave him a private look, winked. Shaking his head slightly, the kid winked back.

Valdes said, "Santiago's mother died five or six years ago." Valdes had to stoop to look into the kid's face. "It was in some kind of accident, wasn't it?"

The kid said, "The house caught on fire. I tried to wake her up, but she was drunk as hell." Monotone, as if he'd told the story way too many times before.

Valdes said, "Santiago's father was a good man. Sergio. I knew Sergio. Not well, but a friend of mine did. In the 'cane fields, he was a mechanic. Fixed the pumps, fixed the harvesters. Always had grease on his arms and his face, and he was a joker, that Sergio. Always making jokes." He stooped again to look at Santiago. "Your father, he was a very clever man. People always said that about him. He was very clever."

The kid didn't react. He might have been hearing a story about a stranger. He had found some fishing line in his pocket and was now playing with it.

"What happened to Sergio is, he . . . you don't mind me telling this, do you, Santiago?" Valdes waited for the kid to shrug again—Why should I care?—before he continued, "For some reason, the housing committee had to find a new house for Sergio, and so . . . wait—what am I thinking? It was because of the fire. *That's* right, this fire, it destroyed his house, so he has to apply to the housing committee for a new place to live. Which meant Sergio had to spend maybe two, maybe three weeks going from office to office, standing in line for hours, then filling out forms, being interviewed—" Valdes stopped, looked at me before he said, "You don't know what it's *like* here," before he continued, "and, of course, he and Santiago had no place to live in the meantime. They're sleeping outside, probably in the yard of this burned-down house.

"So Sergio gets to the final committee. It's his turn. He's waited nearly a month for this. The housing committee . . . it's six party members—my wife and I, we'd been before them—and these six people have complete control. You live where they say you will live. Houses, apartments—they can't be bought or sold. So the committee people, they show Sergio a map, point to three or four housing projects—places the Russians had built—which are the worst places around. Everything poured cement, apartments built on apartments, gray, no grass, no maintenance, probably two or three thousand people living in each project."

I said, "Santiago's father—" I was picturing this clever man, his drunken wife dead, he and his son alone. "—he didn't like that."

Valdes said, "Who would? But Sergio, he's a joker. He looks at the places on the map—he knows those places; we all *know* those places—and then Sergio looks at these six people sitting behind the long table. Party people talking to a man who works in the 'cane fields. The way they stare at you—my wife and I, when we were very young, we'd been there. They make you feel like an insect. So you know what Sergio says?"

I said, "What?"—liking Valdes more and more; I *liked* this kid. If Dewey'd just arrive, I'd have started feeling better about the situation.

Valdes said, "Sergio tells them, 'You know where I'd really like to live?' He's talking to six of the most powerful people in Cuba, keep in mind. Sergio says, 'Out of all these nice places, where my son and I would really like to live is *north* of Havana.' "

Pretty good line. The Gulf Stream. Miami. Cleveland. Anyplace but where he was.

I smiled, looking at Santiago—who was pulling at a thread on his shirt; didn't even seem to be listening. To Valdes, I said, "A man of strength," using the word "*cojones,*" meaning balls . . . looked at him, expecting him to be smiling, too.

Valdes wasn't smiling. Said, "The committee didn't think it was a very funny joke. They sent Sergio out of the room. Made him stand out there, no explanation . . . and he was arrested no more than ten minutes later. The charge would have been . . . I don't know what, maybe treason. They took him to Combinado del Este prison, Havana's largest. He never came to trial because somehow, Sergio, he died in there. Some of the other prisoners—this is what I *heard*—they wanted him to do something he wouldn't, and someone killed him. No one really knows for sure."

Santiago still didn't seem to be hearing any of it. He stretched, shivered a little—very tired—and he said, "*Now* I'm starting to get a little hungry."

To Valdes, I said, "You have any food down here?"

He shook his head. "Back where we're going, when your friend arrives. There is food there. It's a safe place for us."

I said, "That could be in a few minutes, it could be an hour. The boy, he's hungry, maybe there's someplace up on the street. That bar maybe? Where you could still get some food."

Valdes's expression said: Are you serious?

I said, "You think a hundred dollars, U.S., could wake somebody up?"

Santiago was suddenly interested. "Some beans with pork in it, that would be something nice. It doesn't have to be hot. Or some ice cream." The kid looked at me, his eyes a little suspicious, assessing mine . . . reappraisal time; some respect in his expression and a lot of knowledge for someone his age.

But the look Valdes gave me, I didn't like: You think I'm your servant? You think you can buy everything with your American money?

I told Valdes, "The boy's hungry, we're down here waiting around—why not give it a try?" I had fished into my pocket, was holding out a bill.

Santiago said, "And bring a coffee for the gringo." Gave me the little wink again. Said, "Or maybe you'd like a beer?" This kid who'd never been in charge of anything in his life immediately very comfortable taking charge.

Valdes saw the humor in that; he was chuckling as he reached for the hundred—Ben Franklin's big monopoly portrait folded over my finger—then paused, listening.

Voices were echoing down the dark corridor, coming closer, someone talking louder than I would have expected . . . it had to be coming from an entrance different from the other I had seen used. I watched Valdes tense, listening . . . then watched him relax. He didn't take the money as he turned away.

I heard Tomlinson's voice: "Doc . . . hey, Doc." I looked at him as he nodded his head toward the corridor. "That's Taino coming."

Finally seeing him, the first thing I thought was: *Taino?*

He didn't seem to have much Indian in him. A little bit of Arawak, perhaps, with his goshawk nose . . . and the way he stayed within himself, showing nothing, taking things in through black eyes . . . a guy who was above it all and without much patience. Otherwise, he was gray skinned but with a paunchy Castilian face. Probably thirty or so, but looked older, with his wild black hair curling around elongated ears and his black mustache and goatee. Pretty big guy, six two maybe, but looked soft beneath a white guayabera shirt and baggy white slacks. I noticed that he wore strings of beads around his neck and both wrists, and that beads were sewn into the collar of his shirt—red and white plastic beads. He came out of the shadows with two other men who had to walk fast to keep up, as if being hauled along in the guy's slipstream.

He gave me a peremptory glance and was done with me; didn't seem to see the boy at all. Went to the map table, where Tomlinson and Rita had already stepped aside to give him room. Told Valdes, "Get everything together. We're leaving right away," before he looked at Tomlinson and said in Spanish, "How have you been doing with the map? Did you get any messages, any *feelings* concerning where we should look?''

Talking to him as if he were some kind of psychic—the two of them *simpático,* one prophet to another.

Tomlinson made a rocking motion with an open palm. "Nothing definite, man, but some very serious vibes. I just don't feel tuned in the way I need to be.''

I expected Rita to translate—she'd been doing it all evening—but not this time.

No . . . apparently, Taino understood English. He was nodding, thumb and index finger to his lips, giving the problem serious thought. "You have the power; I *know* you have the power.'' He said that as if speaking to himself.

"Power? Oh-h-h-h, have no fear about that one. God wouldn't send me down here without enough juice to get the job done. Thing is . . . what it might be? Those peyote buttons had a very beneficial effect; added just the right kick. Maybe a couple more of those would put me in tiptop shape.'' Being coy about it, as if he were back at Harvard hustling drugs.

Taino was thinking about it. "Perhaps . . . perhaps. But there's also a ceremony that might help. A very special ceremony''—he checked his watch—"we might have time. It has to be done at midnight or noon . . . it's meaningless, any other time. So we have only a few hours because, of course, tomorrow would be too late.''

I wondered about that—it was now around midnight. Christmas Eve. What was so special about Christmas Day to a Santería priest?

Taino had made up his mind. "Yes, that's what we'll do. A sacrifice to Changó. Are you familiar with Changó?''

Tomlinson said, "Like a god? I've met so many, man, they're starting to run together. You know from what solar system?''

Taino wasn't listening. "We will take this map and ask a blessing on it . . . *I'll* do the ceremony, and my apprentices''—he indicated the two men behind him; both very black, very attentive and dressed in pure white—"they'll see to finding several chickens. And a goat, too, perhaps? Mr. Tomlinson will, of course, participate."

I couldn't believe I was listening to this nonsense. I waited a little while longer, becoming impatient, getting madder, while they discussed the details of this voodoo ceremony—"Orlando, we will pour the blood into bowls and you will carry them"—before I'd had enough. Who in the hell was this guy, Taino, to be controlling everyone in the room? While he was still talking, I walked to the table, put my hand on his shoulder. I wasn't at all surprised that he froze, as if, in touching him, I'd committed some blasphemy. He stood very still, looking straight ahead, as I said, "I hate to interrupt, mister, but you people were supposed to bring a friend of mine. Her name's Dewey. I think her well-being is a hell of a lot more important than standing around listening to you plan your party."

I said it in English. If he could understand Tomlinson, he could understand me.

Taino didn't reply. He kept looking straight ahead, everything quiet, then turned and stared at my hand on his shoulder. I gave it a little time then removed it. I expected him to turn and say something to me but, instead, he spoke to Tomlinson: "This is your friend? The one who brought the money?"

Everyone stood listening, very tense . . . except for Rita, who seemed to be enjoying it—what do I care?

Tomlinson said, "Did I forget my manners? You two haven't been formally introduced—" as Taino interrupted him, saying to Valdes: "Have you gotten the money from him yet?"

It seemed to be an awkward point with Valdes. "We never really got around to discussing that . . . issue."

"Then *discuss* that issue. We need it. It's part of our agreement."

Agreement? I looked from Tomlinson to Rita, then back to Tomlinson. He gave me an expression—it's no big deal, man—as Rita said, "That's what I was trying to make you understand earlier. These people are trying to *help* us. You think my great uncle's people are after us because they want to turn what we find over to Castro? No way. They want it for *themselves.* It's them we're hiding from, not the military, not the government. This is personal—we're talking about an old man whom everybody in my family despised."

In a fractured, chaotic Cuba, it was certainly possible that even Angel Santoya—his top men, more likely—were acting independently. That the same might be true of other bureaucrats, other agencies, was a startling realization. Because Castro had chosen to ride Cuba's collapse to the ground, it was not unlikely that a kind of slow-motion anarchy now reigned. It was survival time; every agency, every department, every bureaucrat out for themselves.

It made me think of Rosario. . . .

I said to Rita, "I give them the money, they provide protection. What else?"

To Valdes, Taino said, "Tell him that *Ochoa* will divide the Santoya fortune evenly with the woman, and we will see that all of you have safe passage out of Cuba."

Why did I have the feeling that everyone except for Tomlinson was lying to me?

In Spanish, I said, "Mister, if you want me involved in a discussion, speak to me directly. But I'll tell you something right now: You won't see the first cent until I know Dewey's safe and until Tomlinson's on his sailboat, headed for international waters. You do those two things, yeah, we'll sit down and talk."

Valdes said, "The boat's already been taken care of. It's waiting for you now. The papers, the clearance—whenever he's ready."

"Where?"

"That is something you'll learn later."

"That leaves Dewey. When she gets here, when we're all on Tomlinson's boat, then you'll get the money. Not until then."

To Tomlinson, Taino said, "He is a very irritating man, this friend of yours."

"Doc? Yeah, Doc rides on single rails . . . pisses me off

all the time. With him, it's always like: Why be someone pleasant and interesting when you can be yourself?"

There, that sounded like the old Tomlinson—giving me one of his private digs.

"He didn't know about our agreement?"

I moved a little closer to Taino, breaching that delicate perimeter of personal space. "Unless the agreement's with me, you don't have an agreement. I don't think I'm being unreasonable. Produce my friend, we'll talk."

Taino whirled away, scattering his assistants, arms held aloft—I'm not going to listen to any more of this!—as he snapped, "We are leaving! Valdes, he will ride with you!"

Meaning me, I guessed. Not an ideal situation, allowing ourselves to be split like that: separate, isolate, and destroy. It is an old and effective technique.

But I had no choice.

Which was maybe why I was getting so much satisfaction out of irritating the guy. "Only if you're taking me to Dewey—"

"Yes!"

I had another thought. Looked at Santiago. Where was he more likely to get something to eat? Midnight, alone on the street, or tagging along with me? I called after Taino: "And the boy—he's going, too."

Valdes, still very nervous, started to say, "That's impossible, I'm afraid—" but stopped when Taino yelled, "Do you think I *care* about such details?"

We left by separate exits—me, Valdes, and the boy together, the others taking different corridors. Came out into an alley I'd never been into, streets I didn't recognize.

People still out milling in the shadows. I saw several children huddled beneath cardboard. A few cars; most of them turtling along in the dark, saving their batteries, saving their expensive headlights.

Valdes said, "It's so late, the police may stop us. Please, let me do the talking unless you're asked a direct question. Are you carrying your passport? They'll know you're an American."

I was carrying *a* passport. My real passport was at the Masaguan Embassy along with slightly more than $9,000 in cash. To retrieve either, I'd have to show up personally or someone would have to come with a note signed by me. The note would have to include a telling code word—*Pilar*—or the funds would not be released.

Valdes knew where he was going, and pretty soon I realized that he was trying to fit a key into my rental car. It'd been moved, but it was the same little brown Nissan.

I found that reassuring. I'd left the keys in our room at the Havana Libre. If they had the keys, they probably had Dewey, too.

Valdes said, "I'm supposed to drive," as if apologizing; once again a reasonable man, comfortable with himself now that we were away from Taino. "It's not far. An hour, maybe."

As Santiago scooched himself into the tiny backseat, he asked, "Are they really going to kill some chickens?"

Valdes waited until he had pulled out into the street before he answered. "They probably will. It's what they do." His tone saying that he wasn't a part of that, didn't approve of it, didn't understand it. Then watched him in the dash lights, smiling, when Santiago said, "After they do that. Kill those chickens, I mean. You think they would mind if I cooked one and ate it?"

With the sea off to our right, we took the Malecón to Vedado, then turned onto Fifth Avenue with its broad pavement, iron gates, and wedges of dilapidated mansions showing through branches of laurel trees, the night sea occasionally breaking free of high-rises to flood the northern horizon.

Lots of stars suspended in that Gulf Stream void . . . Florida somewhere out there beneath a Caribbean macrodome . . . then Sanibel Island, tiny on a slick of black ocean, its old white lighthouse strobing . . . a darkened stilthouse, too, with an unattended fish tank; no one around to check salinity or pH or oxygen content. . . .

I thought: *Damn* you, Tomlinson.

Passing through Miramar and Embassy Row—some of the estates converted into tenements now—Valdes drove with both hands tight on the wheel; clutch-bucked the car when pulling away from stop signs.

Automotive skills, I already knew, were among the first casualties of a Third World economy.

At one point, I said to him, "Think you'll like driving once you get the hang of it?"

Valdes, a little sheepish, said, "Before the petroleum crisis, I had a . . . there was another person who always drove me to work. That was before everyone starting using a bicycle."

Now we were on the Coastal Highway and the boy was curled up, asleep, in the back. I decided to try to make some conversation, maybe learn something, as we twisted up the steep hills of Sierra del Rosario toward Mariel Harbor. I started out by telling Valdes about myself, how I knew Tomlinson, what I did for a living, how out of place I felt in these strange circumstances—"I keep pinching myself to see if I'm really *doing* this shit"—saying all the things that we were once taught to say to make our captors see us as humans, to create a bond.

It was the opposite dynamic to making war: dehumanize the enemy.

Now, his turn, I said, "So what do you do when you're not planning to overthrow the government?"

That got a slight smile. He drove for a while, hunched over the steering wheel, before he said, "It's something I shouldn't talk about. It's . . . the way we keep it. No one really knows what anyone else does, who anyone else is." Drove for a while longer before he said, "It's . . . a party technique. A way of protecting information. Are you familiar with the word 'cell,' what it means?"

As in a revolutionary cell and, yeah, I knew exactly what it meant. But said, "Nope, and I don't want to know if you can't tell me. You have any family?"

I listened to him tell me about the wife who'd left him for a man who had an important position in the government, a party official who was really nothing more than a party informant, and who took their two daughters out of his life—"She said I was just too idealistic. . . ."

I listened to him tell me about the family from which he came—"They were half devil, half angel. . . ."—before I said, "I hope this doesn't offend you, but you seem way too educated to believe in this Santería bullshit. You went to college, right? The way you handle yourself, you could be a college professor. Or maybe in charge of some important government department."

I was thinking: Like something to do with shipping?

Silence . . .

We drove a mile, then another mile. I had pretty much decided Valdes wasn't going to answer when he said, "It doesn't matter whether I believe in Santería or not, because . . . well, look at it this way. Thirty, thirty-five years ago, the African religions played no part in the politics of Cuba. Today, they *are* the politics of Cuba. Santería is perfect for Cubans because it mixes Catholicism with the old African religions. The Santeros can go to church and pray to . . . well, say Our Lady the Virgin and it's the same as praying to Oshún. Because the slaves used to have to disguise their gods, understand?"

In a way, I did. Catholic churches were similarly used by the Maya in Central America.

Valdes said, "Fidel's policies key off the predications of the Santería priests. He relies on them to control the masses, yet they also rely on Fidel. It's because the Santería people have always looked upon him as an *elegido,* a leader chosen by God. Are you aware of all the coincidences, all the strange things that tie Fidel to Santería?"

I said, "Not a clue" and sat there looking through the windshield, seeing the countryside—driving through canefields now, a black wall of stalks on both sides—as Valdes listed the reasons. Fidel's revolution triumphed on January first, the holiest of Santería days; the day the *Babalaos* meet and predict the coming year's events. The red and black in the flag chosen by Fidel were the colors of Ellegua, the Santería god of destiny. Many of Castro's men wore red and black beads, as did many Santería believers. But the most powerful and important connection occurred January 8, 1959. Castro was in the middle of a speech when two doves circled him, then one landed on his shoulder. Just sat there, according to Valdes, while the great man continued to speak.

"It was one of the most important events in Cuban history, that ridiculous little bird choosing Fidel's shoulder to land on. To Santería believers, doves are a messenger of Obatalá, the Son of God—the equivalent of Jesus. He's the creator of human hopes and dreams. Imagine the reaction of an audience of Christians if Jesus descended and touched the shoulder of your president. That is *not* an exaggeration. Since that afternoon forty *years* ago, Fidel has been embraced by Santería as the holy man in power. The economy, health care, food shortages—nothing else matters. And he'll remain in power as long as the priests allow him . . . or until Fidel finds a way to demonstrate to the Santería people that he is also a *Babalao,* a more powerful priest."

More powerful? That was no offhand comment. Valdes had thought this all through.

He gave it another long pause before he said, "You are right, I'm very well educated. I'm too well educated to ignore the power of Santería."

I said, "Yes, but if the Santería colors are red and black, why does your guy, Taino, wear red and *white* beads? He had them everywhere."

"Because Taino follows a different god. He's a follower of Changó—remember listening to him? When he was talking about performing the ceremony. Changó's the god of fire and war; a very powerful god, they believe." He hesitated a moment before he added, "The way you asked the question is not quite correct. Taino's not *my* guy."

"So you don't believe?" What I wanted to establish was that Valdes and I had something in common. If things really went bad, I might need him.

He said, "With my mind . . . no. But there are things I've seen, things that have happened . . . like when your friend Tomlinson was tested by Taino—it's a kind of ceremony.

I sat through it expecting the same kinds of . . . dumb conviction? Yes, *dumb* conviction. But then I saw this man . . . this *gringo,* under Taino's spell, touch a map and tell Taino things that a gringo could not possibly know. Cuba's four Santería power places. I didn't know where they are. Only the *Babalaos* know. But I watched this man Tomlinson touch them on the map, one by one."

I was tempted to point out that if Valdes didn't know where these places were, how could he be certain Taino wasn't just putting on a show?

I remained quiet, as he said, "Then Taino asked him to touch the place where Taino was born. This was a test, you understand. And Tomlinson did that."

I said, "You already knew where?"

"Yes, in an eastern province called Oriente, a village called Mayari in the Sierra Maestra. I watched him touch that place on the map. And then your friend said something strange but very convincing. Tomlinson began to smile and he said to Taino, 'Ruz, your father's name is Ruz, and . . . you two have . . .' " Valdes had to think about it for a moment. "No, he said, 'You and Ruz *are* duplicate spirits.' Then your friend told Taino, 'But your powers are greater.' "

Typical Tomlinson gibberish . . . still, something about the combination of places and names nagged at me: Ruz . . . Mayari . . . Sierra Maestra . . .

Why?

I thought about it while I asked Valdes, "How did Taino react to that?"

Valdes said, "Taino became very excited. First, he sees the symbol of *Ochoa* burned into Tomlinson's temple, then he speaks the name of Taino's father; tells him *his* powers are greater. A *Babalao* like Taino, what's he going to think? He is convinced that Tomlinson was sent by Changó."

I was thinking: *Good* . . .

Tomlinson clearly had some leverage with Taino—no small consideration when dealing with a pompous, egocentric crank. And Valdes was a rational man. I could reason with Valdes.

One way or the other, we should be able to work out a deal. I pay them X-amount of U.S. dollars, Tomlinson spends a few more hours—no more than that—pointing at places on a map, in exchange for which they use their contacts to free Tomlinson's boat. Had *already* cleared it, Valdes said. By tomorrow evening, the next day at the latest, Dewey and I would be aboard *No Más,* sailing the twelve miles toward international waters and freedom. And if I had to drag Tomlinson aboard kicking and screaming, I'd do it.

In fact, I'd kind of enjoy it, after what that emaciated little freak had put me through.

As to Rita Santoya . . . ? She could come with us or she could stay in Cuba and play her tough-guy role. Let her decide.

I was feeling pretty good . . . even when we topped a ridge and I looked down into what I knew to be Mariel Harbor. A big lake of a harbor shaped a little like an upside-down dragon's head. The eastern rim, where we now were, was forested highlands. Along the two-and-a-half-mile shoreline was an abandoned naval academy, near which was a sheer bluff said to be a favorite of Fidel's firing squads.

Snake the dissidents away in darkness, line them up on the bluff, shoot them, let them tumble-down rock and cactus two hundred feet into the water, and there wouldn't be much evidence left when the fish and sharks were done.

"In prison," authorities would say. "Still in prison for their crimes."

All it took was Fidel, who was an insomniac, and a telephone beside his bed.

Also along the eastern shore were several industrial-size loading quays, Piers One through Four, a cement factory that once cast a continual gray smog over the area, and a Special Forces training base run by the Russians, called Point Lenin. That, too, had probably been abandoned when the Soviets pulled out.

Across the harbor, across water that was gray beneath

starlight, the shoreline was lower but less uniform. There was mangrove and marshland. An arm of peninsula—I couldn't remember the name of it—was an extended darkness, like an unfinished bridge. Two or three distant lights showing on the peninsula where there had once been a line of wooden barracks . . . looked like campfires, maybe, star-points bright as spider eyes.

I wondered if there was still a small airfield there; wondered if, down by the water, there was still a ragged baseball diamond with its chicken-wire backstop. I was remembering it from 1980, the twelve days I'd spent in Mariel Harbor during the boat lift. A thousand American boats anchored in their own effluvium, tens of thousands of Cuban refugees crowded into holding fields near Pier Three, everyone waiting in the heat and the stink and the boredom, VHF radios and bullhorns blaring, searchlights scanning the harbor at night and the occasional clatter of automatic-weapons fire.

Ten of those twelve days spent watching a forty-two-foot sailboat named *Peregrine* . . . the bright spot of each day being at lunch or late in the afternoon when the airstrip personnel carried their gear to the diamond and played baseball. Cubans, they loved the game . . .

"That's strange." Valdes said it more to himself, looking in the rearview mirror.

"What's strange?"

"To have traffic on the road at this hour. But . . . maybe it's Taino. He drives so fast, though, he usually arrives long before I do."

I turned to look. Didn't see any headlights. Kept watching until I saw a glimmer of windshield or bumper a mile or so back. Not so uncommon to drive in darkness in a country where a headlight cost a month's salary. Still . . . I didn't like it.

"You mind telling me where we're headed? Or is it some kind of revolutionary secret?"

A brief smile from Valdes—Americans, what jokers they were. "The Santería have a retreat on the other side of the harbor; the government people won't come near it. There are buildings where we can sleep. And Taino keeps a cook there. Pretty good food when they can get it. Angosta Airfield, that's what it used to be called."

Angosta Peninsula—*that* was the name.

I was still looking back at the distant vehicle. Was it getting closer?

"Why is it off-limits to government people?"

"It's not off-limits, they just wouldn't go there. It would displease the Santería gods, bring them bad luck because it's been sanctified. Like a holy place, but one that's guarded by . . . something, I can't think of the name. Like evil spirits. One of Taino's jokes is that Fidel couldn't find a Cuban brave enough to follow us into Angosta. Unless he was first invited."

"Is there any other road to Angosta?"

"No. This is the only one."

"You're certain of that?"

"Of course I am."

I was liking it less and less. I was turning around to tell him to speed up, get to Angosta when, up ahead, I saw a brief strobe of brake lights . . . a vehicle turning. To block the narrow road? It was possible. I couldn't tell.

"Stop the car."

The tone of the voice startled Valdes. "What?"

I put my hand on his arm and squeezed. "Stop the car *now*."

He was downshifting, pumping the brake. "But why?"

I was already opening my door. I said, "I'm driving."

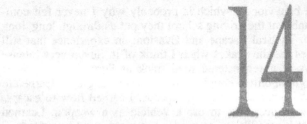

Once behind the wheel, I switched off the lights and punched through the gears, trying to get the Nissan up to speed.

Checked the rearview mirror—yeah, the car was still coming behind us. Not too fast, though.

The road was straight here, visibility pretty good: the macadam was bleached gray by tropic sun, so it stood out nicely between elevated trees on our left and, on our right, rock and vegetation that sloped toward the harbor.

"Why are you doing this?" Valdes was flustered; couldn't figure out what the hell was going on.

"There's a truck ahead."

"So? This is a public road. Cars, trucks . . . I've even seen *tractors* on this road. That's why you're driving so fast?" As if I'd suddenly gone berserk.

I had the cheap little rental up to eighty and Valdes didn't like it. Truth is, I didn't like it either. I am, by habit, a slow and cautious driver. I'm the guy you see from the passing lane, hands relaxed on the wheel, matching the traffic flow, taking in the scenery; the one who slows for every intersection, every blind hill or curve. I never had an interest in that adolescent tangent which lures grown boys into hot-rod behavior . . . which is probably why I never felt comfortable at the driving school they put us through long, long ago, Tactical Escape and Evasion: an experience that still gives me the shakes when I think of it. Seven very intense days at a sequestered road track at Summit Point, West Virginia, only a couple of hours from Langley. I learned to take curves at outrageous speeds. Learned how to escape, how to flee, how to use a vehicle as a weapon. Learned what it was like to be pursued at high speed by experts—*real* experts—who actually enjoyed banging bumpers while doing one-ten, one-twenty, heading into a hairpin turn at night, the blanks in their handguns blazing.

In a class of twelve, I'd finished seventh overall and left that miserable school feeling wobbly, out of my league, but happy as hell just to be alive.

The truck was up ahead, close enough now to see. . . . I waited until I was only a couple of hundred yards away, then I switched on my lights and saw it clearly for the first time: a big stake truck, the kind they used to haul sugarcane. Way too big to ram. It had been pulled across the road, cab pointed toward the harbor, blocking both lanes. I saw the man sitting on the driver's side throw his arm up at the unexpected dazzle of light, as Valdes yelled, "You're going to kill us!"

The man in the truck apparently thought the same thing. I watched him scramble out the door, saw him dive for the ditch just as I grabbed the emergency brake lever and lifted hard. . . .

There was a shriek of melting rubber as the rear tires of the Nissan locked . . . I kept my right hand on the brake lever, left hand on the steering wheel, holding the front tires straight as we continued to skid toward the truck, which was now no more than forty yards ahead. . . .

"Mother of God!" Valdes had his knees up, arms crossed in front of his face—crash position.

My eyes were busy glancing from the truck to the speedometer, truck to the road . . . gauging velocity and timing and distance—all factors in executing what the professionals know as a "boot turn," named after the bootleggers of old.

Turn too soon, we'd probably flip. Turn too late, we'd hit the truck.

I kept the skid under control, fighting it a little with the tires still locked . . . then, when we had slowed to around fifty, I gave the steering wheel a casual quarter-turn . . . felt the car slide sickeningly into a slow motion spin . . . saw headlights pan across ditch weeds and trees and boulders as we pirouetted 180 degrees . . . heard Valdes yell something that I didn't understand as the headlights locked onto open road again—the truck now behind us only a few yards away—and I downshifted into first, released the emergency break . . . and we were driving in the opposite direction without ever having stopped.

Not a great turn, but my old instructor would have approved.

"What are you crazy people *doing?*" The voice of a very angry, sleepy boy—Christ, I'd forgotten that Santiago was back there.

I was charging through the gears again, gaining speed. Yes . . . I could see the car that had been following us. It looked to be a big black Russian Lada coming toward us down the road, now going very slowly, lights still off.

I said to the boy, "Put your seat belt on and hold tight."

"Seat belt, my ass, mister! Stop the car; I'm walking."

Valdes was now beyond panic; he was resigned. To the boy, maybe to me, he said, "The gringo has gone insane. He listens to nothing. Prepare to die."

Because I said it for myself, I answered in English. "That'll be the day."

What I was hoping was that I could take the black car by surprise. Bully them off the road, frighten them with speed. I got the Nissan up to around ninety, the speedometer showing 150 kilometers an hour, and held it there. The car rattled and clattered and missed; the damn thing just wouldn't go any faster.

I still had my lights on; was watching the approaching

car maintain its slow course as it came around a slight curve, precisely down the middle of the road. No sign that the driver was intimidated; no hint that he would pull over enough to let me by.

Was I willing to risk a collision? That's what he seemed to be asking.

Behind me, Santiago yelled, "Holy Mother! You hit that car, I'm going back to Havana. I *mean* it." Still angry.

No . . . I wasn't willing to risk it.

Began to gear down, applying the foot brake.

Valdes said, "*Now* what are you doing?" Like, what insanity is next?

But Valdes didn't understand what was happening; the boy certainly didn't. The methods of terrorism and assassination have been studied and dismantled step-by-step by some bright people who work in very private offices. The simplest terrorist techniques are considered classics for a simple reason: They're the ones that almost always work. From what I'd seen, there was a damn good chance that we were being set up by the passengers of the truck and the car, one being the blocker, the other the shooter. This narrow road, in terrorist terms, was a choke point—a road we *had* to take to reach our destination. The place they chose to trap us was the X-spot—the killing place.

A classic maneuver that is nearly impossible to escape . . . if choke point and X-spot have been wisely chosen.

I was creeping slowly forward as the black car now hit its lights . . . saw that it was still coming down the middle of the road, refusing us passage.

"Perhaps we should stop and speak with them," Valdes said. There was a new quality to his voice—fear. Finally, he was beginning to understand the situation.

I was starting to feel it myself; a sickening sensation. I said, "I don't suppose you're carrying a gun."

"A gun?" As if it were distasteful. "No, of course not. Taino's assistants . . . and sometimes Molinas, they're the only ones who carry guns. Molinas, he likes guns."

Valdes: some revolutionary.

I was almost glad, though. I despised the idea of fitting

a weapon into my hand. Despised the absurdity of it, that mindless potential, and the absurdity of what it implied. I thought: What *is* it about this place?

Mariel . . .

I tried to convince myself there was a plausible explanation for the behavior of the truck and the black car. Yes, they were trying to stop us, no doubt about that. But could both of them simply be blocker cars? No shooters involved? Maybe they were just cops or government security people who wanted to stop us and search us—"Why are you on the road at this hour?"

No one had fired at us from the truck. So far, there had been no shots from the black car.

If a shooter was involved, why weren't they shooting?

I shifted to neutral and coasted to a stop. Twenty, thirty yards ahead of us, the black car also stopped. The driver had his high beams on, now he switched to dim—the polite thing to do . . . or was it an attempt to be intentionally disarming? I watched the car very carefully as Valdes said, "What do they want?" Watched the doors on both sides of the black car open slowly . . . saw two men step out on opposite sides and stand there, showing me their empty hands but not obvious about it. Still . . . why would they make the effort? I pushed the clutch in and shifted into reverse, waiting, as I listened to Valdes say, "See? They only want to talk."

I said, "So why don't they do something?"

Each man remained behind his own door, two silhouettes because of the car lights shining in my eyes.

"Maybe they want us to get out."

"That's what worries me. Any chance these could be some of your own people?"

"*Ochoa?* No . . . why would they stop us here?" As if the question were idiotic.

Why tell him? "You're sure? How it is that Taino trusts a man like you, a nonbeliever?"

"Taino *doesn't* trust me, but why would he do this?"

"Maybe he sees you as a threat; sends the two of us out here in the same car."

Valdes was shaking his head in frustration—why should *that* matter? "You're making too much of this. In Cuba, we get stopped all the time. Wait here. If these men want to talk, I'll talk." As he leaned to find the door handle, I released the clutch experimentally—wanted to make certain reverse was there if I needed it . . . I also wasn't going let Valdes out of the car until I had a better sense of the situation . . . and in that microsecond of movement, the windshield of the Nissan exploded . . . safety glass showering in bright prisms as the crack of a rifle shot registered in my ears . . .

"What's *happening?*"

What was happening was someone was shooting at us from the hill to our right—that registered, too.

I yelled to the boy, "Stay down!" as I floored the Nissan, going full speed in reverse. Valdes was hunched over, his face in his hands. I noted that he might have been hit, whether by glass or a bullet, I couldn't tell. I was counting to myself—thousand-two, thousand-three, thousand-four—then twisted the wheel hard left, spinning the car 180 degrees. I had almost completed the turn when I felt the car jolt, list heavily to the right, and heard the rending sound of raw metal on asphalt—

"Damn it!"

—Shifted into first and tried to drive away . . . saw a comet's tail of sparks as the car attempted to drag itself, exposed axle grinding on pavement—

"Why aren't we *moving?*"

I switched off the engine, yelling to Valdes, "We lost a wheel!" both of us ducking instinctively at the sound of another shot and chunks of rear window that exploded in upon us.

Heard the boy yell, "Get us the hell out of here!" He didn't seem frightened, still sounded mad.

Valdes already had the door open. I reached and dragged the boy over the seat. Waited until Valdes was out, then pushed the boy ahead of me into the gloom of heavy foliage that descended toward the harbor. Heard another shot—*pa-RAP!*—as the three of us began to run . . . then tumble down, down into a darkness . . . sliding, rolling . . . then running again into thick jungle.

I nearly had to tackle Valdes to get him to stop. I grabbed him by the shoulders and said into his ear: "Quiet! Listen a minute—we need to stop; find out if anyone's following us."

It was too dark to be sure if he nodded.

I said, "Were you hit?"

"Something cut me. Maybe the glass. I think I'm bleeding, but just a little."

Santiago stood holding on to my belt. He'd been holding on to my belt most of the way down the bluff. We'd followed what seemed to be a narrow, twisting ravine—apparently the only way to get down on foot. We'd all done some stumbling and falling. I said to him: "You okay?"

"Those bastards were trying to shoot us." He sounded worried but still not scared. Like maybe he'd been through worse.

Valdes stood quietly for a moment, breathing heavily before he whispered, "Why are they *doing* this?"

"You tell me."

"I don't *know* why."

"You're sure it's not Taino?"

"He has no reason. He needs me. He knows he needs me."

"You're going to have to do better than that."

"It's true. Trust me."

"I'm not in a very trusting mood. Tell me why he needs you. Be convincing."

Very long pause. To tell me would be to compromise his anonymity. Finally: "The only way our revolution can get arms and outside funds is through me. I . . . work for a department that deals with merchant shipping."

"If you have a way to bring money and weapons into this country, you're more than just a worker."

"That's true. I'm head of a department."

"For which harbor?"

Again, the long pause. "For all of Cuba."

Jesus . . . in charge of all maritime commerce? That had to be a massive government bureaucracy; almost a Politburo position. Valdes was telling me that he was one of the country's major players. He had to have huge political connections, almost had to be a member of the party.

He was risking all that to help these third-rate revolutionaries? I couldn't decide whether to be impressed or to dismiss him as an idiot. But Valdes had certainly eliminated Taino as a suspect. I said, "See? I'm starting to trust you more already," then stood listening for a moment. There was at least a mile between us and the road . . . no sound at all coming from the ascendant darkness. Why would they have abandoned the attack so quickly?

Still whispering, I said, "What about Angel Santoya's people? Maybe they thought Rita was in the car with us."

"No, it's not them. I'm certain of it."

Something about the way he said that bothered me. A little too confident?

Or maybe it bothered me because it was something I didn't want to hear. If it wasn't Taino, if it wasn't Angel Santoya, then there was only one plausible explanation. It had to be one or more men from a small, select group that was a lot more professional and dangerous than a crazed religious leader or a doddering old man.

It had to be the holdover Russians, Castro's own dirty tricks team and personal hit squad. It had to be *Rojo Seis* . . . Red Six.

But *why?*

That was something else I didn't want to acknowledge. There could be only one reason for killing me—revenge. Revenge for something that had happened nearly two decades ago, probably before those now in charge were even members of the cadre.

It seemed ridiculous; simply made no sense unless . . . unless it was true that the collapse of Cuba's infrastructure was so complete that each agency cell could now operate independently . . . didn't have to answer to anyone, didn't have to ask anyone . . . was free to do whatever it took to survive, free to strike out on its own against any perceived threat.

A team as small as Red Six would venerate its own history . . . and probably never forgive its own losses.

Or maybe it wasn't even that compelling. These days, what role did Cuba play in world politics? No more Angola, no more Nicaragua, no more Grenada—these guys had to be bored, restless as hell; probably lay around on the beach all day having Rambo fantasies, hoping for something interesting to do. Probably young enough and dumb enough to *wish* they'd operated during the days of Vietnam, Mariel, and Star Wars.

Christ, for people like that, nailing me could be like some kind of practice exercise. A live-fire version of hare and hounds; a way to keep their skills sharp. Castro didn't have to have anything to do with it. Nor did politics. With them it would be personal . . . and no one else would ever have to know.

"Shit!"

Valdes whispered, "What's wrong?"

I said, "I think we'd better split up. You take the boy, find somewhere safe and wait it out."

"Because you think I'm the target—that's why you want to be on your own?" Reasonable to suspect and not very flattering.

I said, "If I thought that, *I'd* take the boy. No. It's me they want. You two need to get out of here. Work your way around to Angosta, stay at the Santería place. They might keep the roads under surveillance all night . . . maybe all week. That's what I'm telling you."

I knew he had to be thinking of the hit man in the alley, Rosario; putting it all together.

"But why? The only reason you came was to bring money for Tomlinson."

"I know. But it's more involved than that." I was thinking about Dewey and Tomlinson. Could I rely on Valdes to carry a message? Tell them to catch the first plane out of Havana, no questions asked, and I'd meet them back at Dinkin's Bay. Decided . . . yes, I could depend on Valdes.

He had that quality about him—an idealist, just as his former wife had said, but also rational . . . authentic. Told him, "You and the boy need to get out of here. Trust me."

"Perhaps I'm also not in the mood to trust. I think you should either explain or we shouldn't split up."

I was surprised when Santiago said, "If he promises not to drive anymore, I'd rather stay with the Yankee."

I began to press the issue, then stopped. . . .

Had I heard something?

Yes . . . the sound of a small rock tumbling through rain forest mulch . . . a thudding, muffled, heartbeat sound.

Was someone up there?

Now I heard a twig crack . . . silence . . . then another twig.

No doubt about it, someone was moving slowly down the bluff, coming toward us. Or maybe several people . . .

I took the boy by the shoulder, pressed him to Valdes, then nudged them both downhill toward splotches of gray that were visible through the trees: Mariel Harbor.

I said to Valdes, "Head for the peninsula, I'll catch up. When you get to the water, make some noise. Splash around. Whoever it is, maybe they'll be a little less careful when they pass me."

Valdes hesitated—the guy was so scared he was trembling. "You're not just some guy who came here to help a friend. *Are* you?"

I gave him another little push. "If we get through this, I'll tell you the whole story."

Valdes wasn't the only one trembling. I was beginning to react to it, standing there waiting in the dark, listening to the crunch of twigs, the whisper of moving branches, hearing the bear-heavy sounds of a man who was stalking me, the man intent on killing me . . . beginning to feel panic alarms in all the motor response areas of a very, very tired nervous system.

I had to control the natural instinct to breathe too fast and shallowly. Had to consciously tell myself that fear is meaningless; fear is a handy warning system, nothing more. Repeated words in my head—*stay calm, be patient*—as I waited, listening to the small noises that marked his progression, getting closer to me, closer. Just one man. I was pretty sure it was just one man.

I'd moved down the bluff to the funnel-mouth of the ravine—the natural exit place for someone following us. Was crouched on one knee behind the buttress of a rain forest giant that had somehow escaped the chainsaw. I was now closer to the harbor; near enough to see panels of water through the trees, a few glittering boat lights out there. If the man walked past me, he'd be backlighted; I'd be able to see his silhouette.

Then what?

That was the question: Then *what* . . .

I'd felt around on the ground until I found a couple of chunks of limestone rock and a hefty piece of tree limb. Caveman weaponry against a man with a rifle . . . or who was probably smart enough, well trained enough, to have switched to a handgun for this kind of close quarters, lights-out work. Probably some sort of nine-millimeter semi . . . or maybe a shotgun.

I pictured him standing there, his back to me; pictured me stepping out to nail him . . . imagined what the bullet would feel like when he immediately turned and shot me.

Stay calm . . . be patient.

No . . . a better idea would be to let him walk right past; let him bolt toward the noise that Valdes and the boy would soon make when they reached the water. Give it a few minutes—the whole time, I'd be moving in the opposite direction—then yell at him, let him know where I was, the guy he really wanted, then continue the chase, one on one. Valdes and the boy would make it safely to the Santería compound while I . . . while I spent the next few days running for my life, trying to find a way out of Cuba. . . .

That was a better solution?

Christ!

He was very close now. So close that I could hear the sound his steps made in the spongy rain forest loam. There was a pattern to his movement: Step, step . . . step, step . . . step, step . . . pause to listen. . . .

When he paused, I could hear his breathing . . . the soft *phewing* sound of someone who is exhaling through his mouth, trying to be very quiet. Couldn't have been more than ten, fifteen feet from me. Pictured him, the way he would look: crouched low, weapon pivoting back and forth in synch with the movement of his eyes. Probably wearing some sort of tactical clothing, full cammo with face black; some gung-ho stud who loved the whole uniform, who loved what he was doing.

I had to fight the bizarre urge to just stand up, introduce myself and say, "Hey, let's talk this thing over." Say, "All that stuff they told you? All that stuff they taught you? None of it is . . . *rational.*"

Nor was it valid. His position, my position were both the senseless pantomime of a vanished death dance; a pointless ceremony that was still embraced by a political theater of the absurd. For a thousand millennia we sharpened sticks or rocks into weapons and we stalked and we hunted and we killed because that is what the strongest and the fittest of us did. Those who were incapable did not contribute to the chromosomal mandate because they did not survive. It is what the genetic memory of a thousand millennia told us to do, what it *still* tells us to do.

Necessity plays no role. If the drive is strong enough, necessity can be invented. It is the predicament of our nature that is the imperative, *not* the nature of our predicament. It is deep within us and it is a hunger; a hunger that feeds on meat and feeds on fear and feeds on tribal differences, social, sexual, or visual. Political leaders who want to survive pander to the drive. Political exigencies are the ideal excuse.

But what it always comes down to is young men carrying something in their hands, doing what we have always done, doing it well and with passion, because that is what we *are.* . . .

Yet, I did not call out; attempted nothing as civilized as attempting to introduce myself. Instead, I balled myself tighter against the planked root of the tree, aware that, along with his weapon of choice, it was also possible that he was equipped with a night optics system. I couldn't see him, but he might be able to see me.

We have come so far. . . .

Which is why I crouched low, eyes wide, like some animal frozen in the headlights of a speeding car. I waited. I listened. His movements created a palpable energy wave that seemed to push ahead of him . . . seeped through the darkness like a kind of gas and soon enveloped me. He was that close. . . .

Through the grain of the tree I felt the slightest of vibrations . . . a thud—the butt of a weapon accidentally hitting it?

Yes . . .

He had found my tree; was standing next to it but on the opposite side.

Did he know where I was? He *had* to know. . . .

Moving only my fingertips, I touched the club . . . then dismissed it. Felt until I found the rocks, touched them one by one, then gripped the smallest of them—about the size of an orange. Transferred that to my left hand, then took a slightly larger rock in my right. Held it with a three-fingered grip, like a softball.

I had to do something. I had to act. If I waited for him to attack, I was lost. He'd step away from the tree and shoot me. No muss, no fuss. No contest. I had to attack first. To surprise him was my only chance. . . .

So why wouldn't my legs work? Why couldn't I move?

I heard another small thunk. Yes, he was on the other side of the tree. Probably leaning against it now, letting me sweat it out.

Then I heard something else: a distant voice . . . then the sound of splashing, like someone running through water.

Valdes and Santiago had reached the harbor; were giving up their position for no other reason than I had told them to do it.

So now my stalker would reassess. He would decide that he'd miscalculated; that we already had made it to the water, and he would sprint toward the sound to catch us. . . .

But my stalker did not sprint. He did not move. He waited . . . and I knew that he was waiting for me. I had to move now or die.

I took a deep breath, released it silently. Took another . . . then I was moving without waiting to think it out . . . didn't have to think about it because I knew what to do, just as I've always known what to do, because it's in me, that instinct. The rock in my left hand, I tossed several feet out into the darkness. I waited until it hit, drawing his attention, and I was already moving the opposite way . . . arm back, hand cocked behind my ear . . . and I threw the rock as hard as I could, chest high, at a dark place on the tree's buttress where I knew he had to be. I was already rolling when the rock hit—*waHAP*—and came to my feet, crouched low, expecting to hear gunfire or the groan of a man in pain.

Instead I heard an echoing rain forest silence . . . water dripping, cicadas droning; the squawk of an outraged bird. Then . . . from behind me . . . a voice: "Good move, Ford. Wrong tree."

A man's voice speaking English. A voice that was familiar but that I did not immediately place.

I turned slowly, very slowly, and looked into the jungled void. No one there; the voice seemed to originate from darkness. In the pause that followed, I heard, *thunk*. Then heard it again: *thunk*. The noise that I had convinced myself was the sound of a rifle butt banging the tree.

"Palm nuts," the voice said. "Sounds like wood against wood, doesn't it? Same little trick you tried with the rock."

He left the obvious unspoken: I'd fallen for it, he hadn't.

It was Lenny Geis, the voice. Lenny Geis, the Canadian businessman, the cheerful tour guide, the man with the fiancée back home, the man who was troubled by prostitutes and loneliness, who had been vouched for by bellboys at the Havana Libre, the man who was none of the things he'd seemed to be, who had fooled me twice and was now going to shoot me.

I said, "You're a hell of an actor, Lenny. Or whatever your real name is."

Heard the voice say, "It's like one of those things, those Americanisms, they taught us up there at the training school. The one outside Montreal? The line that goes, 'It takes one to know one.' "

A beam of white light blinked on, blinding me. I used my hands to shield my eyes. The way the light panned across me, very steady, I realized it was one of those mini halogen flashlights that can be mounted beneath the barrel of some weapon. A semiauto pistol, perhaps, or an automatic rifle. What would Geis, a Russian, prefer? Same as everyone else, probably. A Beretta or the superior Sig Sauer—like the one I kept wrapped in oilcloth back in Dinkin's Bay and hadn't used since my last trip to Mariel.

Ludicrous that I should be standing there so calmly, the light now sighted on my chest, speculating on the specifics of hardware.

There was a rustling in the bushes. The flashlight nodded, coming closer. I could now see Geis. He was vaguely illuminated by light reflecting off vines and elephant ear leaves. His face was black. Cammo paint . . . ? No. I watched him reach and strip a black balaclava off his head. Could see his rust-colored hair, one eye wide, looking at me over the sights of a short automatic rifle.

An H&K MP5?

Some ultimate high-tech weapon. Modern times . . .

Geis said, "So . . . the question is: Should I or shouldn't I?" Reflective; didn't seemed to be enjoying it, but didn't seem troubled by it either.

My legs felt weak, watery . . . but a surprising calm had come into my mind. I wondered clinically: In times of extreme fear, does the brain produce some kind of pheromone that acts as a natural sedative?

I said, "Before you do anything, there's something you need to believe—Dewey's just a friend of mine. She's not connected with this . . . business in any way. You make sure she gets back to the States safely, there's some money in it for you."

I was surprised when he answered, "Considering who she's with, yeah, she's going to need a helping hand."

What the hell did that mean?

He stopped now, ten yards or more away, a careful professional distance, the beam of the light once again locked onto my chest.

"You'll see that she gets out of Cuba?"

"Sure. Nice gal. Way too classy for these Cuban goat killers."

"I've got your word on that?"

Taken aback, he didn't reply for a moment. "My *word*? Anybody else asked me that, I'd laugh in their face. But for you—yeah, you bet. You've got my word."

Even holding a gun on me, Geis had an ingratiating genuineness. I could hear him on the street saying, "Us Anglos, we've got to stick together." It was phony, all phony; a learned skill, but even knowing that it was an act, I still wanted to trust him. What choice did I have?

I took a deep breath, my whole body rigid; closed my eyes, expecting him to shoot. After several long seconds, I said, "If you're going to do it, do it."

Small burst of laughter. "You sound eager."

I opened my eyes. He had moved a pace or two closer. Was wearing a black long-sleeved T-shirt and jeans, nothing military except the night optics scope hanging on a lanyard around his neck. Or maybe an infrared thermal scope.

He'd known where I was the entire time.

I said, "It's what you're supposed to do, isn't it?"

"Is that a recommendation . . . or the voice of experience?"

"It's an evaluation. You missed me on the road, you caught me here. So finish the job."

"Missed *you* on the road?" It seemed to amuse him—why? And why was he still talking? "I'm curious about something, Ford. You don't want to answer, fine. But what I'm wondering is, say you were in my position. Would you do it? Right now I'm talking about. Would you shoot?"

"No."

"You seem pretty sure."

"I am."

"Why?"

"Because I wouldn't. Because I grew up."

"Ah . . ." Like he didn't believe me. "What about ten, fifteen years ago?"

"I think . . . I think we both know the answer to that. It's what this whole thing's about, isn't it?"

"Aledia Malinovsky, Nikolai Alekseev—those names ring a bell?"

I nodded. One woman, one man. The woman had been a horrible surprise.

"So you *are* the guy."

He didn't know already?

"You're holding the weapon. You want to ask something, ask."

"I'm asking if you regret it. What you did. That's what it sounds like you're telling me."

I was tempted to go along with him; tell him what he wanted to hear. Maybe he'd spare me. Take me in and have them put me in some hellhole prison . . . in which case maybe I could get word to Juan Rivera, have him ask Pilar to intercede. Would she do it? Did Pilar still care enough?

But no. I'd dealt with the memory of that one night far too long to diminish it all with a lie. I said, "I regret the . . . *necessity* of it."

"Which means you'd do it again."

"Yes."

"The night the sailboat exploded. The whole thing—that's what you're telling me."

The forty-two-foot *Peregrine,* built in Cuba to be sailed among a thousand other Freedom Flotilla boats across the Florida Straits, then anchored in a major U.S. port. The Soviet GRU's absurd and desperate solution to Star Wars: a test boat equipped with a leaded keel, a radio-detonated nuclear explosive therein, and more to follow if the *Peregrine* made it through undiscovered.

Supposedly. I never learned if it was true. I never would.

I said, "Yes. I'd do it again. That's what I'm telling you."

The laughter again as the flashlight beam swung to the ground, then found the tree where I'd been hiding. There was a deep yellow gash in it where the rock had hit. Geis said, "See there, more misinformation. Fidel told me that you couldn't throw; that you're a shitty baseball player."

"He *remembers* that?"

Geis said, "Anything that hurts his ego, the old fool remembers," then fired the weapon twice into the tree—*paRAP-RAP*. He waited for the screams of startled birds to fade before he said, "There. Far as anyone listening's concerned? You're dead."

I was shaking again, the pheromone calm, whatever it was, shocked out of me. "But why? *Why?*"

Geis was moving past me; touched me on the shoulder—I was to follow. "If you'd stood there whining about how guilty you felt, about how they made you do it, just following orders—all that bullshit—then, yeah, no problem. The tree lives, you don't. I've got no . . . patience with people who make excuses. It's like showing disrespect for what we do." He was working his way down the hill toward Mariel Harbor. I stood there dumbly, listening. "Know something else, Ford? You're right. Sooner or later, we all grow up. Nikolai was an idiot, and Aledia Malinovsky, Jesus, what an obnoxious pain in the ass she was. I almost popped her myself once. Red Six, the four of us left, we got drunk one night and actually wrote you a note. Started out, 'Dear Imperialist Brother—Thanks for taking that bitch off our hands.' Like a joke, you know. But we *meant* it."

I was still in shock. "Castro sent you after me because of that goddamn *baseball* game?"

Geis stopped. "He hinted he wouldn't mind if I got the chance. But I set my own agenda, which means you're like zero priority. I didn't even know you were in the car until you started with the tactical turns. Your rental, but I knew Santoya had it. I thought, hey, wait a minute—that's got to be Ford. Adolfo Santoya do a J-turn? Kind of a shitty, amateur kind of J-turn, but Santoya wouldn't have even tried it. He was so bad behind the wheel, the party assigned him a driver."

I almost asked, "Adolfo?" but then I thought: *Valdes.* "Santoya was the mark?"

"What the hell you think? Where's the profit in taking you down? To get Adolfo, I'd've done it, but I didn't want to. Not until I'd had a chance to have this conversation. Let's face it, in our line of work it's hard to find people to talk to." Geis turned. "You coming or aren't you?"

"Wait a minute. He's got a little boy with him."

Geis's silence said, *So . . . ?*

"You expect me to tag along and watch you kill them both? I'm not going to do that."

He took a couple of steps up the hill, close to me. "You're not going to just tag along, you're going to *help* me. You spent some time with that group, maybe you picked up some information I don't have."

"I don't know anything."

"When I sounded you out in the street in Old Havana, *that's* when you didn't know anything. By now, a guy like you, you're bound to have collected a little bit of information. You've been trained, remember? And you're going to tell me."

I said, "Nope. I won't do that."

"Yes, you will. Know why? Adolfo's planning to assassinate my boss. That's why. Him and that Santería idiot, Taino. They even try it, Dewey, your buddy Tomlinson, anyone within a couple of miles, they're going to be executed. Like maybe three days jail time, just so the guards can have some fun, then put up against a wall. Your pretty little Dewey. You want to see that happen?"

"Kill *Castro*?"

Geis put his hand on my shoulder and started me down the hill. "The moment Rita found a way to sneak in here, I knew it. Trouble is, I can't get my idiot boss to believe me. Know why? Because he's become a fucking goat killer, no smarter than the rest of them."

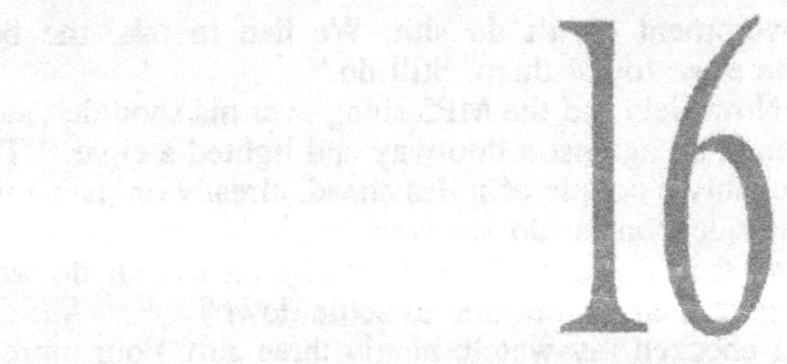

Geis said, "We either missed them or they traveled a lot faster than we did."

We'd spent the last two hours picking our way around the southern rim of the harbor: rain forest, then plowed waist deep through marsh—"Watch out for snakes; the bastards are thick in here"—then walked through a couple of clearings that had gone to weed until we came to a line of low CBS buildings, windows boarded, everything dark.

Pier Three, where they had loaded small boats with 120,000 refugees, was behind us. The narrow mouth of the harbor was off to our right, north, a couple of miles away.

Geis had kept his eye to the scope around his neck, a thermal sensor. Saw nothing. Just in case, he wanted me to call out the names of Valdes—Adolfo Santoya—and the boy, try to lure them in. I'd refused.

"You don't trust me? I won't shoot either one. Promise."

"That's right, I don't trust you."

Harsh laughter. "Every time we talk, I feel like we've got more and more in common. Hey, know what I'd like to do? Next time we sit down, I'd like to hear about the benefit program they had set up for you guys. For us, the government didn't do shit. We had to take the benefits where we found them. Still do."

Now Geis had the MP5 slung over his shoulder; stopped, leaned up against a doorway and lighted a cigar. "They're probably a couple of miles ahead, already on the peninsula. The question is, do we want to go barging in there now, have that Taino ready and waiting on us? Or do we want to give them some time to settle down?"

I checked my watch: nearly three a.m. Four more hours and the winter sun would be up.

Christmas Eve . . .

I looked across the harbor to Angosta Peninsula. No fires showing, everything dark; no boat lights out on the water, either . . . but one boat, way in the distance, under way and moving. A sailboat? Yes, a sailboat. I could see the delicate triangulation of its mast against the stars. Could hear the diesel *pop-poppa-pop* of its tiny engine straining against the tide.

I remembered Tomlinson saying that *No Más* was in Mariel Harbor, anchored as if she were waiting for him. Remembered Adolfo Santoya saying the boat was ready, everything cleared.

Could it be?

To Geis, I said, "Maybe we should hike back to the road, have one of your partners drive us to Havana. You want to stop the Santoyas? You've got Castro's whole army to back you up. Surround the place, smoke them out, and arrest them."

Geis said, "Those aren't my partners; they're flunkies I hired. Pay them a few bucks, they'll do anything you tell them to do. Besides, you don't understand the situation or you wouldn't even suggest something like that. Surround the place?" Like I was being silly.

"Because of who you're after. He's too well connected." Maybe Angel Santoya was now so powerful, the only way to deal with his wayward grandson was through covert action. Geis acting alone.

"Adolfo? No one in Cuba is that powerful. Jesus, what bullshit story did those people sell you?"

"That he was a department head; in charge of shipping for Cuba. That Rita had come back to retrieve the family fortune—didn't say anything about being her cousin. Just that Angel Santoya's people were after her, wanted it all for themselves."

"Yeah, well . . . everything's true but the last part. Angel Santoya, the old son-of-a-bitch, died three months ago. I can see why'd they'd want people to think that, sure. They've got to explain being followed some way. But the only person after them is me."

"To save Castro. It's not the money."

"Damn right it's the money; it's got everything to do with money. What, you think I'm being patriotic? If there really is a family fortune, I want it."

"And you don't want to share it. That's why you won't have them arrested."

"Partly, yeah. Why make it a public matter? But mostly, I want to keep my crazy boss alive. If Fidel gets whacked, I'm out of a job. I've got a pretty nice life here. Beach house down on the Isle of Pines, my suite at the Havana Libre. No one knows who I am but everyone does exactly what I tell them to do. A month off a year to go anywhere I want to go, brush up my languages. That prostitute I told you about? It's true. She comes to the hotel for only one reason. One of the most beautiful women in the world.

"What, I'm going to go back and freeze in fucking Moscow? Or Montreal? Believe me, five years training in that place, dealing with those asshole Canucks, it was enough. You know what I'm saying. The rest of the world, having money just makes you rich. But in a place like Cuba, it makes you God."

I didn't want to hear any more. I wanted to be away from him. Was it that I found Geis so repelling . . . or just so uncomfortably familiar? I said, "Then let's talk money. I've got nine thousand, cash. I can get it for you tomorrow. You cut me loose now, I walk to the Santería compound alone, get Dewey and Tomlinson, and we're out of here."

"You get back with Taino's people, you're not going anywhere. That's what you don't understand."

"They like Tomlinson. They think he's helping him; him and his psychic powers. They're not going to hurt me or Dewey as long as they think they need Tomlinson."

Geis said, *"Oh?"* letting me know that I was already providing information, whether I wanted to or not. Then he said, "Tomlinson's going to get all three of you killed. Tell me this, last night, when you went down that alley? Did some gorilla jump you, try to rob you?"

"He tried to kill me."

"There you go. A guy named Rosario. He used to do some stuff for us. That guy, Jesus, he'd sneak up on cows, neighborhood dogs at night, and cut their throats just to stay in practice. Rosario, he *likes* it. Now he works for the priests. Taino put him onto you. Taino would burn his own mother if he thought it would get him a little more money or a little more power. He's like the fifth or sixth most powerful priest in Cuba, and he wants to be first. So what's new?"

"Bullshit. Taino's people tried to rescue me. I'm pretty sure they killed the guy you're talking about."

"You think Taino would tell anybody? He has you popped, takes the money, his own people still think he's a great guy. What's he care what happens to you or anybody else. He's just like Fidel; all those power-hungry assholes. He's got a public agenda and a private agenda. What you better hope is, Dewey's not on Taino's private agenda." Geis puffed on his cigar before he added, "So you going to think it over, or are you going to help me?"

I stood there feeling sick; cornered. Finally said, "God *damn* it."

Geis said, "Good decision," then turned suddenly and kicked open the door of the building. He had the light of his rifle on, shining it around: some kind of old mess hall; a few cans of food sitting on shelves, dust everywhere, the tiny ruby eyes of rats looking out at us. Was this Point Lenin, the old special forces base? Geis said, "First thing we do, we get something to eat. Maybe sleep a little bit, too."

I was exhausted. When was the last time I'd slept?

Dewey and I had had a short nap at the Havana Libre—this after making love. But my last real sleep was . . . Panama City.

It seemed as if we had flown out of Panama City weeks ago, not the day before.

I said, "You don't have to worry. I'm not going to sneak off and I'm not going to try to take your weapon." Telling him that in advance so he wouldn't be tempted to tie me.

The man was looking at cans, holding them up to the light. Black beans; something else that might be spinach. "Damn right you're not," he said. "I'm your ticket out of here, your only way. That's why I trust you a lot more than you trust me."

When I awoke, the sun was casting dust streamers through cracks in the boarded windows. I'd folded some newspapers, old copies of *Granma,* into a pallet and had slept on the floor, my back to a wall.

I'd been dreaming about something . . . what? Something to do with Dewey; one of those anxiety-ridden dreams that suddenly lost detail as it collapsed then blended into a general feeling of dread.

Rolled, stood, checked my watch: seven forty-five a.m. I'd slept for less than three hours. I'd talked with Geis until first gray light, telling him what I knew about the *Ochoas,* what I knew about Rita Santoya. That she was looking for something that Taino wanted her to find, but her grandmother's directions were wrong. So they were now depending on Tomlinson's psychic vision to lead them to it. I told him the names of the villages I remembered, La Esperanza and Candelaria, but that Rita had said she'd already spent two days in Candelaria and claimed she didn't find a thing.

Geis had asked, "You really think he's got those kinds of powers?"

"Tomlinson? No, of course not. It's nonsense."

"Total bullshit, I agree. What it is, I think someone's trying to buy time. They tell you what it is they're after?"

"Money for their revolution."

"That too," he had said.

"What else would it be?"

"Something a lot more important than money. At least, that's what the Santoyas want them to believe."

"Meaning you think they're intentionally misleading Taino."

"At least one of them is. If they knew where it was, they'd have it by now."

"Have *what*?"

"It's voodoo bullshit. Magic. That kind of crap. Trouble is, Fidel's gone so nuts he believes it, too."

Geis wouldn't explain. Told me, "If you need to know, I'll tell you. Standard procedure, right?"

I thought back to Geis's tour of Old Havana, the way he'd probed for a reaction, telling us things so he could read our faces, find out what we knew. I had a pretty good idea what it was they were looking for. But if he didn't want to come right out and tell me, I'd go along with it. He was right. Standard procedure.

I was having trouble reconciling my impression of the man I knew as Valdes with the man I was hearing about, Adolfo Santoya. Yes, I could see him arranging a meeting with Rita, trying to reunite with the estranged branch of his family. Could see him trying to rise above the reputation of his much-hated grandfather. He was that much of an idealist. Maybe could see him planning to assassinate Castro; whatever it took to save his country. But to intentionally mislead for profit? It seemed unlikely. Or I had misread him . . . not that I hadn't misread people before.

The last couple of years, it seemed, I'd been doing more and more of that. . . .

But Geis had told me, "You may be right about Adolfo. He's a straight arrow. When he disappeared a week or so ago, went underground, people figured he was dead or something. But neither one of us knows the girl, right? That family's got a bad side; maybe she inherited the full dose." When he chided, "Wasn't it her father who pulled a gun on Fidel a few years back? At some baseball game?" I did not reply.

And that's the way he had left it.

Now I put on my glasses and looked around. Big abandoned cafeteria, a couple of signs on the wall in Russian. Geis's newspaper pallet was empty. I went outside, urinated. No sign of the man.

Geis was gone.

I walked down the beach looking out over the harbor: a trash line of plastic bottles and broken glass edging a breathing azimuth of dishwater gray. A few boats on moorings to the south, a few more across the harbor near the peninsula. The boats had a dilapidated look, like junked cargo trucks adrift. For a harbor this size to be idle illustrated Cuba's alienation; it was a dead spot in the mall of international shopping.

I decided to keep on heading south, see if *No Más* was among the anchored boats. If Geis didn't appear, I'd just keep on walking. Go straight to the peninsula. Dangerous or not, I wanted to find Dewey. She was a tough woman, a powerful individualist in her way, but she was no more equipped to deal with the potentialities of a Third World country than I was equipped to deal with the social pressures of professional sports.

And that fuzzy dream had left me uneasy, worried about her.

I pictured Taino trying to bully her with one of his egocentric tirades; saw his expression when Dewey told him to go fuck himself—he spoke English; he'd understand. Or maybe Molinas. Molinas, with his broken nose, might try to use Dewey to get even with me. I pictured Dewey freezing him with those sled dog eyes of hers, telling him to get the hell away.

Yeah, she could probably handle it. A primary characteristic of successful women is their ability to deal quickly with the lingering stupidities of men. The smart ones accomplish it so effortlessly that they can drive a pin through the heart without bruising an ego. Dewey had spent a lifetime perfecting that.

Yet . . . there was a softness in her, particularly now. She had been attempting an emotional transition with an eagerness that approached panic—not uncommon for a wronged lover. More difficult for her, for anyone in her position, was the psychological transition she was attempting . . . *inviting,* really, for I was unconvinced that she was really driven to be anything other than the kind and decent person she was by nature. Her behavior of late was, at best, experimental and, at worst, a kind of controlled hysteria designed to distance her from the woman she had loved and who had badly hurt her.

Dewey was not at her strongest. No doubt about that. That was the woman I worried about. Worse, I, her friend, had been complicitous through my weakness every damn step of the way.

Ahead, at the narrowing base of the harbor, I could see mangroves hunched over a breach in an expanding mudflat: a river; the Rio Bongo on the chart I had once memorized. Could see several people, one man and some children, trotting along the bank of the river, animated; excited about something.

I picked up my pace; pretty soon was jogging.

What I was worried about was that Geis had found Adolfo Santoya, and that nice kid, Santiago.

But no . . .

No sign of Geis. The attraction was a West Indian manatee with calf, the two of them trying to fight their way upriver against a boiling tidal current. The man and the children were following along pointing, occasionally stopping to tug at something.

Even from a distance, I could see the whiskered nose of the female breach the water's surface, followed by the cetacean curve of her arched back—unscarred, rubber gray, tapered like a small boat—then out of the water she lifted the huge fluke tail . . . hesitated a moment, then soundlessly found purchase in the water-mass, the thrust of tail creating a circular slick as she submerged; a slick in which surfaced the calf, nostrils flaring to breathe. Her baby was the size of a very large stuffed toy. Couldn't have weighed more than forty pounds. The mother probably weighed close to nine hundred.

As I got closer, I saw that the man was holding a frayed length of blue nylon rope that was attached to a Styrofoam float. The working section of the rope extended into the river, bellied with the tide, then disappeared underwater in the direction of the manatee. My first impression was that the animal had gotten tangled in a lobster trap line. It is a common occurrence in Florida. Over the years, I have helped free several. They swim around dragging the float which, ultimately, gets tangled with something else—another trap or a mangrove limb—and the animal dies.

I stopped on the mud flat and watched the people watching the manatee. A father with his children, I decided. A tiny man with splayed feet and a four-day growth of beard. He had a cigarette rolled from a corn husk sticking from the corner of his mouth. His kids ranged from seven to maybe twelve years old. Two little boys and an older girl, all of them wearing nothing but ragged shorts; each with the toothpick legs and distended bellies that I have come to associate with malnutrition. He probably lived in the thatched roof palm shack I could see through the mangroves. Beachcomber junk lying around the yard, a campfire smoldering out front. Take a photograph from the right angle, use the photograph in some coffee table book with appropriate inspirational quotes, the shack could become someone's fantasy ideal of a simple life.

But simple lives are seldom ideal.

I watched the manatee surface again; watched the man dig his heels in the mud and give a tremendous pull. The line still didn't come free. Didn't he realize that he had to first give the rope slack? Allow it to untangle gradually?

The children were the first to notice me approaching. I startled the boys so badly they both sprinted for the trees. The little girl stood her ground, though; went shyly to her father and clung to his leg, which is when he glanced over his shoulder and saw me. For a moment, I thought he was going to run, too. He had a look on his face: nervous, frightened; a guy who'd taken some beatings. But he reconsidered, calling, "Sir, if you could spare a few minutes, is it possible that you could help me?" Very formal: a peasant speaking to his superior.

I took the rope from him; immediately allowed it to go slack as I began to explain that I might have to get into the water—the entire time, he was nodding eagerly—and that if he handled the rope more gently, it was a better way and that we would have more luck because he would not frighten the animal so much . . . and then I stopped talking.

The manatee was on the surface again, the calf nosing close beside her, and I saw for the first time the homemade harpoon in the mother's side, black blood blooming out into the gray water. A bamboo harpoon with a brazed steel head; the shaft of the harpoon fluttering in the tidal rip like certain elongated barnacles that cling to the backs of whales. I watched the animal list sideways, its mouth open wide; heard a gasping, grunting noise that I'd never heard a manatee make before, and it registered in my memory as the sound that this species makes when desperate and in great pain; my knowledge of biology expanded.

I stood there idiotically holding the rope, as the man said, "Yes, if you get into the water, perhaps you will frighten her to the shore. I cannot swim or I would offer . . . and lately, I have not been well. It seems as if I have lost my strength. But if I can get close enough, I will use my machete. I am still fairly good with a machete."

For the animal, he used the word *manatí*, a name handed down from the original Spanish. He seemed very pleased that I was so willing to take charge.

"You eat these things?" I wanted to drop the rope and escape; get the hell away from this place, this world that kept trying to suck me back into its own dark vortex.

"Only when we are very lucky," the man said. "My wife and my children, it has been so long since we've had meat. This will be a wonderful—" He hesitated, realizing that he didn't know who I was. He stared at me with large brown eyes that were flecked with splotches of milky blue. Was I a tourist? Or was I some holdover Russian? "It will be a wonderful night," he finished lamely, but I knew he had intended to say wonderful Christmas.

Geis said, "You're not going to like what I'm going to tell you."

I knew it was about Dewey and I didn't want to hear it. I said, "Why should anything change now?"

I'd walked back to the abandoned special forces base; had been in the cafeteria for twenty minutes or so when Geis came in. I'd decided that he was right; he was my ticket out; that I had no hope of collecting Dewey and Tomlinson and getting back to the States without him.

I had paused on the way back long enough to confirm that *No Más* was not among the boats moored in this part of the harbor. Had that been Tomlinson I saw sailing out under cover of darkness? Or maybe Adolfo Santoya with the boy? They could have heard the shots, assumed I'd been killed, and chosen an unlikely means of escape. Santoya had arranged to have the boat cleared. He would have known where it was.

Or *No Más* could be on the other side of the harbor, gathering barnacles, anchored with other confiscated boats near Angosta Peninsula.

Geis was looking at me, then looked away. Something in the corner had caught his attention. He bent down and picked up a wad of newspapers. Held it between two fingers as if he were handling a soiled diaper. "Jesus Christ," he said, "you cut yourself shaving?"

"It's not my blood." Nor was it human blood. I'd used the newspapers to finish cleaning my hands after I'd left the happy little man and his children on the riverbank. When reduced to the context of survival, my view of nature is pragmatic, not romantic. Even so, I didn't want to talk about it, didn't want to think about it, certainly wasn't going to tell Geis. I said, "You were about to give me bad news."

"I decided to make an early-morning reconnaissance on the Santería compound. You know, see if they had any guards posted—sometimes they use some of those *Abakua*, freaks, the ones I told you about. Don't want them drinking any blood from our skulls. Right? Just wanted to get a feel for the place before we made any moves."

I thought: Yeah, and shoot Adolfo and Rita if he got the chance.

Geis said, "But guess what? The place is deserted. Nobody home but this old woman who said she was a cook. Oh, that reminds me—" He reached into his field satchel and tossed me a soggy banana leaf that was tied like a bandanna. Inside was cold rice mixed with black beans and fried plantains. I began to eat even though I didn't feel like eating. Listened to Geis say, "The cook, she didn't want to talk. Had to use all my charm, but she finally told me that Taino and his people pulled out late last night. Looks like they didn't care if you and your buddy Adolfo showed up or not."

"Was Dewey with them?"

"Yep. A blonde that tall, these people don't forget."

He was right; not good news, though I had expected worse. But we had the names of a couple of towns—Candelaria and La Esperanza—and we could track them down. I started to ask a question, but Geis interrupted. "Wait. I'm not so sure that's all the bad news."

Said, "What do you mean?"

He reached into the satchel again and tossed something

to me . . . something small and silken. I caught it and held it up as he said, "They seem a little fancy for a *Cubana* to own. You recognize them?"

A pair of bikini underwear, nearly new but both sides had been ripped away from the elastic band so that now it was a single piece of cloth. The underwear was jade green. Dewey had told me about buying it in Madrid.

I took a deep breath, then another, trying to stem the rage I was feeling . . . then wasn't so sure I wanted the rage to disappear. "Where did you find these?"

"One of the rooms. The cook told me the blond woman, as they were leaving, seemed pretty upset, but that the Miami-Cuban—she meant Rita—was taking care of her. So at least they haven't killed her yet."

"Yet?"

Geis said, "They're hers?"

"Yes."

"Well . . . assuming what we're both thinking happened actually happened, I doubt if Taino's dumb enough to let an American girl go back to the States and tell the kind of story she might tell. Fidel wouldn't like it. It's better she just disappears."

I began to pace; had to move. "Why in the hell would they do . . . *that* to Dewey?"

"I liked the girl, but she had a pretty smart mouth on her. Taino—remember me *telling* you about these people?—Taino, one of his followers gets out of line, they might wake up with blood and chicken feathers on them or they might wake up with their legs on fire. It happens. I've seen the bodies. The priests don't tolerate disobedience from men, how you think Taino's going to react if a woman gives him a hard time?"

"That's no reason. With Tomlinson there?"

"Maybe he realized the Santoyas were feeding him a line of bullshit and gave up on Tomlinson. Or maybe the guy came through, finally pointed to a place on the map, so they figured they didn't need to keep him or anybody else happy anymore. They pulled out without you or Adolfo for a reason. They were in a hurry to get someplace."

I was making myself think it through; to be anything but clinical was to think about Dewey, what had happened to her, what was going to happen. Said, "Last night, when you were waiting for us on the hill, did you see their vehicles leave? No cars passed us, either direction."

Geis said, "I was sort of wondering about that myself." Meaning that he hadn't.

"Those two villages, Candelaria and La Esperanza, is one of them on the water?"

"Yeah, well, there're a couple of Esperanzas. But one of them, it's west, down the coast about eighty kilometers. It's on the water. Like a fishing village with some islands off it."

"Can you drive to those islands?"

"Shit, the roads in that section are so bad you can barely drive to Esperanza."

Which explained why Taino and company hadn't left by car; they'd gone by sea.

I threw open the door so hard that its window shattered. "We need to find a boat. Can you get us a boat?"

The expression on Geis's face illustrated a hard-edged amusement—you're giving orders? "A boat? Sure, I can get a boat—but not officially. Between you and me, Fidel didn't exactly sign off on this little project of mine. He doesn't want me screwing with one of his favorite *Babalaos.*"

Something else he had refused to tell me about. But he would tell me. I would make him tell me everything.

I said, "Then I'll find a boat for us unofficially."

I found what I was looking for aboard a scarred-up Grand Banks, a forty-six-footer, that hadn't been in Mariel Harbor long enough to be thoroughly scavenged. On the stern, the port of registry read *Grand Cayman,* so the owners had probably made the same mistake Tomlinson had—strayed too close—or maybe got nailed by the Cubans for carrying drugs.

That would have been a double windfall for Cuban authorities. They had a boat to keep and sell, same with the drugs.

It had taken awhile to find what I wanted. I had stripped to my underwear and swum out to the little pod of confiscated boats while Geis sat in among trees, smoking a cigar. First, I climbed aboard a shrimp boat out of Brownsville, Texas. The thing had been completely stripped. Nothing usable, nothing of value left aboard. Checked the fuel tanks. Empty.

Tried a beat-up wooden sailboat next, about a thirty-two-footer. It still had its canvas, but everything else was gone. The sailboat could be useful, but I wasn't going to attempt to sail it along fifty miles of Cuban coastline. There wasn't time.

Before I slipped over the transom of the sailboat and headed for the Grand Banks, I took another look toward shore. Couldn't see Geis but knew he would still be there. It was the reasonable thing for him to do.

At first it had bothered me that he had agreed so quickly to my plan . . . but then I realized that I provided the perfect cover or an ideal alibi for him. He had said himself that Castro didn't believe there was a plot to assassinate him. But there had to be more to it than that. It had to have something to do with Taino, or maybe all Santeria priests. It was possible that Castro had forbidden Geis to take any kind of action whatsoever against a *Babalao,* but Geis, being Geis, was finding a way to circumvent those orders. Whatever happened next, from stealing a boat to murder, he could place the blame squarely on me. Could say he'd been on my trail the whole time but got to me just a little late.

That was fine. He could use me; I would be using him.

The galley and staterooms of the Grand Banks were a mess. The authorities had torn the vessel apart looking for something—yeah, it was probably drugs—but hadn't yet come back to finish stripping out the valuables. Which is the only reason that a sixteen-foot Avon inflatable, with a hard-shell deck, still hung from davits, ready to be swung off the stern and lowered. It had two six-gallon gas tanks in it, both nearly empty.

Trouble was, there was no motor on the boat. I assumed the Cubans had already taken it but searched the aft storage lockers anyway . . . and found a beat-up forty-horsepower Mercury outboard wrapped in plastic sheeting.

A spare motor. Anyone who owned a Grand Banks would have had something new and flashy on their runabout. But the old forty would do if I could get the thing started. Too much engine for a boat as light as the Avon, but I preferred to have it overpowered rather than underpowered.

I crab-walked the motor to the stern and screwed it tight to the little boat's transom. Checked the oil plug and cowling before attaching the fuel line and lowering the boat into the water. I pumped the fuel-line bulb hard, pulled the choke, then yanked the starter rope.

It took me five or six tries, but when the carburetor was getting a steady flow of gas, the engine caught and held, gurgling, missing, blowing blue smoke out its exhaust. It probably had some water in the gas from condensation.

I ran the boat to shore, where Geis stood waiting.

"I'll be damned," he said. Quite a surprise—I'd done what I'd said I was going to do.

"We're going to need fuel. There's not much more than a pint in either one of these tanks."

"Fuel, that's always a problem. But we've got something a little more pressing than that. There's a two-man coast guard outpost at the mouth of the harbor, the *Guardia Frontera*. We try to run past them without stopping, don't have some official papers to show them, we're going to have patrol boats after us."

I'd already considered that. What I thought might work is that I'd swim back to the sailboat, cut the anchor line and raise the sails. Lash the rudder so the boat would sail north toward the mouth of the harbor, then dive overboard. Sooner or later, the men at the coast guard station would notice her and come out to investigate. With their attention diverted, we might be able to slip past them and out to sea.

But Geis said, "Yeah, but where we gonna get fuel once we leave Mariel?" He was looking at a coil of rope on the deck of the Avon. "I think I've got a better idea."

"What's that?"

He used the automatic rifle to gesture. "Put your hands out in front of you, let me tie you up. I'll tell them you're my prisoner, that I'm in a hurry."

"They're not going to believe that. If I were under arrest, you'd take me to Havana by car, not boat."

Geis's smile told me how naive I was. I watched him turn his head to look toward the abandoned naval academy, as he said, "See that cliff? Sometimes they take prisoners up there, sometimes they take them for boat rides. Depends on how important the person is and if he's actually been arrested or not." He laid his weapon across a log and came toward the Avon. "Now—you want to hand me that rope?"

There were four men at the *Guardia Frontera* outpost, not two. They had been sitting around in cane-back chairs but now stood as they noticed us approach. Their office was a one-room block building that sat out over the water on cement pilings, everything painted military green. A small patrol cruiser, gray with big white numbers, was bumpered off a pier that jutted away from the platform; some kind of high-bowed cutter with a 50-caliber machine gun was mounted forward and another aft near the red, white, and blue lone-star flag of Cuba.

Geis was sitting in the back of the inflatable, steering. He nudged me and whispered, "*There's* the boat I'd like to take . . . only it would attract too much attention." He didn't seem to be joking, like he was actually thinking it over.

"That would be crazy."

Small snort of laughter. "If you'd stayed in the business longer, you wouldn't worry about little things like that." Now he brought the Avon around, starboard side against a floating dock where a couple of dinghies and a dugout canoe were tied. He was already calling orders to the four men, bluffing it out in loud Spanish: "I'm going to need some gasoline right away. And a bottle of water. A couple of bottles, if you have it . . . yes, and some cigars, too. I'll pay—for the cigars, I mean. Not for the gas. Come on! I'm in a hurry."

He was so convincing that, for a moment, I thought Geis knew the men, that he'd given them orders before. One of them was already hustling toward a big gas storage tank that stood higher than the block building.

But no . . .

The officer in charge—he had red lieutenant's bars sewn into his epaulets—wasn't intimidated; not much, anyway. The officious type, with his uniform neatly pressed and an attitude, wearing a .45 in a webbed holster. He stood there with his hands on his hips; told his men to stop what they were doing—one was getting water for us now—before he asked Geis, "Who *are* you?"

"You don't need to know who I am." Geis was reaching into his back pocket; took out a laminated card. "All you need to know is this."

I saw the lieutenant's face blanch slightly as he read the card, then handed it back. I wondered what it said—probably something about the office of the president and please extend every courtesy to this man. . . . A typical clandestine device. But the guy still wasn't going to allow himself to be bullied. "Then you must have your department telephone me and ask for these things. You will need a proper requisition. We can't just hand gasoline out without the proper forms."

A bureaucrat.

Geis, the MP5 slung over his shoulder with the barrel down, looking pissed off and bearish, threw a line around a cleat and stepped onto the dock. "Mister, I'm not going to stand here and repeat myself. I don't have time. Get the gas, get the water—or I'm going to make a telephone call and have you arrested."

In Cuba, that word—*arrested*—has so much weight because it has so many meanings. I was watching the lieutenant's face and saw it jar him. "I'm not saying you can't have what you need, please understand." But then he regained his composure, adding, "As to the phone, it's for official use only. I can't allow unauthorized personnel to make or receive calls."

Geis's face was getting red. I wondered if that, too, was a device; part of his many acts. I watched him advance toward the lieutenant, as he said, "What I understand is that I have a prisoner and I'm in a hurry and you are interfering with my orders which come from the Maximum Leader himself."

Maximum Leader—Castro's title of preference.

But the officer wasn't going to budge. His men were listening, judging him, judging his behavior. He said, "But I, too, have my orders. You come to me, you're carrying an illegal weapon. You're in a boat that I recognize; you've stolen it. You don't offer your name or the nature of your business. You could be anyone. And you have no forms! But here's what I will do. I will telephone my superior officer and he will say if you may have the things you need."

Geis watched the officer disappear into the office before turning to me and saying in English, "If his boss has half a brain, we'll get the gas. These people are scared of their own shadows. Mention arrested? They fall apart."

I said, "I don't like it. Let's get out of here." I didn't, either. Didn't like the contest of egos Geis had gotten into with the officer; didn't like the way the three guardsmen were standing in a tight klatch, eyeing us. Two of them with side arms, their hands resting on the grips.

Geis was shaking his head. "Hey—it was your idea to take a boat. You going to give up so easily?"

"We can find fuel someplace else. Or find another boat. You don't have access to a boat?"

"Three of them. Two back in Havana, another at *Cojímar*. But that would add thirty, forty miles to the trip. You want to take the time?" Geis seemed to be enjoying my uneasiness. Acting as if he could play it one way or another; didn't matter to him. I didn't like that either. All I wanted to do was get down the coast and try to find Dewey, but

Geis was treating it as sport. He loved this sort of thing. It was his life. Everything else was just role-playing. These sorts of situations were probably the only time he felt . . . *real.*

I said, "When we pull out of here, you and I need to have a talk."

"Sure. Anything you say." Still enjoying it, but something predatory in his tone now. "Before I untie your hands or after?" Then he looked away when he heard the lieutenant call, "Excuse me, sir."

The lieutenant was standing in the doorway of the office, still holding the telephone. He put his hand over the mouthpiece as he said, "My captain says that we can give you fifteen liters of gasoline, but only if you promise to have your department send us a letter of requisition."

"As soon as I get back to Havana," Geis said. He gave me a private wink as he added, "You have my word on that."

"But there may be a problem. The man with you—is he an American? My captain says that the police have been directed to find and detain a large American man who fits the description of your prisoner. It came in the bulletins this morning. Apparently he damaged his room at the Havana Libre and left without paying his bill."

Geis had crossed the floating dock and was now going up the steps toward the office. "Is your captain a complete idiot? Tell him not to worry about it. This man was with me last night, he didn't damage anything."

The lieutenant said something into the phone, then put his hand over the mouthpiece again. Thought about it a moment, his expression changing, before he said, "My captain asks how do you know the damage occurred last night?"

Geis was still walking toward him. The three guardsmen were moving, too; spreading out a little, sensing trouble. They kept moving as Geis said, "The man's already my prisoner. What the hell difference does it make when he damaged anything? Just get my goddamn gasoline so I can get out of here!" I noticed that Geis had changed his grip on the automatic rifle; had his hand on the trigger guard, the weapon still upside down and slung over his shoulder, but the barrel slightly higher now. A very subtle change. I thought: *Jesus.*

I watched the lieutenant say something into the phone, disappearing into the office as he did. Then he reappeared a few seconds later, his right hand pulling the .45 from its holster, crouching, his dark eyes very bright . . . and Geis shot him with a three-round burst without seeming to move the rifle, the lieutenant's chest fluttering with black starbursts that launched him backwards into the room. I was still looking at the empty doorway as Geis continued to fire—down on one knee now—pivoting toward the three guardsmen whose bodies appeared momentarily electrified, one by one, as the rifle's ambit swept across them, arms and legs flailing as if attempting flight, each man frozen for a microsecond in a wasted posture of defense, small clouds of red mist lingering in the air as they were thrown across the platform . . . then one of the men attempted to crawl toward the water until Geis shot him with another burst. The other two men lay contorted, still; appeared as if they were liquefying in the heat, melting into the crimson cement.

"Shit—forgot about one little detail." Geis was standing now, talking to himself. I watched him sprint into the office, worried about something . . . then came out much more relaxed, unwrapping a fresh cigar. Tilted it into his mouth. Looked pleased. "It's okay. No cause for alarm. He'd already hung up the phone." He lit the cigar, then calmly took a fresh magazine from his satchel and punched it into the automatic rifle.

I thought: For a *hotel bill?*

At some time during the shooting, or maybe in the silence that followed, I had stepped from the boat to the dock. Had also ripped my wrists free of the rope. Couldn't remember doing it. Looked at Geis standing among the bodies. He was smoking, looking at the sky, looking at the water; his little vacation time. "You're insane. You really are, Geis. You're nuts."

He puffed on the cigar, gave me a private look. "Yeah, well, that's what they said about Charles Manson."

A joke?

He gave me a smile—*of course* it was a joke.

I knelt by one of the guardsmen and touched my fingers to his jugular. Dead. Heard Geis say, "Take their money, their weapons, anything else valuable you can find," as I moved to the next man, then the third. Felt a frail pulse . . . then nothing. I was almost glad. Tell Geis that one was still alive, and he'd walk over and finish the job.

I said, "I think you've already robbed them of enough," as I stepped into the office. The lieutenant was dead, too. All dead.

"Fine. I'll do it; damn right I will. Can you believe that asshole? Said I couldn't even use the phone. All over Cuba—hell, it was the same in *Canada*—you wait in some government line and the person you're waiting to see always ends up being the same sort of jerk. The lieutenant, but with a different face." Listened to him say, "Every fucking country I've been in, that's the kind of asshole who screws up the works. Government paper-shufflers. Things would go a lot smoother, be a lot more profitable, if they just left it to people like you and me. People who can get things done."

I was standing, looking up the dirt road that wound into the rain forest. There was a donkey tied in the shade of a mango tree, a couple of bicycles, and a rusted Lada painted military green. No one else around. The harbor was quiet, no activity, but a couple of boats out on the Gulf Stream. A sportfisherman trolling—had to be out of Marina Hemingway—and an oil tanker several miles out.

I said, "How are you going to explain this?"

Geis was collecting the side arms and ammunition in a pile. Money and cigars, he put in his pocket. Turned to me and said, "You know how much they had between them? Three dollars U.S., plus some bullshit Cuban pesos that no one even bothers using anymore."

"These men are going to be relieved in a few hours. Tomorrow morning at the latest. How are you going to lie your way out of this one?"

He had gone from man to man, very quick and meticulous; also collected his wasted shell casings. "What do you mean lie? That's the great thing about my job. It's the only honest work around. If I've got a reason to do something, I *do* it. What? I'm supposed to stand there and let that idiot arrest you? I told him I was under direct orders of the Maximum Leader and he still gave me a hard time."

"You explain it to Castro and he makes everything okay."

"That's about the size of it. He's done it more than once. I'm involved with national security. That covers a lot of ground."

"Then get him on the phone. Tell him. Tell him we don't want every boat and plane in the country hunting for us, because that's what's going to happen if we don't take care of it right now."

Geis had the pistol belts over his arm, was carrying them down to the Zodiac. "I'd like to do that, Ford. I really would. But the thing is, the old man and I, we sort of had a falling-out about this Santería business. And I just don't want him to know I'm on the job."

Yeah, I was his cover; brought along to take the blame. No doubt about it now.

He said, "But that'll change come tonight or tomorrow when he sees that I was right and he was wrong. After that, everything will be official again. The old man's number-one guy. Until then, it's just you and me. We're on our own."

Because there was nothing else I could do, I went and found a couple of jerry cans and filled them with gas. When I got back to the dock, Geis was standing at the front wall of the building. In blood, he'd written one large number, one large letter: *8A*.

Said to me, "There? That make you feel any better? Let them think the revolutionaries did it."

I started down the steps toward the Avon. Noticed that

Geis was staring at the patrol boat. Told him, "If you take that, you're going without me."

"It'd be a lot faster. A lot more comfortable, too."

Was he serious? No . . . Letting his playful side show; a man happy in his work. He said, "But I guess I should trust your superior aquatic skills. Hey—want to blow it up just for old times' sake?"

I was in the skiff, transferring fuel. If I pulled away and left him, would he shoot? Of course he would shoot.

He said, "I suppose you want to drive, too."

"That's right. I'm driving." I capped a jerry can and started the outboard. As Geis stepped aboard, he held something out to me—the .45, an American-made Browning. The lieutenant, with his ego, had probably enjoyed flashing it around.

I hesitated—what the hell was Geis trying to prove?—then took the weapon. As I pulled away from the dock, I twisted the tiller throttle into neutral for a moment, listening. Up at the office, was the telephone ringing?

Geis seemed to hear something, too. He said, "If we're going to go, let's go."

The northern coast of Cuba: bluffs and lowlands, gray and parrot green; a vectoring shoreline that is awash in the sea mass from which it rises. I ran the Avon as fast as I could make it go—forty, forty-five miles an hour—until the water changed beneath us; changed from a turbid brown to purple-black in shafts of clear sunlight, and I throttled back on hill-sized swells because I knew that Mariel was behind us.

The breeze was freshening out of the east, seas five to seven feet but not capping, the bulk of Cuba providing us wind-shadow.

"You want some advice, I'd stay way outside that reef line. You try to run between the shore and all that coral, you'll kill the boat and probably kill us, too."

I didn't want Geis's advice. But I did need his knowledge.

"You ever try it?"

"Hell no. But then I was always in a boat that made sense. Not in one of these little pieces of shit." The guy was settled back, arms thrown over the rubber-hard tubes of the Avon as if it were a couch. Still enjoying himself.

"But you do know this section of coast. You'll be able

to point out La Esperanza when we get there."

"You get me there alive, I'll recognize it. And if something does happen to me"—he was reaching into his day pack—"you got this. Don't say I never gave you anything."

It was a topographical map, not a coastal chart. But that was fine if it covered enough area. I slowed the boat but still had to battle the wind to get the map open and folded to the right sector. I held it in a tight little square and returned to speed, glancing from open water ahead to the coast of Cuba drawn in relief.

It showed the village of La Esperanza—a tiny place right at sea level, with a marked channel to the northwest just off an appendage of land called Punta Lavandera. But it was all lowland; no headlands that could be easily recognized. If I passed by Punta Lavandera, what landmark would I look for?

There was a large island just off La Esperanza that ran east and west, then jagged southwest. A very strangely shaped island. Its name was Cayo de Soto. Cayo de Soto was maybe six or seven miles long, curved like an arched prawn, the eastern point creating the prawn's horn, the broader southwestern section the prawn's tail. No lighthouse on the eastern point of the island—a good place to put one—but I would know my location by the size and odd shape of the island and be able to turn into a bay . . . a place called the Bay of Playuelas.

I folded the map, then put it into my pants pocket. I steered for a while, trying to ignore the back of Geis's head, focusing on wave rhythms and optimum speed, seeing the bottom through a water stratum that thinned and deepened, jade tinted and clear, buoying us above deserts of white sand, mesas of coral, our boat shadow following the demarcations of light and depth far, far below.

Then for no reason that made sense, I thought: *Lighthouse.*

Why did a lighthouse come to mind?

I thought about the map. There were several landmarks but no lighthouses. So why *lighthouse?*

I kept steering, heading west. That word would come into my mind, stay for a while, then fade.

But it kept returning.

Lighthouse . . .

I drove and let my subconscious work on it.

We were a mile or so off the reef line that fenced mainland Cuba from open sea, two miles or so from what was now jungled shoreline. I figured we'd been traveling an hour and a half or so—it was now nearly three p.m.—and that we'd covered thirty, maybe thirty-five miles. Saw thatched-roofed shacks built among coconut palms on the beach. A lone man on a horse. Listened to Geis tell me about his prostitute in Havana—"Everything I told you was the truth; about her, about Castro, about Cuba, everything. That's the only way to convince guys like us"—but I kept thinking: *Lighthouse?*

Finally, I took out the map and looked at it again. I paid particular attention to Cayo de Soto. Yes, the eastern point of the island would be a good place for a lighthouse, but why did that strike a chord?

I had almost put the map away a second time when I realized what the connection was. Made myself look away, then look again. Months later, I would find myself reviewing a map of coastal Cuba just to be certain I hadn't imagined it: Cayo de Soto, shaped like an arched prawn, was the inverted twin of Sanibel Island. It was as if someone had inked a map, folded it, and stamped a carbon copy of Sanibel on the northern coast of Cuba. Sat there at latitude 22 degrees 45.7 minutes north, longitude 83 degrees 50.5 minutes west, for anyone with a chart to see.

The islands of Florida and the Caribbean are often similar in shape. Forces of tide and wind are immutable, so the landmasses they contour become a repetition of theme.

But not Sanibel.

Sanibel, because it was formed over the millennia by an unusual confluence of river and tidal flow, was very different.

So was Cayo de Soto.

The lighthouse meant nothing—it was the distinctive eastern point of the island that had keyed the memory electrodes. And, perhaps, the smaller islands clustered around the prawn's belly . . . and the narrow Blind Pass–sized opening at the western end. But none of that was as compelling as the amoeba-shaped bay—a Cuban version of Dinkin's Bay—sitting just below the hump of the arched prawn. Sanibel's mangrove littoral was on the northern side, Cayo de Soto's on the south, but they were duplicates other than that. It was so obvious that I wondered why I hadn't noticed it immediately.

To me it was a geographical oddity. To a mystic like Tomlinson, under the influence of peyote and pressured to pick a spot on a map near La Esperanza, the similarities would register subconsciously—as they had with me—or consciously . . . something he would interpret as a divine message.

I put the map away and said to Geis, "I know where they are."

Geis, for some reason, seemed concerned. He was looking past me off our stern. "I was hoping you'd noticed. Hotshot boatsman that you are."

What did that mean?

I glanced over my shoulder and saw a cruiser a mile or so away, closing on us. A high-bowed patrol boat; the *Guardia Frontera.*

"Slow down, let them pass us. Or stop and let them ask us for papers—what the hell do we care?"

Meaning he would talk us out of it. Or shoot our way out of it.

I twisted the throttle for maximum speed. "I'm not stopping. We can outrun them."

"The patrol boat, maybe. But not them."

I glanced over my other shoulder and saw some kind of small power boat—it looked like a Whaler—so overpowered that its engine threw a rooster tail of spray behind it.

I turned sharply toward the reef line. Said, "We can try."

• • •

The reef appeared as an extended hedge of black upon which ocean rollers exploded, throwing white spume that created a jagged and shifting border westward, down the coast. The way the sunlight caught the surf line, the breakers appeared to be moving in slow motion, like polar ice, mica and silver. I had to find a way through the coral into the calmer, much shallower water that lay between the mainland and the reef.

"Stop, goddamn it! If we run, they'll open fire without asking any questions. For all we know, they just want to search us because they're bored." Geis had turned to face me; he was sitting on the wooden decking, his back against the bow. Already, we were taking some spray and his shirt, his red hair were soaked.

"Know what I think, Geis? I think they found those bodies back in Mariel and they're going to shoot no matter what."

"Then why's the fucking patrol boat already pulling off?"

I took a quick look behind us. It was true. The cruiser appeared to have slowed and changed course. It seemed to be turning out to sea. Would they give up so easily if they had found the four dead guardsmen? It seemed unlikely.

But the power boat was still on us, vectoring like a bullet. Less than a half mile behind and closing fast.

"And choppers—you don't think they'd dispatch a chopper after us if they knew? Hell yes, they would. Cuba's still got an air force and those boys love to shoot. They wouldn't miss a chance like this. A moving target? *Shit.*" As if he'd have enjoyed the chance himself.

I turned my eyes toward the sky: high white mackerel clouds; sea birds kiting in the Gulf Stream breeze. No aircraft.

Maybe Geis was right. . . .

But what if they *had* found the bodies? Or what if someone found them while the *Guardia Frontera* had us stopped? The patrol boat would undoubtedly have a radio.

It was possible that the Whaler had one, too. I wasn't going to risk it.

I looked past Geis; he was still scanning the surf line, looking for an opening. It appeared to be a solid line of coral, some of it exposed to the wind. Hit it at speed, the engine would be ripped off our boat and we'd be catapulted out, cut to pieces. I pictured us on foot, fighting the breakers, getting sliced apart with every step while the men in the Whaler took their time; sat off and opened fire.

"Listen, you dumbass Yankee"—Geis was reaching for the fuel tank—"if you won't stop us, I will." He got his hands on the fuel hose, was trying to rip it off, when I pivoted and hit him hard between the ear and the jaw. He sat back dumbly, trying to blink his vision clear. I watched him move his hands—for the automatic rifle still slung over his shoulder, I thought—but no; only to feel his jaw. "Goddamn," he said, "that really fucking hurt!"

My left hand was on the throttle; the .45 Browning was on the wet deck, my right hand touching it. "You try something like that again, I'll throw you out of the boat. Or I'll shoot you."

Still wiggling his jaw, he studied my eyes—no doubt; I meant it. Said, "Either one, try to throw me out or shoot me, that's okay. But don't you ever hit me again. Not and expect to live, anyway." His eyes telling me, yeah, he meant it, too.

I moved my right hand from the deck to the safety lashing on the Avon's pontoon, holding tight. I was running parallel to the reef now, far enough off to avoid the breakers, but the surge and lift of every wave tilted us crazily to the left, our port side, causing the outboard's propeller to scream when it broke free of the water.

"They're going to stick their bow right up our ass, Ford. If you're going to outrun them, do it!" Geis was squatting now, looking behind us, both hands gripping the boat. A new objective, a new Geis—suddenly the cheerleader. "Three guys in uniform . . . yeah, they're *Guardia.* And one of them's bringing out a rifle . . . shit, no, it's one of those damn baby machine pistols."

I swung my head for just a moment—the Whaler was no more than sixty yards back; too much of a blur to confirm what Geis was seeing. I was concentrating on the reef: a wall of brown staghorn coral; flashes of reds and greens as the waves broke over it. There had to be some kind of tidal cut. . . .

But there wasn't. None that I could see . . . not with my damn glasses coated with salt spray.

"He's bringing his weapon up, Ford. Trying to aim in this shit. The son-of-a-bitch, he's—well, fuck him, I can play that game, too." Now Geis was trying to unsling his MP5, bouncing around in the bow, his feet slipping, landing hard on his butt. "Stop this goddamn boat so I can shoot!"

"Hang on! I'm going to try and jump the reef."

"*What?*"

"I catch one of these waves just right, I think I can jump us over the lip. We make it, there's no way they can follow us."

I wasn't certain I believed it, but I was starting to panic. My muscles had gone rigid, expecting to feel the impact of a bullet at any moment.

"If you're going to do it, *do* it. Shit!"

I was watching the swells rolling in off to my right. Pretty big swells, six- to seven-footers, that seemed to absorb elevation and pitch as they glided onto the reef. I was also studying the reef, looking for the narrowest band of staghorn. It didn't seem to be much more than eight or nine feet wide here. I saw a large, glassy roller ahead and off to my right, way out, and I turned the boat toward it. Pounded full speed at what I hoped was a precise point of intersection, then I pulled the tiller hard toward me, turning sharply toward the coral . . . looked ahead and could see nothing but white spray . . . looked behind us and saw the wave gathering mass and height, and I twisted the throttle open, trying to match our speed to the speed of the wave. Heard Geis yell something loud and in Russian—an instinct probably keyed by fear—as the wave lifted us easily, carrying us crest-high, then surfed us onto the coral . . . then over and partway across it, where we banged down bottom-hard, engine tilted upward and kicking until I shifted to neutral.

We were frozen there a moment, hard aground, but then the next decaying surge lifted us . . . lifted us a little more . . . and then I powered into deeper water and back onto plane.

Geis yelled, "I'll give you this—you're a hell of a lot better in a boat than you are in a car."

My heart was pounding. We'd actually made it? I said, "I know."

The Whaler had stopped, was dolphining in the rollers, trying to hold its position off the reef: three men in uniform, just as Geis had said, one of them with a weapon aimed at us. I watched the man trying to balance himself as he leaned toward us; heard nothing because of the surf, but saw a line of angulated geysers streak the water ahead of us.

"Shit, now they're shooting at us." We were in flat water; Geis had no trouble shouldering his automatic rifle, but I reached and batted the barrel away.

"Stay down! If you return fire, they're going to follow us whether they know about Mariel or not. And probably call in help."

"They shoot us now, what the fuck difference does it make?" He gave me a look—don't interfere again—and raised the weapon. I ducked low, expecting him to shoot . . . but he didn't. Heard him yell, "They're moving. They're under way now." He was motioning to me, like get *going*.

I had been zigzagging toward the mainland, trying to vary my speed and heading to make a more difficult target. Now I swung west, running fifty yards or so offshore. That little bit of distance, the air had changed. The rain forest was on hillsides above us and I could smell wet earth and leaves; brackish odors that were incongruous with the sea fans and flower-bright coral heads that blurred beneath us through the veneer of water.

The Whaler was still on the Gulf Stream side, two miles off and ahead of us. It was working its way along the reef, trying to find a passage in. I watched the boat slow, retrace its own wake, then power bow-high toward the coral.

"He thinks he's got an opening," Geis said. "If he makes it, we're going to have to do something quick. Maybe beach this thing and hope they try to follow us up into the jungle." He was looking in his satchel; plenty of ammunition since he'd plundered the base at Mariel. He said, "You think they're *that* dumb?"

I was watching the boat snaking its way through the coral. It stopped a couple of times with the engine trimmed . . . but no, they were through. Saw the Whaler lift and flatten, gaining speed. They were coming at us.

I pulled out the map. "Take a look. Is that a river up ahead?" I could see a delta of white sand; a break in the shoreline.

Geis took the map and held it low out of the wind, calmly unfolding it as I yelled, "Where the hell you think we are? Maybe fifteen, twenty kilometers from La Esperanza?"

"Farther than that." He was taking his time; didn't seem to be in any rush. I said, "You mind hurrying a little bit?"

"Then we're probably off La Mulata—this shitty little village up ahead. Dogs and snot-nosed kids; I've been through there. Yeah, there's not a river, but there's like a creek that comes out, kind of winds its way back in."

"To where? The village?"

Geis held the map out toward me. "What the hell you mean where? It's a fucking creek. It leads to nowhere!"

"Does it dead-end?"

"*Someplace* it does."

I could see the mouth of the creek now: coconut palms throwing shadows on white sand and a conduit of dark water that vanished into the trees. The Whaler was blowing its rooster-tail wake once again, a mile or so away. I tried to estimate how close they'd be behind us if we beat them to the creek—a hundred yards, maybe less.

"We're going to try the creek," I said. "Maybe we can lose them in the creek."

"Goddamn it, that boat's too fast. Let's stop—find a place up on that hill. Three of them, two of us. Then we take their boat, stop flying around in this little rubber piece of shit.''

I didn't reply. I swung out just enough to avoid the sandbar, then turned hard into the opening through the trees.

At first, it was too deep and wide to be called a creek, then was immediately too narrow to be called a river. One of those black-water tidal streams that creates its own cavern through shadows and overhanging trees. Probably thirty feet wide, with rocks sticking out of the mud banks; higher banks set back in, overgrown, showing that the course of the creek sometimes flooded and changed, winding its way out of the headlands.

I never slowed down. I kept the Avon doing at least forty until I came to the first turn. Cut the inside bank a little too close, a little too fast, and the boat nearly walked into trees on the other side.

I paid no attention to Geis when he yelled, ''You want to fucking die, stop and let them do it! Hell, I'll *help.*''

I kept pushing the limits of the boat, knowing that I had to put more distance between us and the Whaler. I'd assembled the scaffolding of the plan when I noticed the creek; now I was trying to put it together in my head. I needed to be a couple of hundred yards ahead of them for it to have a chance of working. It was a very narrow creek with lots of twists and turns . . . and an outgoing tidal current.

Maybe . . . it might . . .

Geis was nearly on his belly, fighting to stay in the boat. Limbs were swinging past overhead . . . white birds exploding out of the tree canopy . . . cormorants, with gargoyle wings and cobra eyes, flushing ahead in panic.

Because I hesitated, I did not stop after a series of turns that would have been ideal. What I needed was a place in the creek that had a stretch of fast straightaway, then a ninety-degree bend . . . and I needed it before the creek narrowed much more.

I went through a series of S-turns, the wall of trees squeezing so close that I had to duck low to keep from getting knocked backwards out of the boat. For a terrible half-minute, the creek continued to narrow; I thought we had reached a dead end and were trapped. But then the partition of trees veered away, the waterway reflected a broadening expanse of sunlight, and we were into another long stretch—the straightaway I'd been waiting for.

I got the Avon up to full speed before I kicked at one of the big khaki jerry cans and yelled, "Get that thing open. Get ready to dump it."

Geis looked at me blankly for a moment, then his expression changed. Now he was nodding, smiling—I like it; I *like* it.

At the next bend, I banked wide, made the turn—a sharp right turn—ran upstream twenty yards or so, then immediately throttled down off-plane. Got the boat under control and steered toward the northern bank, the side invisible from the straightaway, and ran the boat under some trees. Geis had already wrestled the jerry can onto the downstream gunwale and was about to begin pouring, but I held my hand up. Said, "Wait."

Sat there listening for a moment. I could hear the Whaler's outboard screaming, echoing through the forest; could hear indistinct words in loud Spanish—three men with guns, excited by the chase. They were closer than I thought they would be.

Geis said, "I'm not waiting."

I told him, "Pour it."

I watched him dump the gas, nearly ten gallons, into the creek. I felt an odd regret for the fish larvae we were killing; all the microspecies. Watched the gasoline pool and bead on the surface, a gelatinous slick of petroleum purple and green; watched the slick drift with the current toward the sharp bend in the creek.

Geis had his lighter out. Had a book of matches, too; had already twisted the open flap into a kind of fuse.

"Not yet," I said. "When I tell you."

I reached and grabbed a limb above us and swung the Avon around so that our bow was facing downstream, the direction from which we'd come.

Geis eyed me nervously. "You're not going to run us back through this shit. Not until it's out."

I held up a warning finger. *"Listen."*

The Whaler was very close now; it sounded like a fast Japanese dirt bike coming at us on a collision course through the trees. They were on the straightaway, gaining speed after the S-turns, yet I couldn't spring the trap too soon. I'd risk giving them time to react.

I kept saying, "Wait . . . wait . . . wait. . . ." until, through the trees, I saw a flash of gray—the Whaler passing and banking into the turn—and then I yelled, "Now!"

Geis didn't rush it; he gave it a professional air as he used his lighter to light the matchbook, then lobbed the little torch downstream.

The creek flamed . . . petered . . . flamed again . . . then the bend in the creek *whoofed* and exploded just as the bow of the Whaler came swooping into view. I saw the face of the driver briefly—his eyes hugely wide—as he gunned the boat in a panic, driving the boat into the flames, then clear of the flames undamaged, but much too fast . . . and I watched the three men throw their arms up as the Whaler missed the turn and careened up the bank into thin trees and bushes, tilting sideways, threatening to flip . . . and watched the men go tumbling over the bow as the boat impacted and settled on its side, the engine's lower unit ripped away . . . everything at high speed, like a video being fast-forwarded.

I had pushed the Avon out into the creek; already had the outboard started. Geis was on his feet. Had his rifle. He was studying the men: one lay somewhere in the bushes—I could hear him groaning—but the other two were already up, working their way groggily toward the injured man.

"Hang on to something," I said.

"I'm thinking about what I should do. Maybe talk to these guys, see why they were chasing us."

I knew how Geis talked. He valued silence so much in others.

I said, "We're going," as I twisted the throttle enough to make Geis sit . . . then I got the inflatable up to full speed before we scattered the remainder of the flames and turned down the creek seaward.

"We should have at least checked to see if they had a radio. If they called in a description of us, every military vessel in the area's going to be looking for this boat."

I said, "How far's that little village you told me about?"

"La Mulata? La Mulata's not on the water. I never said that."

"Then what's the next village on the water?"

"Probably Cayo Paraíso. It's where the islands begin on this coast. It's not too far—but shit, anyone sees us . . ."

"When we get to Cayo Paraíso, we'll find another boat."

19

Geis told me, "Fidel has a thing about Taino—Jesus, the guy's real name is Ramón Estevez; such a dipshit I guess he asked the Santería gods to find him another name. You know, give him something jazzy. Make himself feel important."

At Cayo Paraíso, a crescent island, palm and bleached shacks at the base of mountains, we'd hidden the Avon in a thicket of mangroves, then walked to the village. Geis had wanted to commandeer the largest boat on the island, a rotting lobster boat, probably forty-some feet with a cabin. But because I wanted to approach Cayo de Soto quietly, I'd settled on a raw-wood fishing smack with hand-hewn dagger boards and rudder. It had a single mast with a spinnaker pole, plus a little one-cylinder diesel engine if the wind failed us.

An additional advantage was that patrol boats would be less inclined to stop such a craft—a couple of locals out fishing for food. Not in any hurry.

Yet I was in a hurry. Whenever I thought of Dewey, it was like a sickness inside me. I wanted to be there; get her the hell away from a world she didn't know or had ever suspected. It was less true of Tomlinson. He, or his injury—

maybe his illness—had gotten us into this mess. But, though I was less sympathetic, I was still worried about the guy. Sappy greeting cards aside, friendship is defined, not measured, by one's willingness to go to the aid of another. It is an obligation that blends conscience and accountability. Very, very few are worthy of the word. Tomlinson is. Lately, he'd been behaving like a selfish, drug-addled dilettante, which I, his friend, would happily tell him . . . the moment we got away and were safe.

If he and Dewey were on Cayo de Soto.

That was another constant worry.

I kept telling myself, they'll be there. They *had* to be there. I knew Tomlinson all too well; knew how his mind worked.

She'll be there. . . .

But to find them, I had to stay smart; couldn't rush it. The fishing smack's lack of speed was a serious drawback, but the trade-off seemed necessary if I was to make it to the island at all.

The old man who owned the boat had asked for a hundred dollars, U.S. I'd given him two hundred and told him, in a couple of days, maybe he and his grandchildren should go looking in the mangroves. Maybe he'd find a replacement.

"If this son-of-a-bitch sinks," Geis had said dourly, as he stepped down off the dock, "we'll both drown." Meaning the sailboat.

The old man had given me a few days' supply of water and a couple of chunks of salted shark. I had been stowing it aboard. "If it sinks," I'd told Geis, "I want to die knowing what the hell's going on. That's why you're going to spend the next ten miles or so talking. If you won't talk, get out. Steal the lobster boat. I'll take this and go alone."

Geis had looked at me—me, his fall guy if Castro required an explanation. Why had he disobeyed orders? Because he'd been on the trail of the American spy, that's why. The one who'd murdered the four guardsmen and injured others; the one who was tracking Taino, maybe even wanted to take another shot at the Maximum Leader himself.

Geis had thought about it a moment before he said, "Thing is, I've gotten kind of fond of you. Like I said back at the Havana Libre, when you showed up, it was like being in jail and getting a visitor. You know the feeling?"

"That was a guy named Lenny Geis talking. Not you."

"You got a problem with the name? I'll choose another, any name you want. But me, I've gotten kind of fond of that, too."

Lenny.

He had been smiling when he added, "No offense, but I think it's a hell of a lot better than the name you used. That time you came to Havana to play baseball? I followed that Iran-Contra business; watched that Marine on television those Senators tried to nail. The same last name you used, man! I thought, Can't those people think of anything *original?*"

Now Cayo Paraíso was nearly two hours behind us and Geis was talking about Taino and Castro. He'd told me, "Because of what we might be walking into, I guess we're still on a strictly need-to-know basis. Which means you *need* to know." He sat there speaking softly in the darkness, the tip of his cigar glowing bright orange whenever he paused.

It was a little after nine p.m. With the wind behind us, we were fishtailing along wing-and-wing, jib and headsail on opposite sides, making pretty good bottom speed. Maybe five knots—fast in that old boat. Above us, stars illustrated the basin of deep space, rotating above the mast as if the universe were being drained slowly, slowly into some celestial whirlpool.

Ahead, I could see a white rind of beach and a charcoal elevation that was the eastern point of Cayo de Soto. I'd been steering toward it for the last maddening hour, and only now did it seem slightly closer.

I sat with the wooden tiller under my arm and listened to Geis say, "Like I told you, Fidel has a thing about Ramón . . . Taino . . . whatever the hell you want to call him. What it is—and Fidel never told me this, I checked around and found it out for myself. Taino is Fidel's illegitimate kid. One of the many."

I remembered how the names Ruz, Mayari, Sierra Maestra had stuck in my memory; the names Tomlinson had supposedly divined. They had something to do with Castro. Maybe a family name among them. Fidel Ruz Castro? And where he was born. I wasn't sure; it didn't matter—but it suggested that Tomlinson knew more about Taino than he had volunteered. I said, "Castro doesn't seem like the kind of man who keeps track of illegitimate children."

"Hell, no. He's probably got forty, fifty—hell, a couple hundred. Who knows? But the thing about Taino is, he's got power. Fidel likes that. He *respects* it. His only legitimate son is a lazy dope. Fidel tried to hide him away by appointing him head of the Cuban Atomic Energy Commission. That's like being appointed head of Ireland's space program. But Taino's just like Fidel. He's ruthless. Got to the top by lying, killing—shit, that's *nothing*—the kind of guy who looks at people but sees ants. What Fidel thinks about Taino is, hey, a chip off the old block."

I remembered that Tomlinson had said they were duplicate spirits, Taino and his father. Remembered that he'd said that Taino's powers were stronger—whatever that meant. I said, "Castro didn't tell you this."

"No. I already told you he didn't. It's just me putting the pieces together. But Fidel, he likes to talk. Up until about two weeks ago, he talked to me all the time. I've seen the man alone, face-to-face, maybe twice in the twelve years I've been here. But what he'd do was call me. Started maybe two years ago. And always late at night, because the guy can't sleep, and he'd just ramble. Name a subject, he'd ramble. At first, I thought, why the hell's he calling me? Then I realized—I'm a Russian. The only Russian left in the country. A Russian could never hold a position of power in Cuba. No way; the *Cubanos,* they wouldn't stand for it. See? No matter how much I knew, how much I had against him, I wasn't a *threat.* Another thing, I've got a secure phone line and I've got top security clearance. So he could say any damn thing that popped into his mind and he didn't have to worry about it. When you think about it, if a guy like Fidel's got a lot of shit he wants to get off his chest, I'm the perfect choice."

Lately, Geis told me, Castro had a lot to get off his chest. I sat steering, feeling the boat lift and surf on the dark waves, hearing wind in the rigging, my eyes fixed on the beach ahead, as Geis told me about it. The picture of Fidel Castro that emerged was that of a man who was paranoid, egomaniacal, and who had lost touch with reality. The failed economy, the food shortages, the gas shortages, the failed tobacco crop, the political isolation—why were people blaming *him?* During the last secret ballot, several members of his own politburo had actually voted against him. First time in history his election wasn't unanimous—and he was going to find out who the traitors were and destroy them. Had Geis heard the whispers? People were saying that he was losing control of Cuba. But it wasn't true! Here is what he would do to prove to them that it wasn't true.

"I don't suppose you ever read much by Stalin?" Geis asked me. "We had to read it. One line stuck with me was this thing Stalin said: 'Only religion can keep the masses satisfied to live in hunger and ignorance.' Know who told me the same thing about a year ago? Fidel—but said it like he'd made it up himself. That's when he started talking about Santería and Taino. Taino's idea was they could unify the country if Fidel started taking the national religion a little more seriously. Couple of months pass and I realize that Fidel has slipped over the edge; he's *believing* this shit. Talking about which god is in charge of what; how the tobacco crop failed because the idiotic priests hadn't made the right sacrifices, hadn't read the omens correctly. That's one thing about Fidel—no matter what the subject, everybody's an idiot but him."

Taino the anti-Castro revolutionary?

Geis made a fluttering sound of disgust. "Taino likes to pretend he's working for Fidel. He's an informant. *Ochoa,* the name, it was Taino's idea—this big white guy pretending he's mostly Arawak. Who's going to suspect the head man? It's like a big sting operation: let the traitors find us instead of us having to go looking for them. As long as they're not a threat, let the names keep piling up and arrest them all at once."

"Then you were lying to me. You don't believe Taino is conspiring to kill Castro."

"Hell, yes, I believe it. Adolfo Santoya, too. Trouble is, I couldn't get Fidel to believe it. Tells me, 'Taino is a great *Babalao,* a brilliant man like me—are you questioning the personal judgment of the Maximum Leader?' " Geis was lighting another cigar. "Why else would I be here, riding in this shitty sailboat with you? It's because Fidel got so mad arguing about it. Told his own security people that I was crazy. Okay, I'm crazy. What do they care? Except for one crazy Russian, everybody in the goddamn country wants the man dead. He tells them to ignore a plot to assassinate him, they couldn't be happier. Then what's Fidel do? He turns around and fires *me.*"

What I wanted to do was start the little diesel engine to navigate the last half mile to shore—had to be some sandbars and coral around; tough at night under sail—but I didn't want to risk the noise.

"Damn right you don't," Geis said. "That stuff about Tomlinson being attracted to some kind of identical island . . . Jesus, has everyone gone stupid? But if they *are* here, they'll have those voodoo people I told you about posted around. Like bodyguards. The *Abakua.* To get into their secret society—what it really is is a gang—they get pissed on, drink blood. All this weird, secret stuff. Bite the heads off rats, eat babies? Whatever they're told to do. But don't sell them short. They hear us, they'll kill us. In a country where guns are illegal, they've gotten real handy with machetes."

I said, "You never said anything about that. Why bodyguards? They go looking for the Santoya fortune, why would they want extra people around?" I stared at Geis.

He was sitting forward of the mast, looking at the island—silhouetted forest and beach rising, then sinking beyond the bow. For some reason, he hadn't told me what I had already guessed. I thought about it before I said, "What they're really after is Columbus's casket. They want those medallions." Fidel, whose power had been consolidated by a white dove, was looking for another harbinger to reestablish his authority.

I wondered: Why doesn't Geis want to tell me?

Geis was nodding, not looking at me. "Taino, you're damn right that's what he's after. Fidel, too. The people in this country really do believe in magic. They run their fucking lives by signs, omens, all that shit. Put Yara Hatuey's medallion around Fidel's neck—a symbol like that?—the people would accept him as president *and* head priest. Tell them, after all these years, the gods chose him to find it. How are the other priests going to argue? Taino's angle, what he knows is, whoever wears it has obviously been chosen to be in control."

"Your deep interest in the church; I can see a reason now. What makes them so sure the casket wasn't taken to Spain? You're the one who said it was a legend. Maybe—"

"That was just a way of . . . believe me, they *know* it wasn't taken to Spain. Remember when we were at the Plaza de la Catedral? The part I left out was, back in nineteen hundred, it was the most powerful family in Cuba that made sure Columbus's bones never left the island. The Santoya family. People looked for the damn thing for sixty years, but the only ones who knew where it was were a few of the Santoya men.

"Then Rita's grandfather got into such a fight with Angel, he found it and moved the thing just before Fidel came to power. Angel's people went through just about every mausoleum in the country—I guess it was originally hidden someplace like that—but no luck. Taino, people like him, have been waiting a long time for one of Eduardo Santoya's grandkids to come back and lead them to it."

I said, "So why didn't Rita lead them to it? She sits around watching Tomlinson eat peyote, point at a map.

That makes no sense. Why the charade? I think her grandmother really did screw up the directions. Rita has no idea where it is. She sees the scar on Tomlinson's temple—everybody falls in love with Tomlinson. She listens to a lot of convincing talk about mysticism and magic, or maybe she finds out she really does like the idea of playing revolutionary. She decides why not find out? Can he do it?''

Geis said, ''Rita? No, what I think is . . . I'll tell you, I took one look at her and think, Jesus, she's Angel Santoya all over again. Those eyes of hers, like gun barrels. With her, I think it's strictly the money . . . which is why I expect her to be gone by the time we catch up with them. The only reason Rita would stick around is because she was still looking for it herself. Looking for something; doing it on her own *privately*. Or because she wanted to buy herself some time. That's what I've thought right along. She wanted a few extra days, so she had to play along. Up until yesterday, Adolfo was still officially in charge of shipping. Whatever he told his people to do, they'd do. Maybe she was waiting for a freighter to take her out. Maybe they were both waiting.''

I thought: *Panama.*

I had tacked to starboard and was now running just off the beach. Everyplace I thought there might be reef or a bar, there was a reef or a bar—could hear the rollers breaking in the shoal areas as I dodged them. Cayo de Soto's similarities to Sanibel were only that. Similarities. Yet they were consistent enough that I began to acquire confidence in my knowledge of sea bottom and topography. Arriving here by boat—if he had arrived at all—Tomlinson would have experienced the same eerie sense of mirror image, only it would be stronger in him. He would accept every likeness as a directive; a kind of homing signal from God. His spiritual home had always been and would always be Dinkin's Bay—the shallow-water lake located in the eastern mangrove littoral of Sanibel Island.

Cayo de Soto's duplicate bay would be the first place he'd go. He'd expect to find what he wanted to find right there. I knew the man. Had heard all his theories on parallelism and the symmetry of life. He'd once asked me, "Have you ever looked down and noticed that urine spirals *precisely* like a DNA helix?" And had once told me, "Shadow universes exist—that's a scientific truth. So is repetition of design. So isn't it illogical *not* to believe that every planet, every dimension, every *thing* has a shadow duplicate?"

No, I didn't think that it was logical, but I did believe it was that kind of reasoning that would lead Tomlinson and his group to the bay. Which is why I wanted to sail inland. Wanted to confirm that there were boats there. Hoped to pull into the bay and see the familiar night outline of *No Más* sitting at anchor.

But I couldn't. I had to stay on the seaward side of the island. Had to run down the beach an approximate distance, anchor, then hike across the island to the bay. All because Geis had said Taino might have brought guards to patrol the place—the *Abakua.* Said if they saw us, they would kill us. Which he still hadn't explained.

I had asked, "Is it because you expect Castro to be there?" I'd been anticipating that. Would a paranoiac trust someone so like himself to deliver a thing of great value?

Geis's reply was not an answer: "The *Abakua?* Fidel's their main competition in the crime business. They hate the man; would love to take him apart one piece at a time. If they're *there,* it's not to protect Fidel."

Now, closing on the beach, I told Geis, "Dig through that mess in the bow and see if you can find a couple of anchors."

Geis had been watching the shoreline; watching me work our way through the shoals. On his feet now and moving, he said, "Ford—I'm impressed, I've got to tell you. The way you handle these waters, it's as if you'd been here before."

Cayo de Soto was a black thing elevated; a dinosaur shape afloat. No lights showing: beach . . . dark trees . . . wind. It might have been Sanibel at the time of the Spanish conquest. It might have been a thousand years before. Cut the electrical umbilical and the eyes are quick to readjust to primal light.

I said, "In a way, I have."

I was looking to the northwest at a blazing white star. . . .

More likely, a planet. Venus . . . ? Maybe Jupiter—a solitary ball that flamed above a moonless sea.

I was crouched on a sand dune among bushes wondering if the damn thing, all by itself, provided too much backlight to cross the beach unseen. It seemed out of place in terms of my amateur's knowledge of astronomy.

Or maybe a plane with its landing lights triggered, too far out to be heard.

Yes, it had to be a plane. . . .

Geis was beside me. He had the black balaclava hood on; back in tactical uniform. Automatic rifle, his field satchel, webbed belt. Ready for business—although he had made it clear he thought we were wasting our time on Cayo de Soto. Now he had the thermal scope monocular to his eye, scanning the area. Looked to the east. Whispered, "Look what you found us—couple of raccoons . . . a dog, maybe. Nice work, Ford."

Probably out scavenging turtle eggs.

I waited while Geis scanned the casuarina forest ahead of us. Heard him say, "All clear there. Lots and lots of cold-blooded pine trees." Next the thread of beach that stretched westward. That took longer. He looked through the scope, looked with both eyes, then used the scope again. Finally, he said, "Well, well, well . . . we've got company. One man, I think. About a hundred meters out. Must have been in the woods because I didn't pick him up right away."

I raised my head enough to see down the beach: a lone figure on the pale sand. He seemed to be coming pretty fast.

"Is there a village on this island?"

"Probably. But . . . maybe not, too. One of these islands, maybe it was this one, it used to be a leper colony. Back when they needed them fifty, sixty years ago. I can't remember the name."

It was the first I'd heard of that.

Geis had put the monocular away, now was unslinging his rifle. "I think this guy saw our boat. Wants to check us out."

I put a warning hand on his arm. "You're not going to shoot him."

"Give me some credit. That would make too much noise." As if that were the only consideration. Ironically, on the boat trip to Cayo Paraíso, he had told me, "The greatest thing about working in Cuba? It's a place that never requires a silencer. Honest work, just as I told you." Now maybe he was rethinking it. I didn't react for a moment when he said, "Mind if I give a few orders now that we're on land?"

Finally: "I'm open to suggestions."

"What I'm going to do is slide over to the other side of this dune and away a little bit. Spread us out some. If he gets too close to you, I'll take him. You do the same."

He was belly-crawling over the dune before I could answer.

I watched the man on the beach come closer. He was dressed in white—not a good sign. The Santeros, they seemed to favor white. When he was abreast of me, I also saw that he carried something in his hand. There was starlight on the water, and when he turned just right I saw that it was a long, curved cane knife. He was tapping the flat part of the blade on his leg as he stopped and stared at the fishing smack—a dim shape bucking on the slow rollers. I thought he might produce a flashlight and search the boat . . . but no, in Cuba flashlights were probably only slightly less rare than flashlight batteries. Then he turned and looked in my direction.

I pressed tight to the sand dune, my eyes on him. He stood there; seemed to be staring back at me. Was I visible in my khaki cargo pants and dark blue polo shirt? He took a few steps toward me . . . hesitated. Took a few more . . . then began to angle away to my right.

It was the direction in which Geis had gone.

I raised my head just enough to see what it was that had caught the man's attention: a gray shape on the next dune.

Was it Geis?

Saw something tiny and bright reflecting light. The lens of the thermal monocular, probably.

Damn it.

Yes . . . it was Geis.

The man with the cane knife was walking slowly toward him. I got my hands under me, ready to push up and move. I expected Geis to react, but he didn't. I hoped he would react; take care of it himself. But no, he lay motionless as he was approached.

Didn't he realize that he had been seen?

The man was closing—no doubt about it now—only twenty yards or so away, and I was up, crouched . . . I began to move toward the man, not really sure what I would do. The .45 Browning was wedged into the back of my belt, and I drew it as I started toward him. Maybe tackle and club him. I thought: Tackle a guy carrying a machete?

The man was moving faster now . . . stopped abruptly—had he noticed me? No, more like he had confirmed something. I heard him give a loud yell—a war scream—as he raised the cane knife over his head and began to run toward Geis, who still had not reacted.

I hadn't expected the man to run. The surprise of it froze

me for a moment; just long enough so that now there was no way I could intercept him. Even so, I was sprinting heavily over the sand, shortening the distance, the man with the knife so focused on Geis that he didn't hear me . . . so I shouted, "HOLD IT!" to get his attention . . . which caused the man to slow slightly, the machete still raised . . . and I had the Browning up, pointing it at him as he began to swing downward at Geis, who finally, finally was reacting.

My finger was on the trigger but wouldn't move, then I removed it from the trigger as I watched the bear shape of Geis collide with the man, knocking him backwards . . . then the two of them were on the ground, rolling, swinging their arms . . . now one was atop the other using only one hand . . . drew his arm back, hammered it into the man on the bottom; hammered again; hammered once . . . twice . . . and stopped. Then I watched one of them get slowly to his feet as the other man lay still.

I'd stopped running. Still had the Browning pointed. "Lenny?"

Heard a winded growl: "Who the fuck you expect?" Then heard, "What an idiot, huh? You timed that pretty good. Thought I was going to have to shoot him."

He was kneeling now, wiping something in the brush. Then he returned to the dune on which he'd been lying and found the automatic rifle. He had his hand over the halogen sight light when he switched it on so that only a muted beam came through. He said, "This son-of-a-bitch was going to cut me in half. I'm lying there thinking: Where's Ford? Turns out you're not stupid. Only shoot when you have to."

He was moving the light over a dead man. Pasty white face with dark stripes painted under the eyes, down the chin. Long arms and body, his knees drawn up to his chest as if frozen in a spasm. Probably late teens with a buzzed tough-guy beard, barefooted, wearing cheap white pants and guayabera shirt that showed two soaked red splotches. There was a third—more like a black puncture—where his jaw and neck met.

I wanted to say *I wouldn't have shot.*

Instead, I listened to Geis tell me, "He's an *Abakua.* See the face paint? The assholes wear face paint. Like a bunch of fucking savages. And the beads."

Red and white beads as a necklace. One bead of each color pierced into the dead man's nose, his ears. Same beads that Taino wore; follower of the god Changó.

Now Geis was going through his pockets. "I used my knife on him. Got a good angle on the first try but hit him a couple of more times just to make sure. A Glock. Pretty nice knife. I'll show it to you when we get time."

I didn't want to see it. I didn't want to see it because I had an old Glock attack knife hidden away with some other things in my stilthouse on Dinkin's Bay. If they were alike, I didn't want to know.

I watched Geis, feeling a growing animus toward him and everything about him . . . or maybe it was just fear reconstructed into anger. I asked him, "Do you rob everyone you kill?" but said more with my tone of voice.

He was taking two dirty one-dollar bills from a leather billfold, then looking at the photographs: an elderly man and woman beneath a tree; head and shoulders of a teenage girl with a chubby face. Said, "Goddamn right. Think I do this shit for free?" as he removed something from an inside compartment beneath the photos—an aluminum condom packet. He seemed pleased by that. "The little bastard was already screwing around on his girlfriend. But this I can use. Even rubbers are tough to find in Havana."

He switched off the light and stood. Used the thermal scope to scan the area again—nothing—before he said, "A guy's got to be thorough, right?" Finally reacting to the tone of my question. "When they found Aledia Malinovsky, she was picked clean. All she had was her clothes and her shoes. Unless you count the hole in the back of her head."

I was walking toward the casuarina forest. The bay would be through those trees, over a long stretch of coastal ridge. Less than a mile away. If the *Abakua* were here, Taino was here.

Behind me, I heard Geis say, "That's why I enjoy our little talks. I know you can relate."

I could see *No Más*. . . .

An old white-hulled Morgan sailboat floating at anchor, port side to me, a couple of hundred yards off the shallow mangrove hedge, right where it would have been anchored in Dinkin's Bay.

No doubt about it . . . Tomlinson had sailed her here. Only he would return to such a precise water place; his homing instincts as accurate as a satellite-positioning system.

Unlike on Sanibel, the interior sand ridge of Cayo de Soto extended to the bay and was elevated above it. Geis and I lay on our bellies in the thick cover of Brazilian pepper bushes and oak. I had a pretty good view of the brackish lake and the clearing below. Other than the shape of the bay, and *No Más* suspended on dark water, there was nothing else familiar about it. Where the marina should have been was the burned-out scaffolding of what had once been a large building. The foundation was of rock; had faded paint showing through the char.

It had burned years ago.

Behind it and to our right were three stone huts, the roofs of all but one torn away. The clearing, overgrown with weeds, expanded toward the water, where there were the remains of a deep-water dock. Two large vessels were tied there, both cruisers. A much larger yacht was moored off what had once been a loading platform.

Not that my brain recorded all this immediately. No. When Geis and I had topped the ridgeline, the first thing I saw—and watched for several minutes before noticing anything else—was the people below. All the activity. What they were doing.

Taino needed light. He had had his people build a massive fire at the center of the clearing. There was a second fire blazing off to the left in what I at first thought was the toppled debris of another stone building . . . but then realized was a cemetery. A lot of plaster crypts showing above the weeds. Easier to see when one of Taino's men—there were four or five working in the cemetery—called for more light and the cruisers swung spotlights on them.

What the men were doing was going from crypt to crypt, using a sledgehammer to break the plaster away. Then they'd use a crowbar or stout limbs to pry open coffin lids.

It was a slow process. They had to feel around inside the coffins, holding up pieces of this and that. They would throw the pieces aside, then fish their hands into the coffins again. The men were not happy in their work. They had rags tied around their faces—to keep out the odor; keep out the germs or the imagined spirits.

Why, on a remote island, would there be a cemetery with airtight crypts?

The abandoned leper colony . .

Geis had watched them for a time, then whispered, "They haven't found him yet." He meant Columbus; the medallions.

I whispered, "No, and they won't."

Of course they wouldn't. They'd been led here for no other reason than that Tomlinson had found a place on a map that had called him home. When they completed their search, when they realized that Tomlinson was useless, they would get rid of him. He had witnessed too much. And Dewey, too—if they hadn't killed her already.

"I don't see your friends. Don't see Rita or Adolfo, either." Geis was looking through a small pair of binoculars; had been looking for quite a while. "That's bad for you, but maybe worse for me."

What did he mean by that?

He passed the binoculars across—apparently, he wanted me to find out for myself.

I removed my glasses and refocused the binoculars. First checked the men working in the cemetery. Cool December night, but they had their shirts off, sweating. They'd been at it for a while. Maybe most of the day, judging from the piles of plaster that covered the field. I tried to gauge how many more crypts they had to open before they were done. A dozen, perhaps. An hour's work; not much more.

If Tomlinson and Dewey were still alive, I had to find them and get them out soon.

I looked at the six men standing in the center of the clearing, the light of the fire illuminating their bodies in vertical halves. Taino was there. He was wearing a white robe over slacks and a white cap. A big man surrounded by other men; two dressed similarly, and I guessed they were *Babalaos,* like Taino. I recognized two of his assistants—Orlando and Molinas—everyone dressed in white, wearing their beads. Watched Taino throw something onto the ground. Wooden discs, they looked like, dark on one side, white on the other. He threw them near what appeared to be the statuette of some Catholic saint . . . also a black statuette shaped like a child's doll. I could see that Taino was talking while he studied the discs.

I checked the three stone cottages. There was a light showing through the gun port–sized window of one. The others were dark.

No sign of Dewey or Tomlinson. Didn't see Santiago, either. What had happened to the boy?

Was it possible they were still aboard *No Más?*

I checked the boat. No one above deck; no lights showing below. Looking at *No Más,* seeing it close-up and in such a familiar setting, catalyzed in me an uncharacteristic spike of emotion, and I swept the field glasses away.

Geis said, "He's not the reason the *Abakua* are here. It's because whenever there's an important Santería ceremony, they always carry along a few to stand guard. That's how I knew. So heathens like us won't sneak in and peek. They couldn't go looking for something like Columbus without doing it up right. Making offerings to the gods, throwing the coconut shells to get direction. See those bowls sitting around? They've got blood in them. Gifts, like liquor and tobacco. They'll keep filling them up and dumping them until the gods finally come through."

I still didn't understand. "*Who's* not the reason?"

"You didn't see him?" Geis took the binoculars for a moment. Held them to his eyes, then handed them back.

"Take a look at the other big guy. The one right there . . . or wait. . . . Now Taino's blocking him."

I knew then who he meant.

I looked beyond Taino and saw the man's back, his shoulders, the graying hair above the white guayabera shirt that probably smelled of cigars. I saw the attitude, the way he enlarged his own space, no one addressing him directly but deferring to him by avoiding eye contact and allowing him room. I saw the beard when he turned away from the fire; read impatience in his movements, an imposing quality; not very happy with events, a displeasure that radiated from him and seemed to diminish the physical size of the five men nearby . . . all but Taino. Taino continued to throw and study the coconut husks. He, too, created his own space; the two of them, he and Fidel Castro, standing close but in their own orbits.

"That yacht's Fidel's. He travels with a captain, a mate, and a cook. All three of them are working in the cemetery. Not a single goddamn security man with him."

Geis had his mouth close to my ear. I continued to watch through the binoculars.

"It's because of what Taino told him: You've got to go before the gods . . . no, you've got to *stand* before the gods with open hands and an open heart. Which means no weapons. Taino says the word, the *Abakua,* they'd hack him to pieces with their machetes. Jesus, what a setup. It's like the guy's asking to be put out of his misery."

I watched Castro say something to Taino. Watched Taino say something to his two fellow priests before he assumed a thoughtful pose. He was looking at the coconut husks as if the answer were in them. Castro said something else; used big hand gestures. He probably was not pleased that he had come so far to be coronated with the medallion of Yara Hatuey . . . but no medallion.

Geis said, "We've got to move. I've got to account for Adolfo. For all I know, he's off in the trees right now trying to figure which end of the rifle to aim. If he gets a shot off,

Taino'll have them chop up everyone around just to prove he wasn't involved."

I said, "You've got the thermal scope. Use it." Then looked to see that he already was.

I checked the perimeter of the clearing. Saw what might have been one of the *Abákua* standing back in among shadows near the tree line. Saw a third now walking near the stone cottages.

A guard?

Then I saw another, smaller shape near the water but away from the docks . . . someone child sized—maybe Santiago—sitting on what appeared to be a broken plaster grotto. What was a kid doing there? The statue inside the grotto had been torn away, but the soft foundation remained. A place for the lepers to pray or maybe feed the birds.

Birds . . . ?

I'd just seen some birds. As I swept the binoculars past the cottages, I'd seen white-crowned pigeons spooking from their roosting place among the trees, scattering high above the firelight.

I took a last look at Castro—Why had the other men moved away, leaving him to stand alone in front of the fire?

Separate, isolate, destroy. . . .

I pushed the binoculars toward Geis. "You're right, we need to move. I think Adolfo's right below us."

I was pretty sure I knew where Dewey and Tomlinson were, too.

As we worked our way through the trees down the ridge, I heard what, at first, I thought were gunshots . . . then realized that they were the tentative beats of a drum.

A rim-shot sound. Like a mallet striking a hollow log.

Startled, Geis hissed, "Shit!" and began to run . . . then nearly stopped: *"Oh."*

He was about ten paces ahead of me. He headed downhill again, moving quickly but making very little noise. Kept my eyes on his back as the drumbeat continued . . . a drumbeat that soon marked the rhythm of a man's deep voice; a voice with a singsong imperiousness: *Nangare, Nangare, Nangare, Nangare, Nangare . . .*

A voice that was answered by other men's voices in chorus: *Nangoreo . . . Nangoreo . . . Nangoreo . . . Nangoreo . . . Nangoreo . . . Olorum Mafoiu . . . Olorum Mafoiu . . . Olorum Mafoiu. . . .*

Taino was leading his people in a chant.

Or was that Castro's lone voice?

The ridge flattened toward the clearing. Mostly scrub-oak trees and pines through which I could now see the gray shapes of the cottages . . . could see the remains of the burned-out building and the fire beyond . . . could see that

Castro remained alone in front of the fire, head tilted upward, palms out in some kind of ceremonial stance while, nearer to us, the chant continued: *Nangoreo . . . Nangoreo . . . Nangoreo . . . Nangoreo . . . Jimaguas . . . Jimaguas . . . Jimaguas. . . .*

Geis had stopped abruptly. Stood there crouched, frozen.

Why?

He held his hand up, touched a finger to his eye—*look*—and pointed.

Ahead of us, in a thicket of trees, stood a man. He had his back to us; was silhouetted by the fire. I could also see the silhouette of a rifle barrel extended over the limb of the tree against which the man was braced.

Let my eyes focus on the silhouette . . . then refocus beyond the limb, some forty yards away—his target, Fidel Castro.

The light was poor. I couldn't see that it was Adolfo Santoya, but I knew it was he—the man I knew as Valdes, and liked—so I continued walking. I wanted to get in front of Geis. Wanted to grab Santoya from behind and talk some sense into him before Geis had the chance to use the knife I could now see him reaching to unsheathe. Heard Geis hiss at me as I passed him; felt him press something into my hand—the knife—and I carried it with me as I took my time, putting one slow stride in front of another, watching Santoya.

But, as I drew closer, I noticed that there was something very strange about the way Santoya was standing. He seemed to sag there, his head thrown back. There was no movement; no nervous shifting or lifting of hands, no swatting of bugs . . . much too calm for an amateur to do what he planned to do.

Now I put my hand up, telling Geis to stop. I stood there for a few seconds before I whispered, "*Valdes.*" The name he would associate with my voice.

The man did not respond.

I turned to Geis; touched my eye, then my chest—body heat. Waited until he had checked the area with the thermal monocular. Watched him hold up two fingers, his fist, then flash four fingers followed by five: two men, not moving, forty or fifty meters away. They were in the tree line to our right.

Less carefully, I approached the man with the rifle. Said the name again—*Valdes*—and I knew that he was dead even before I touched his shoulder . . . then pulled on his shoulder, and his body came loose from the crotch of the tree in which his head was wedged, though his head remained.

The tree had made a handy chopping block.

His eyes still wide open, his face drained white, Adolfo Santoya remained staring at the man he had wanted to assassinate. One more Santoya from a family who had all been failures at that task. He had given up everything to help his country—an idealist—but he'd been caught by surprise from the rear.

I took a quick look behind me; pure instinct mixed with horror.

"Either one of the *Abakua* got overeager, or Taino's got someone doing my work for me." Geis was standing there. Waited—was he going to rob Adolfo, too? No. He hardly paid the corpse any attention, as he whispered, "This must mean Taino's going to do it himself. He's got no other reason to have Adolfo killed. Say the gods ordered him; get his priests to agree. Maybe that's what this ceremony is about, only Fidel doesn't know."

Meaning kill Castro. Geis's attitude was: New target, same job.

He said, "I'll try to find some high ground, get a good field of fire. The moment he makes his move, I'll open up. That'll make my boss real happy." He grinned, lifted Adolfo's head by the hair, said, "This will, too"—before he dropped it on the ground.

Just a good day all around.

I had moved away from the tree, its odor. I said, "I'm going to check that cottage, the one with the light. If they're in there, could you postpone whatever it is you're going to do until I get them on the boat? We'll try to sail out."

I knew that Geis was calculating my worth to him. Me, his alibi—but did he need an alibi now with Adolfo dead, a rifle nearby?

Finally, he said, "What I'll try to do is get things happening when you're *on* the boat. A little diversion to give you some time. Call it professional courtesy." Looked at Santoya's corpse before he added, "But I don't think you're going to find them in the cottage. Or anywhere else."

He was wrong.

With Geis covering me, I crossed from the trees to the cottage and peeked into the gun port–sized window.

Tomlinson was there; he stood in the corner twisting a strand of long hair—an old nervous habit. Rita was there, too; she had her hands in her lap, sitting on the floor. And Dewey was sitting beside her . . . though, for a moment, I wanted to believe she was someone else. It was because of the way she looked; what they had done to Dewey's face . . .

Looking from side to side for the guards I knew were nearby, I removed the bar from the padlock hinge and shouldered the door open and closed it tight behind me. I stepped into the little room—probably a sleeping hut years ago—and it seemed that all I could see in the light of a single burning candle was Dewey. I saw her one good gray-blue eye open wide in terror, then in relief when she realized it was me; watched her comb a shaking hand through her blond hair, a familiar gesture that I found heartbreaking—let's pretty ourselves up a little—and then she was on her feet and in my arms, her bruised and swollen face on my shoulder, crying uncontrollably, her body trembling beneath my fingers. She was wearing the tattered remains of the black dress she'd worn two nights before.

"It's okay now, Dewey. We're going to be okay. I'm going to get you out." I tried to smile at her . . . a failed gesture of my own.

I stood there as she held me, her body spasming, then felt her recoil away unexpectedly: her left eye swollen closed from someone's fist, her lips and left ear the color of bloated grapes. It made it painful for her to speak. I listened helplessly as she sobbed, "How could you bring me to a place like this, Doc? You knew what it was like and you let me come anyway." Confused by it all; she genuinely wanted to understand. "And I heard them say you'd killed someone here years ago. You never told me that, but you *still* brought me. You lied to me; you knew and you *lied*."

I pulled her back to me, whispering, "You're right. I'm so sorry," because I *did* know and I had been stupid, had let her convince me, and now it was something that we would have to live with—if we did live—and that would forever change our relationship, and our lives. Innocence cannot be lost; it can only be taken. My bad judgment had taken far too much from her; had taken it all.

Tomlinson was approaching us, a scarecrow man with his baggy brown shirt and his hippie hair. I flashed him a warning glance—stay the hell away. There was no smile on his face now. Looking into his eyes was like looking into the windows of an abandoned house in a winter field. Yet there was a mildness about him and a disposition of serenity that I found infuriating. He looked at Rita before he said, "They did it to her because I finally had to tell them I couldn't find what I was supposed to find. I tried, man; I really tried, but there was nothing I could do because it was our . . . karma. What? Let Castro's twin spirit stay in power for another forty years? I chose the greater good, man. The greater good, believe me." Then added the next more softly: "The worst thing, Doc, it's your karma, too."

I wasn't going to listen to it. Said, "We don't have time for your bullshit Ping-Pong talk. All I want to know is who did this."

"It doesn't matter who did it. It happened, it's over."

If I hadn't been holding Dewey, I would have swung him up against the wall. "It does matter, goddamn it! Now *tell* me."

Tomlinson's painful expression said, yeah, to someone

like myself it would matter. "It was Taino," he said finally. "And maybe Molinas, too."

Dewey's face was warm against my ear, and I heard her whisper: "Those bastards. It's because I wouldn't quit fighting. I never quit fighting." Some anger in her voice now; that was good.

I looked at Rita—still in jeans and black T-shirt. By tricking Tomlinson, she'd begun the whole rotten chain of events. I said to her, "You're still here? Is it because you didn't find what you were looking for? Or maybe you just missed your boat."

She eyed me steadily, no fear in her but there was some anger . . . or maybe just resolve. "I would have been long gone . . . but I stayed to help her. You know, someone to share the load when the men started getting drunk. Someone who doesn't fight." She was telling me something that was unexpected in light of all her lies; she told me something else when she took Dewey gently by the elbow and allowed me to free my arms. Her voice was different with Dewey. She said, "Are you okay?"

I felt ridiculously close to tears when Dewey answered, "Well . . . shit, I don't know. If the big bastard gets us out of here . . . and it's not like I play golf with my face."

From outside, I heard a rustling sound, then an esophageal grunt. Geis was out there. Had he taken one of the guards? I glanced through the window—darkness; the drumming chants; nothing else. Geis had probably pulled the guard into the bushes and was robbing him.

I help my palm up to Tomlinson—*quiet.* Yanked him to me and whispered in his ear. I was telling him that the four of us were going to work our way through the trees, back to his sailboat, and we were going to sail out of the bay, then motor *and* sail a crow-flies course to international waters—twelve miles and we would be safe. I was also telling him that, from now on, he would do *exactly* what I told him to do, no questions tolerated . . . but I stopped abruptly when I heard an incongruously polite tap at the door. Listened . . . and heard it again. A person tapping—may I come in?

I pulled the .45 from my belt and waved everyone to the blind corner of the room as I slowly cracked the door . . . and there stood Lenny Geis. He had his black hood off, red Mayberry hair and mustache glistening with sweat, and he was looking at me with a perplexed but slightly amused expression . . . a this-is-our-private-little joke-expression . . . and I backed away as he shoved the MP5 rifle into my hands. I watched him take three robot steps into the room, twist, lose the support of his legs . . . and then he fell backward onto the dirt floor, landing in a way that drove a wooden shaft completely through his chest and pierced the black shirt he wore.

His arms limp, his mouth open, he moved his eyes enough to see the serrated bone point on the end of the shaft—watched the surprise of that register—and then his eyes looked to me as he gasped, "An . . . *arrow?*" with an inflection that said, Can you *believe* this shit? then his eyes glazed over, two coals blinking out, and he lay still.

Dewey was asking, "Lenny? Is that Lenny?" as I returned to the door—saw two figures in white standing among the trees. I turned and said to Tomlinson, "When I start shooting, stay here and count to sixty. Then go directly to your boat. Start the engine and get the hell out of here. Don't stop, don't hesitate, don't wait for me."

I held my hand up when he tried to reply. "Don't argue! I'll meet you back in Dinkin's Bay."

Then I turned and fired a burst of warning shots over the heads of the two figures in white; watched them scramble back into the trees. As I sprinted out the door, I heard Tomlinson call after me, "Find the boy! You need the boy!"

One more lunacy from a man whom Dewey had once described as maybe the wisest person she knew . . .

The chanting, the drumming, had stopped; I could feel the silence created by the unexpected gunshots as I ran toward the fire at the center of the clearing. Taino was still there, standing with Molinas, Orlando, and the two other priests . . . Castro, too, set off to the side but down on one knee as if he'd been ducking . . . and I knew that part of the reason they remained frozen was the shock of hearing shots and realizing that Castro had not been hit.

When they noticed me coming, I slowed to a walk. I didn't want to panic anyone. I wanted to communicate an air of being calm and in control. They'd run from a crazy man. Better off to take their chances running than stand there and be shot.

I could feel their eyes watching me as I entered the perimeter of firelight. I had the automatic rifle in my left hand. It was aimed at Taino. I had the .45 Browning in my right. It was aimed at Castro. I saw Castro's expression change, then change again—yes, he was afraid . . . and yes, he recognized me. He gave me a searing look; began to speak, but I interrupted loudly, though I did not yell. People in control never yell.

I said, "No one talks but me—not a word! I'm here to make a deal." I looked at Taino. He'd been backing away, trying to get Molinas and the others in front of him as a shield. I motioned with the rifle—don't move!—then said, "If anyone attacks me or tries to interfere with my friends, I'll shoot Taino first, then I'll open fire on the rest of you. You understand me?"

I watched the priests nod. They understood; were frightened enough to agree to anything. Molinas, his nose still crooked, was nodding right along with them.

I continued, "But if you do exactly as you're told, the only person I'm going to shoot is him." And I looked at Castro.

There was a long, nervous silence. Were they supposed to answer? Did anyone have the *courage* to answer? Then everyone listened to Taino say agreeably, "May I speak?"

I made Taino call all his people to him; made them approach the fire and put down their weapons. Then I ordered them to sit with their backs to me, no moving, no talking.

And we sat there and waited in the silence of black sky and meteors.

I had once loved silence, but not now. My wandering thoughts had a single destination, the reconstruction of a single lovely face . . . and so I did not allow my thoughts to wander. I kept them on business. Survival—that was now my only business.

There were fifteen men in my little group, but I knew there was at least one, maybe two, of the *Abakua* missing.

There was no bow and arrow among the little pile of cane knives.

They were probably out there in the trees . . . or maybe working their way around to the water . . . watching me, awaiting their chance. Were I in their position, I would have been making similar moves.

The missing *Abakua* worried me, because I knew what I was going to do; what I *had* to do, because I no longer had the inclination or the energy to resist it.

I could remember Tomlinson's words: *Fighting your own nature—that's your karma.*

Well . . . I don't believe in karma. The realities of nature, however, cannot be argued, nor can the instincts that guide each and every successful species. Members of an animal community survive because, instinctually, they are accountable to the needs of their own species. Members that did not behave accountably could not survive—nor should they survive.

What would the *Abakua* do when I acted upon my own instincts?

They would act upon their own—naturally.

Now I was sitting near the fire with my back against a big gumbo limbo tree; kept checking my watch. It had been more than two hours since I'd heard the little diesel engine in *No Más* clatter to life. More than two hours since I had watched the old sailboat hunt her way out of the bay, then vanish through a distant wall of mangroves toward dazzling starlight to the northwest.

Was two hours enough? They had only twelve miles to travel.

Yes . . . probably; even if it wasn't, they were close enough. I'd been prolonging it, postponing the inevitable. I pictured Tomlinson at the wheel of *No Más*—or maybe Rita—sailing the long beam reach into international waters and safety. Imagined Dewey sitting at the VHF radio below, waiting for word from Tomlinson: "Call Key West Coast Guard, tell them we're in danger and need an escort." He was sailor enough and smart enough to do exactly that.

But would Dewey be able to function after what she'd been through?

Probably . . . She was a strong, strong woman; more importantly, a good person, and the good ones always find a way to endure. I pictured her, my lost friend—for she was certainly lost to me now—out there gathering herself, drawing on all that strength, already beginning the slow, slow process of putting the broken pieces back together.

At least, that is what I imagined. It is what I hoped. It was what I wanted, not just for her sake, but for my own.

As Tomlinson had said, Guilt is the curse of those who care. . . .

I got to my feet and checked my watch a final time: five minutes until midnight; almost Christmas in Cuba. Then I signaled Taino, Molinas, and the priests to get up; Castro, too, and I waved him toward me. "Get over here!"

But tyrants, I had already learned, made rotten hostages.

Castro didn't budge; he stood there hunched like an old silverback gorilla. "What do you want? What right do you have to order me around!"

At different times over the two hours, I'd had to fire a total of three warning shots past the man's ear just to make him sit still and be quiet. Before the third, he had snapped at me, "You were a shitty catcher! I think you were the worst catcher I ever had!" And I had replied, "Well you're a shitty president and a shittier excuse for a pitcher, and pitchers aren't supposed to think," before putting a round so close to his head that he would feel the atmospheric shock of the slug's passage.

Now I was tempted to fire a fourth, but said instead, "I saved your life tonight. The least you could do is cooperate." I was looking into the face of Taino when I said it; saw surprise, then anger.

I kept looking at Taino as I said to Castro, "Send a man to your yacht and have them call in a helicopter. You and I are flying back to Havana. Everything your Russian bodyguard told you was true. He and I were working together. That's what I mean—we saved your life tonight."

I heard Geis's real name for the first time when Castro whispered it: "Leonid?"

I nodded toward the stone cottages. "He's in there dead. They killed him. There were three assassins; your investigators will find their bodies. Now get going!"

I watched Castro think about that. Maybe he believed me, maybe he didn't, but he liked the idea of calling in his air force. But before Castro strutted off—he'd make the call himself—he whispered the name again in a kind of haze of realization: *"Leonid?"*

Lenny . . . the man I found repugnant because he insisted we had so much in common; but he'd been right; I knew it to my marrow, and if I wasn't certain then, I proved it to myself when I turned to Taino and said, "Remember the tall girl, Dewey? She was one of the most decent people I've ever met. And she was my friend."

As I said it—she was my *friend*—I watched the involuntary smugness that came into Taino's eyes . . . and then I saw the smugness change to fear because he was looking at me, seeing what was in my face . . . and then I shot him before he could move or speak—a clean head shot from a good angle, but I added another to the chest just to make sure.

I used the Browning because a handgun seemed more personal.

It was not unlike the dream that haunted me: a human head vanishing in an explosion of iridescent vapor. But unlike the dream, I could see the residue of Taino's face fade from gray to white, could see his white robes sponging scarlet, could watch his quivering hands stiffen and go still.

I waited for a moment, taking my time, but not too much time, because now I *wanted* Taino's people to panic. I wanted them to run off into the night and leave their Stone Age weapons behind.

So I swung the sights onto Molinas, who had dropped to his knees, arms crossed in front of his face . . . but then I hesitated . . . hesitated because Taino's shocked followers were behaving in a way that I had not anticipated.

They were screaming at me—I hadn't expected that. I also hadn't expected them to surge toward Taino's fallen body.

Were they insane?

Then they were pushing toward me idiotically; coming at me in a rage. Couldn't they see that I had an automatic weapon and could kill them all? So I fired two more rounds into the tree limbs above me to freeze them . . . and then everyone did stop because of what happened next. There was the sound of the breaking of a tree limb overhead . . . a muffled scream . . . and from out of the dark leaves, amid a feather-veil of startled white-crowned doves, a little boy fell to the ground at my feet.

I stood there as stunned as the priests, as stunned as everyone else who was now watching him closely . . . watched Santiago, illuminated by the golden firelight, stand quickly, brush some of the feathers off his clothes . . . then heard him say to me in a gush of relief, "Holy Mother, that was close!" as he straightened two aged medallions that hung around his neck on a single new cord of fishing line.

One of the medallions was a crusted green—a St. Christopher's medal? The other looked to be made of obsidian . . . some kind of polished black stone that had been carved into a swirling figure-eight . . . or the symbol of infinity.

I was looking at the reverent expressions on the faces of the priests . . . saw the same countenance in the eyes of the men who, a moment ago, had been mobbing me. A child falls among them from a tree of white doves, and he is wearing ornaments that the gods refused to reveal to them. Yes . . . *yes* . . . this was something important. . . .

I felt Santiago touch my elbow. "You idiot, were you trying to shoot me?"

I was still watching the faces of the priests. Said, "Huh . . . ? No . . . no I wasn't trying to shoot you. What the hell were you doing in that tree?"

The boy was breathing heavily, still frightened. "Because the strange Yankee said I was supposed to watch over you. But maybe he didn't mean *high* over you. And try to help you, only I don't know how. Maybe that tree wasn't such a good spot."

Very slowly, I moved my hand and patted his shoulder. Said, "No, it was the perfect spot," listening to Santiago's words being passed through the crowd—I was not to be harmed; the child had said it.

The two priests—white robes and white hats, just like Taino's—were on their knees now, chanting something, staring at us. The other men had bunched up around Santiago, wanting to touch the medallions, or maybe touch the boy, but their veneration was like a shyness and they maintained a respectful distance.

All but Molinas. I surveyed the clearing . . . then the cemetery . . . then looked toward the docks where Castro's yacht was moored.

Molinas was gone. He was probably out there in the jungle now, running for his life. I could follow him. Maybe I *should* follow him—track the man down, kill him, then try to escape to international waters in the fishing smack. Fidel Castro, who had debased so many and so much, would not endure personal debasement, so it was probably better than what awaited me back in Havana.

Or was it?

I released a long, heavy breath, then tossed the Browning and the rifle to the ground. I put my hand on Santiago's shoulder and walked him through the parting wall of men . . . was nearly to the docks before I asked what I knew I had to ask: "Were they in the grotto?"

He touched his fingers to the medallions. *These?* "They

were right where the other Yankee told me to look. He's a very strange Yankee. He can do magic tricks. He says that he can heal people."

I looked at the figure of Fidel Castro standing on the bridge of his yacht—a man who was back in control—and then I stared at the Gulf Stream darkness beyond. I said, "I would love to believe that."

Epilogue

On the first official working day of the first month of the new year, I was standing among the commercial docks and rusted warehouses that line French Canal in Colón, Panama; had been standing there for more than an hour because I was waiting to see an old friend.

Two friends, really. Two ladies . . .

I had no other reason to be in that nasty little city. No one in their right mind would want to spend time unnecessarily in Colón, because it is one of those drunken-sailor destinations: ratty bars and prostitute curb-stations and way too much traffic on broken streets that were never designed to handle the burden of what Colón has become—Central America's busiest, tackiest, and probably most dangerous duty-free seaport.

Which is why I was eager to finish my business and get the hell away from there. I wanted to catch my ride back to the isolated beach house I had rented east of Coco Solo. A nice little house up on stilts with a porch that framed its own seascape. Nothing behind the house but an ascending jungle canopy from which the wild cries of howler monkeys awoke me each morning at first light. Nothing to the sides but empty beach . . . and an interesting lagoon in which I had already begun to collect some unusual littoral specimens. I'd found some striped tunicates there, an interesting species because, unlike some other tunicates, they are solitary creatures. They clump on rocks or mounds of sea grass and grow there alone, feeding by filtering water and, as they do so, clean way more water than organisms that size could be expected to clean.

"The duality of design," Tomlinson had replied, when I told him what I'd been doing. He'd been speaking by phone from Dinkin's Bay; had reconfirmed that he and Dewey and Rita had made it to Key West safely . . . which is where he had left them to sail back to Sanibel. Then he had said, "This's going to sound strange, man, but guess what? I don't have a clue who you're with. And I didn't know where you were till you told me. I thought Castro, that asshole, might have you in prison. But *Panama*—far out."

Nope, not prison. I'd spent a day, a night, and part of the next day at the State Security complex in Havana, *Villa Marista,* hoping that Santiago's renown would spread quickly enough through Cuba to save me from the killing bluff at Mariel. The prospect didn't even qualify as tenuous hope. Castro being Castro, the idea was, in fact, an exercise in absurd optimism. If the Maximum Leader wanted me dead, no child wearing sacred medallions could stop it. Each time my cell door opened, I looked up expecting to see the face of my executioner. On a Thursday afternoon, though, the door opened and I was shocked to see a face so unexpected that I thought I might be hallucinating. After that, it was a matter of mustering political clout to negotiate my release.

But because I didn't want to burden Tomlinson with all the sensitive details, I had replied, "You didn't know I was in Panama? What's so strange about that?"

I could hear some of the old excitement in his voice. "It's because this whole last year, I *knew* things, man. I could look at you and I knew where you'd been. I knew where you were going, who you were going to meet. Not that I ever knew what was actually going to *happen.* But now . . . it's like I've lost my powers. Like maybe that whole gig in Cuba burned them all up. It was so damn *heavy*. You think?"

I'd told him, "If that means you're going to start behaving normally, then I hope so."

When he answered, his voice turned sad and a little wistful. "Me too, man. Seriously—the whole scene was getting to be a drag. The omniscient are friendless for a damn good reason."

So Tomlinson now knew where I was, but he didn't know whom I was with. That's the way I wanted it. It's the way it had to be; the only way it was possible to work out security and logistics. Which is why I had chosen the rental car that now pulled up and stopped at the curb beside me. Some kind of Japanese model; the chunkiest, safest, most nondescript rental car I could find. Its windows were tinted almost black. Tinted windows, very important.

I left my spot by the warehouse and was smiling involuntarily as I walked over to the car. I waited for the driver's window to open and then I leaned in and kissed the copper-dark lips, touched the raven hair, traced the handsome Indio face and cheeks of the woman with whom I'd rendezvoused clandestinely two days earlier and was now sharing my beach house. And then I stood and asked Pilar Fuentes Balserio, the sovereign of Masagua, a commoner's question: "All done shopping?"

Which earned me the regal smile. "I have everything we need, I think. Know what? I had a good time. I really did, Marion. It's fun acting like a woman again." Then she turned from me, studied the warehouse I had been watching, then looked back into my eyes.

The way her eyes bore in, the way she looked at me . . .

It was one of her many rare qualities; a gift that she seemed to reserve for me, just for me . . . a quality that I had never forgotten, that I would never forget.

She became serious. "Have they come out yet?"

"No. But they're in there. A buddy of mine knows all the shipping schedules, and her friend's name was on the manifest. They should be leaving anytime."

She had asked me before, now asked again: "Are you certain you don't want to speak to her; to let her know you're here?" Pilar wasn't pressing me, but was telling me that it was okay if I wanted to.

Three days before, Dewey had gotten my message from her service and dialed the number I had left. She had told me, "I need some time, Doc. In my way, I will always, always . . . *care* for you as a friend. But I need some distance. And I need some space to try to put all of this behind me. I hate to say it, but seeing you would bring back . . . too much."

I told Pilar, "No, I don't want her to know. I just want to see her, make sure she's all right."

"Then you'd better get in the car because the doors are opening. The warehouse doors—see? Better hurry."

I hustled around to the passenger's side, watching the double-wide barn doors slide away, and I ducked in beside Pilar and saw through tinted glass an old white Chrylser convertible pull out with Rita at the wheel, Dewey sitting beside her. It was a striking car; a classic that Geis would have treasured—a two-door roadster with red leather upholstery; the kind of car a famous writer could drive around Cuba while dreaming up stories about big fish and African beaches. I also noted that the car was sitting low on its springs. Nothing lead-heavy in the trunk, but things heavy enough. Things that, like the car, were probably very valuable and not too big to be hidden away in one of *Candelaria*'s mausoleums.

I wondered: What else did shrewd Rita find?

Pilar looked at them a moment before she said, "She's beautiful. She really is. And Marion—her face . . . she must heal remarkably fast."

Dewey *did* look good. She had a blue scarf around her neck. I watched her tilt her head back and laugh, reacting to something Rita had said. Watched Rita look both ways, adjust the radio knob, then turn left onto the street and drive away from us.

I sat there in silence watching the blond hair and the fluttering scarf, thinking things that I, too, did not care to remember . . . until Pilar reached into the backseat, dug through some sacks, and dropped into my lap something that genuinely surprised me—a Rawlings Heart of the Hide catcher's glove; the Gold Glove series.

She said very softly, "It came with his luggage. This afternoon. He's already at the house waiting for us, and he says he wants to throw. It may be a little awkward at first. Are you sure it's okay?"

She wasn't talking about Gen. Juan Rivera.

I had turned my face away from her; I was looking at the glove. I looked at it for quite a while, then I put it on and tapped my fist into the pocket. I waited awhile longer—I couldn't trust my voice—before I said, "Sure. Anything for the woman who came to Cuba and rescued me."